MARRIAGE AND MAYHEM

MARRIAGE AND MAYHEM

A LEXIE STARR MYSTERY, BOOK 7

JEANNE GLIDEWELL

Book and cover design by eBook Prep
www.ebookprep.com

April, 2019
ISBN: 978-1-64457-001-2

ePublishing Works!
644 Shrewsbury Commons Ave
Ste 249
Shrewsbury PA 17361
United States of America

www.epublishingworks.com
Phone: 866-846-5123

In the midst of writing this seventh Lexie Starr mystery (not including The Spirit of the Season, a holiday novella) my husband and I moved to Rockport, Texas, into a full-time waterfront home on the coastal bend, having lost our winter home there to Hurricane Harvey the previous August. With a picture-perfect view of the sun rising over Salt Lake from our back deck, to the breath-taking sight of the sun setting over Copano Bay from our rooftop deck, I feel blessed to have such an idyllic place to write, even though it meant leaving a lot of family and friends behind in Kansas. On the very day I completed Marriage and Mayhem, my new great-niece, Everly Rose Goodman, made her entrance into the world. Everly arrived on my sister, Sarah Goodman's, sixty-second birth-day. I think it's awesome that Everly and her Grandma GiGi will always share this special day. My sister, and only sibling, who retired just a few weeks prior to Everly's birth, has always been my most ardent supporter when it comes to my writing, and my most loyal ally when it came to growing up in what wasn't always the easiest childhood. I'd like to dedicate this novel to her and wish her a happy retirement and many wonderful years of sharing, and celebrating, September 25th with her new little birthday buddy.

FROM THE DESK OF JEANNE GLIDEWELL

Dear readers,

Although I intended to end the Lexie Starr series with *Cozy Camping*, I received numerous messages from readers requesting another installment. It seems that after Wendy Starr and Andy Van Patten became engaged at the end of *A Rip Roaring Good Time* (my first Ripple Effect mystery), many of my readers wanted to see these two love birds get married. Not wanting to disappoint my loyal readers or leave a stone unturned, I wrote *Marriage and Mayhem*, the story behind Wendy and Andy's wedding.

As you may imagine, the wedding does not go exactly as planned, and absolute mayhem erupts at the drop of a pin. Or in this case, the drop of a very large best man.

I hope you enjoy this latest adventure as much as I did writing it.

Happy reading,

Jeanne

P.S. As usual, I apologize in advance for any words I have made up for lack of having a better, dictionary-sanctioned, word at my disposal. It's a bad habit that I have no intention of kicking. I'm hoping if I use the word often enough, I'll bring Funk and Wagnall around to my way of thinking.

PROLOGUE

Wedding Day - August 25, 2018

"Nine-one-one. Do you have an emergency?"

"Yes, ma'am." My voice quivered uncontrollably. "We need an ambulance. Right away!"

"What is your name and the nature of your emergency?"

"My name is Lexie Starr. In the middle of my daughter's wedding, one of the groomsmen collapsed to the ground."

"Is he breathing, ma'am?"

I glanced over to watch Raven Kostaki perform chest compressions on Bubba Slippknott. "Someone's doing CPR, but he doesn't seem to be responding."

"What is your address? I'll dispatch assistance immediately. Continue administering CPR until help arrives. Does he have a pulse?" The operator's voice was calm and matter-of-fact. Doesn't she realize this was a life-or-death situation?

"I'm not sure." I recited the address and implored her to ask the ambulance driver to hurry. "We need them here A.S.A.P."

"Help is on the way, ma'am."

I swear I could actually hear the woman's eyes roll over the phone. But I realized she couldn't allow herself to become overly distressed every time she took an emergency call, or she'd soon develop severe hypertension.

Moments earlier, Reverend Bob Zimmerman, minister of the local Methodist Church, had asked if anyone had any objections to the union of Andy Van Patten, my husband's nephew, and Wendy, my thirty-one-year-old daughter.

"Erg, I, uh—" The six-foot-eight best man tried to speak, then took a step back and keeled over like a tree toppled by a chainsaw.

"Well, that was a rather dramatic objection," Reverend Bob, as the cleric preferred to be called, said with a chuckle.

At first everyone laughed, thinking Bubba had either fainted from the exhilaration of the moment, or was acting out a rather tasteless prank for everyone's amusement. However, it soon became apparent it was no joke, nor had Bubba merely passed out.

I studied the scene in front of me. Some wedding guests ran around like squirrels looking for nuts to bury. Others looked as if they'd been dipped in a vat of nitrogen and were frozen in time. The groom wore an expression of disbelief. He'd clearly anticipated he'd be kissing his new bride right about now instead of looking down at his best man's lifeless body.

Wyatt Johnston, our good friend and one of Rockdale's finest detectives for sixteen years, stepped around Gunnar Wilde to tend to Bubba, who lay motionless on the ground. Kneeling down, he checked his fellow groomsman for a pulse and respirations. He looked up at me and shook his head.

ONE

Four weeks prior to the wedding

A ndy Van Patten, Wendy's fiancé, delivered her to the inn on his way to a farm auction early in the morning. I woke up to the sound of their voices talking and laughing in the kitchen. The auction was scheduled to begin at six. *Who goes shopping at that time of day unless it's Black Friday?* I had to wonder. Apparently, like farmers, farm auction attendees liked to get up with the chickens while the rest of us still lounged around in bed, as I'm certain God had intended us to do.

Andy had forty minutes to spare and he and Wendy had decided to spend that time together at the inn. When he'd relocated to the Midwest from the east coast over a year ago to be closer to his Uncle Stone, Andy had purchased a cattle ranch near Atchison, Kansas, which was less than an hour's drive from Rockdale. He was now hoping to get a good deal on a newer model John Deere tractor to be auctioned off at the estate sale.

As we chatted at the kitchen table, I downed cup after cup of strong Columbian brewed coffee until I could literally hear my own heart pounding in a rapid staccato. It reminded me of the sound of

Tony Montana's "little friend", an M16 automatic assault rifle, that he used to spray hundreds of bullets at the Columbian drug cartel's henchmen toward the end of the movie *Scarface*. I really did need to cut back on the caffeine a bit, as my primary doctor had gently suggested at my last checkup. In fact, I couldn't recall an appointment when she hadn't suggested it.

Andy and Wendy sipped their coffee and discussed their upcoming nuptials while I looked online for a chicken enchilada recipe I planned to serve that evening to the Clevengers from Arizona, and the Masseys from Texas, who'd be checking in that afternoon. The Alexandria Inn went above and beyond the duty expected from most B&B owners, serving not only breakfast to our guests, but dinner as well. There were days I wished I'd never started that tradition. Setting the bar so high during the inn's inception had only added pressure on Stone and me not to fall short of meeting those standards in all the days that followed. This was one of those days I regretted our desire to be as accommodating as conceivably possible.

I enjoyed cooking, but that doesn't mean I was good at it. In fact, not long ago I'd almost killed a man with an undercooked chicken. On another recent occasion, I'd made a commendable attempt at burning down the inn with a nuked-to-death baked potato that had ignited inside the microwave oven. Fortunately, Stone had put the fire out before it could spread. If nothing else, when it came to meal preparation I deserved a "C-" for effort.

I had poured the rest of my coffee down the drain after I noticed my fingers were trembling like an aspen leaf in a gale-force wind. I then checked to ensure I had shredded cheddar cheese in the fridge. While I gathered the ingredients I was going to need later on, I'd listened in on Wendy and Andy's conversation.

From the very beginning, Andy had balked at the idea of being intricately involved with planning the wedding. He told Wendy the very thought of spending three hours choosing between green napkins with a white imprint or white napkins with a green imprint made his blood run cold. I could relate, as my blood had already cooled to room temperature just thinking about it.

"I'm sorry, honey," Andy had said. "But the entire process of planning a wedding is way more than I can handle. It's your day, and I want everything to be exactly the way you want it. So I'm fine with whatever decisions you make. It makes no difference to me if the napkins are pink with an orange imprint or green with purple polka-dots. In fact, I'd be okay with just passing around a roll of paper towels. And the refreshments at the reception could consist of nothing but beer nuts, cold pizza, and shots of tequila for all I care."

Naturally, the soon-to-be groom had to back-track after spouting those last several comments, but he was eventually able to bring Wendy around to his way of thinking.

"You're right, Andy. The intricate details of planning our wedding would drive you crazy. You'd be nuttier than grandma's fruitcake before I got you to the altar. I may end up being that nutty myself by the time this wedding is over and done with."

"'Over and done with?'" Andy asked with a grin. After chuckling good-naturedly, he added, "Baby, you make marrying me sound so incredibly romantic."

"You know what I mean, you big goofball," Wendy replied as she touched up her cherry red lipstick. She then planted a big kiss on his cheek, leaving a perfect imprint of her lips.

With the enchilada ingredients lined up on the counter like little soldiers, I sat back down with the kids at the kitchen table and laughed at Wendy's antics. It was heart-warming to see my daughter so over the moon about marrying the love of her life. I may be a bit biased, but I didn't think she could have found a better man than Andy, who'd not only inherited the Van Pattens' good looks, but also their kind hearts and thoughtfulness.

I tuned back in to their discussion in time to hear Andy say, "Besides, I know your mom is dying to help you with the wedding. Every bride's mother wants to be involved in the planning, and I don't want to take that enjoyment away from her."

If Wendy had not been sitting across from me, with a smile plastered across her face, I'd have clocked my future son-in-law in the noggin with the frozen chicken I'd just removed from the freezer to thaw out for supper.

TWO

"Really, Mom? You think I look like a 'skinny snowman' in this wedding dress?" The expression on Wendy's face was that of a woman who'd just been told she was too unattractive to risk producing offspring, lest she pass that hideous "ugly" gene down to her children. Perhaps honesty wasn't always the best policy, but I didn't want to lie and let her buy a wedding dress that didn't do justice to her beautiful figure.

"It was the best comparison to something white I could come up with at a moment's notice. I'm sorry, but you did ask me to be brutally honest."

Wendy stared at me in horror. Evidently, I'd taken the "brutal" part of her request a little too seriously. My mind raced for a way to escape from the hole I'd dug for myself. The result found me even deeper in the crevice. "I meant to say you looked like a well-rounded snowman, not a skinny one."

A lone tear ran down Wendy's cheek. "I don't want to look like any kind of snowman, Mom. I want to look like a beautiful bride. I've tried on over a dozen dresses, and you haven't liked the way I looked in any of them."

"Not true, sweetheart. Even though it's too expensive, I thought you looked lovely in the cashmere silk dress with the pearl-studded neckline."

"Yeah, right."

"How many times have I told you I'd kill to have your figure?" I asked. Standing four inches shorter than Wendy's five-foot-seven, and with quite a bit more posterior padding, my height, shape, and curly mop of blond-highlighted brown hair were in sharp contrast to her slender build and long, straight auburn tresses. Lucky for her, she'd taken after her father. Wendy had always been thin, so I was happy she'd recently put some much-needed meat on her bones.

"Thanks, Mom." Her response sounded neither appreciative nor sincere.

"I'm just saying I don't think you should invest half-a-year's salary in a dress you'll likely wear only once."

Wendy glanced at the price tag on the gown she wore. "I know this is over my budget, but I haven't found a reasonably priced wedding gown I look good in."

"There are other bridal shops offering beautiful wedding gowns for far less money. You'd surely get a better price if you shopped in a less ritzy neighborhood."

We were at a designer bridal shop on the County Club Plaza, a fifteen-block section along Brush Creek in Kansas City, Missouri. The affluent shopping district was known for its beautiful Spanish architecture and numerous fountains. During the holidays, every building was outlined with Christmas lights, horse-drawn carriages click-clacked down the streets, and the air held the scent of cranberries and pine needles, with just a hint of horse manure. It was truly a magical place where many of the wealthier locals shopped.

But the holidays were still four months away, and I wasn't feeling the magic. It was a typical mid-July day; hot and sticky. What I felt at the moment was a bead of sweat rolling down my spine. The dampness from perspiration making my shorts stick to my thighs like a sand burr was making me cranky. The fact Wendy was having trouble accepting that we just weren't in the right tax bracket to shop on the lovely Plaza wasn't helping any.

With pouty lips, Wendy's voice had a woe-be-gone inflection to

JEANNE GLIDEWELL

it as she spoke. "Yeah, there's nothing like wearing a cheap ugly dress on the biggest day of your life. Should we try the dollar store next?"

"Don't be so melodramatic, Wendy. You've been awfully moody recently. Are you sure you aren't pregnant?"

"For the umpteenth time, Mother, I'm not pregnant. You know I'm on the pill."

Wendy's indignant voice and snippy attitude were obvious signs I should back off and let the subject drop. Unfortunately, my mouth failed to get the memo. "That doesn't mean anything, honey. I was on the pill when I got pregnant with you."

"Oh, really? I was an accident? So you didn't even want——"

"Now, wait a darned minute, missy!" I was indignant now, too. "Just because your father and I weren't planning to get pregnant at the time doesn't mean that finding out we were going to be parents wasn't the happiest day of our lives. I just wish Chester was still alive to see what a successful and beautiful woman his daughter's become. He would've been so proud to walk you down the aisle."

"Yeah, I wish he was still here, too." Wendy's voice now sounded melancholy. I hadn't intended to sadden her. I was relieved when her mood rebounded swiftly. "But Stone's been like a father to me since the day I met him. I'm pleased to have him stand in for Daddy."

"Good. Stone's looking forward to it, as well."

Stone Van Patten and I had married a year and a half ago, although I'd kept my maiden name, Alexandria Marie Starr, or more simply, Lexie. Stone and I own a bed and breakfast in Rockdale, Missouri, that he named the Alexandria Inn after me. Wendy and Stone's nephew, Andy, were scheduled to be married on August twenty-fifth in the very gazebo Stone had built for our own wedding on the lodging facility's back lawn.

As much as I hate to admit it, I could hardly wait to see the taillights of Andy's truck when they drove off to begin their honeymoon. Hours and hours of mind-numbing details and non-life-threatening decisions, like whether to serve butter mints or mixed nuts in the bowl next to the guest book, nearly bored the frigging life out of me. So why had I volunteered to help plan their wedding? Because that's what loving mothers do—damn it!

I might have enjoyed the process of spending quality time with my daughter while planning her wedding if not for three things: my daughter could be exceedingly melodramatic, my daughter was a perpetual nit-picking perfectionist, and my daughter was extremely moody when under pressure.

I loved Wendy more than life itself, but planning the most important day of her life seemed to bring out all three of those innate traits in spades. If there was one tiny little glitch in the wedding ceremony, Wendy was sure to have a meltdown of epic proportions. I'd, no doubt, be the one held responsible for whatever caused the hiccup in her and Andy's nuptials. Knowing this put great pressure on me to make sure every single detail was flawless.

But there was no time to dwell on the tedious and drawn-out process ahead. I needed to keep my daughter focused so we could make progress on our lengthy list of tasks. To hurry things along, I decided to suggest we try out a bridal shop in Shawnee, Kansas, the town we'd both been living in when I'd first met Stone.

"Wendy, let's try this shop called the Hitching Post on Quivira Road. I've heard their prices are incredibly reasonable. I'd hate to see you two be one of those couples who are still making payments on a wedding dress after the ink on their divorce settlement has begun to fade."

Bad choice of words, and I regretted them even before my lips stopped flapping. I may have forgotten to mention that undue stress tends to make me engage my mouth before I've put my brain into gear, which in turn makes my good sense fly out the window like a trapped falcon.

The first meltdown of what would undoubtedly be many, had officially begun when a blubbering Wendy started ranting loud enough for every shopper in the store to hear. "No wonder you want me to go cheap on my dress! You think our marriage is doomed to go down the toilet faster than a dead goldfish."

"Whoa! Calm down, dear. You're making a scene. I wasn't inferring I thought your marriage was destined to fail. You two were absolutely meant for each other. I just meant it'd be a shame to have a debt hanging over your heads when it's not necessary."

I studied Wendy for a moment and could tell she was taking in every word, so I continued trying to talk some sense into her. In retrospect, my decision to keep talking was yet another ill-advised one.

"I'm certain we can find a gown at the Hitching Post that doesn't cost as much or make you look hippier than you actually are, like that dress you have on now."

After an audible gasp, Wendy screeched, "Now you're saying I look like a fat-assed brideglobzilla?"

"No, of course not, dear. Don't be ridiculous. Besides, I don't think brideglobzilla is a real word." I said in an attempt to change the subject. My bad decisions were stacking up faster than the discarded wedding gowns on the chair beside me.

"'Hippier' is not a real word, either, Mother, but that's beside the point. The point is I have less than a month to get ready for my wedding." Wendy was flustered—madder than a hornet who'd just been drenched in Raid—and I knew she was overwhelmed with frustration. As if the fabric was searing her skin, she clawed at it in an effort to undress and I feared she was going to rip the expensive gown she'd been modeling.

"Relax, sweetheart. You're being overly sensitive. Your derriere is anything but fat. In fact, your figure is exquisite. We still have plenty of time to get all the details worked out. After all, I planned my wedding to Stone in no more than forty-five minutes."

"Maybe so, but you guys are old."

"Excuse me? I'm only fifty-one."

"I'm sorry, Mom. I apologize for being offensive, but this is my first marriage, and Andy's too. Both you and Stone had previous marriages, so you weren't expected to have a ceremony that's, um, well…"

"Insanely over-the-top?" I asked, rather than point out it was actually her second marriage too.

Wendy shook her head and sighed loudly.

At this point, I'd have welcomed having masked gunmen

storm the building. A distraction, along with half a roll of duct tape over my mouth, would have benefited my cause. Unfortunately for me, no one on the Country Club Plaza was in the mood for terrorizing a bridal shop that afternoon. I could feel myself sinking another foot down into the swiftly deepening pit I'd been shoveling for myself for the last twenty minutes or so. I should have focused on the quicksand swallowing me up rather than adding another bad decision to the overflowing heap I'd already accumulated. Unable to contain my annoyance any longer, I asked, "What about your ill-fated marriage to Clayton Pitt?"

"Are you really going to throw that in my face? I could have been killed in that fiasco. Besides, that marriage was annulled, so it doesn't count."

It was true Wendy's life had been put in danger just months following her and Clay's wedding day. Fortunately for her, however, she had a mother who didn't have the sense God gave a dandelion when it came to protecting her offspring. On the fateful day in question, I had thrown caution to the wind and saved her from a gun-wielding maniac.

I certainly didn't cast any blame on my daughter for the unraveling of her marriage. I was lucky she was still alive and such a vital part of my life. But my point is, despite the fact her marriage to Clay had dissolved quicker than a stick of butter in boiling water, the ceremony had been elaborate and pricey—and at my expense. I certainly hadn't been issued a refund check for the wedding when the annulment was granted. However, with Wendy's emotions in overdrive, I chose to take the high road and not rain on Wendy's self-pity parade. "I know, darling."

"I heard Sally and Stephen Morgan's wedding cost over forty grand, and he'd been married before," Wendy said.

"And do you know why you heard that?" I asked, not appreciating her huffy tone. "It's because everyone was talking about it—for all the wrong reasons. The few people I chatted with all agreed it was a frivolous waste of money. Having all the guests raise a toast to the newly wedded couple with eight-hundred dollar

11

bottles of rare champagne in solid-gold rimmed goblets as a dozen doves were released into the air was plum crazy if you ask me."

"I didn't ask you."

Ignoring Wendy's rude retort, I continued. "The Morgans are hardly wealthy. They'll be lucky to have paid off their wedding debt by the time they have their children's college tuitions to worry about."

"Well, yeah. That's probably true."

"What I'm trying to say—and so far making a real mess of—who cares how elaborate the ceremony is? The most important objective is to join you and Andy in holy matrimony, isn't it?"

"Yeah." A hint of a smile appeared on Wendy's face. "It *would* be a lot easier and cheaper to just fly to Vegas and elope."

"Now you're talking. Stone and I will even spring for the ladder." We both laughed at my quip. "It can be your wedding gift from us."

"Don't tempt me."

I put my arm around Wendy's shoulders as I spoke in a soft voice. "I wouldn't actually want you two to elope, but the ceremony doesn't have to be overly extravagant or ridiculously expensive. Not to mention, you seem to be putting way too much stress on yourself." *And me, as well*, I thought.

"I know. I just want our wedding to be a day we'll never forget."

I gave my daughter a warm hug. "No matter how elaborate or how simple it is, I promise your wedding day will be one you'll never, ever forget."

I didn't know it at the time, but my words of encouragement could not have been more prophetic. As it would turn out, it'd be a day no one who attended the ceremony would ever forget—no matter how hard they tried.

THREE

Even though Wendy, who served as the county's chief medical examiner, could be moody and emotional at times, she was usually a fairly laid-back, level-headed woman. After she became engaged to Andy Van Patten, she had gradually taken on a "Dr. Jekyll and Mr. Hyde" kind of demeanor. I sensed that my words to her in the bridal shop were falling on deaf ears, and I was correct. As if I hadn't spoken, Wendy continued to whine.

"You were right. I do look like a snowman. A lumpy one."

"I never said lumpy——"

"I look absolutely atrocious." As Wendy spoke, she did a complete 360. She stared at the elongated mirror as she rotated. Finally she stopped and gazed at her backside in the mirror's reflection. "Actually, I'd look more like an ugly duckling than a snowman, waddling from side to side as I walked down the aisle. Get a good look at all this extra junk in my trunk, Mom, because it's not going to be around for much longer. I need to shed twenty pounds in the next month. How long do you reckon a person can fast before becoming critically ill?"

"Don't be silly. You don't need to lose a single pound. You're a very attractive woman and at the perfect weight for your height."

"Yeah, right." Wendy's tone was sarcastic. We'd driven to the Hitching Post in western Shawnee. Wendy had been rambling on incessantly, upset about her appearance, since we'd walked out of the upscale bridal shop on the Plaza. Continuously assuring her she had a beautiful face and figure was beginning to get tiresome.

"Relax, Wendy. As I said before, you're a stunning woman and would look better in a gunny sack than most people would in an Oscar de la Renta gown. Your physique is quite enviable, and I think you should show it off with the perfect dress. There is not one spare ounce of junk in your trunk, as you put it. In fact, you needed to put on a few pounds and I'm glad Andy has helped you accomplish that. So let's put that little ugly-duckling monster torturing you to bed once and for all. All right?"

"Okay. You're right. You must think I'm beginning to act like a drama queen. Don't you?"

Beginning to? That was an understatement if I'd ever heard one. I merely shook my head in response.

"Am I starting to drive you crazy, Mom?"

"No, of course not, sweetheart." *That bat-crap-crazy ship sailed three hours ago with my bone-weary body aboard it,* is what I really wanted to say. But the maternal instinct in me—the one that had been in hibernation since about two seconds after I'd volunteered to assist in planning the wedding—came back into the picture just seconds before I made some edgy comment that would have only upset my daughter further. "You are understandably anxious about your upcoming wedding. Who wouldn't be?"

"That's true." I could see the tension fade from Wendy's face. Then she turned to scrutinize her backside in the mirror once more. After the tension faded from her face, a disgusted grimace emerged. "Yikes!"

"I'm no fashion expert, by any means," I said, before I had to assure Wendy about her looks for the fortieth time. "But my advice is to buy the gown that makes you feel the most beautiful, the most comfortable and the happiest. If you feel beautiful, you will look even more stunning."

"Yeah. You're probably right." Wendy studied herself in the

mirror with a pensive expression. "You're also correct that this gown doesn't do a thing for me."

Oh, thank God! Uncomfortably warm, I dabbed at the sweat on my cheek with a Kleenex. I couldn't tell if I was having a hot flash or the store was trying to lower their electric bill. I watched silently as Wendy hung up the white wedding dress with the short lacy hoop skirt that made her look like a life-sized ballerina who was ready to spin like a top when some little girl raised the lid of the jewelry box her grandmother had gifted her with at Christmas. I was relieved to hear Wendy's next comment.

"This won't work. It just isn't the look I'm going for."

"I agree. I know anything goes in this day and age, but the shorter dress just doesn't do your figure justice, or have the proper look to it." *Unless you're going for the ballerina look,* I wanted to add. "Keep looking at the full-length gowns. You'll find the perfect one, I'm sure."

"I did kind of like the way that last one I tried on looked on me."

"I did too. You looked drop-dead gorgeous in it. It's my number-one choice, by far. And the price is reasonable. Don't you agree?"

"Yes, very reasonable," Wendy replied. She went back to the dressing room to put the straight-line silk dress with the spaghetti straps back on. She turned slowly, scrutinizing the dress in the mirror from every angle before exclaiming, "This is the one. I think Andy will love the way it looks on me."

"He'll love it. It's exquisite on you and flatters your figure beautifully." I was so exhausted from dress shopping, I might have said the same thing had she been wearing the aforementioned gunny sack. But, in all honesty, I had to agree it was the perfect dress for Wendy.

"I'm going to buy it right now so it doesn't get snatched up by some other bride-to-be. Besides, I can't waste much more time selecting a wedding gown because there are a zillion other details we need to get worked out."

"Good idea, dear. Do you need help paying for the dress?"

"No, but thanks for the offer. We're in good shape financially, and we've set aside enough to pay for the entire wedding if, as you cautioned earlier, we don't go overboard. Besides, you paid for my first wedding to Clay. It wouldn't be right to ask you to chip in on my second one, too. Helping me to plan the rest of the ceremony and reception is more than enough assistance from you."

Wendy's remark gave me an inspiration, and I wondered why I hadn't thought of it earlier. "Why don't you let me hire an expert to assist you? Instead of a ladder to elope, an experienced wedding planner would be an ideal wedding present. Stone has something else in mind he'd like to give you guys, so I'll let him do his own thing independent of me. I think a wedding planner would take a lot more responsibility and pressure off of your shoulders than I ever could."

"Hmm…" Wendy murmured as she mused over the suggestion.

"I will help out as much as possible, too, of course, but it'd be nice to have an expert to guide us as we make plans. Business at the inn has doubled in the last couple of weeks, and I know you've been busier than normal at work, too." This wasn't a fabrication just to appease my daughter. Although it wasn't unusual for us to have all seven of our suites full at the same time, we only had two suites rented out this week. But that's twice what we'd had the first half of July, with only one suite occupied each week. That's double the business, any way you look at it.

Wendy's agreement came in the form of a nod. "I've been buried in work too. I don't know why so many people had to pick this spring and summer to drop dead."

"Other than that unfortunate Vietnam veteran who committed suicide last week, I don't think people necessarily pick when they're going to 'drop dead', as you put it." I was a bit taken aback by Wendy's insensitivity. I'd yet to get used to the idea that she made a living off of other people dying. I doubted I ever would. The very thought of it made me nauseous. The fact she appeared to take great pleasure in discussing the ins and outs of every autopsy had a tendency to make me want to upchuck my latest meal.

My daughter was not typically thoughtless or dispassionate, but she was acting like a spoiled brat that day. It reminded me of when she was ten and refused to share her dolls with two less fortunate young girls she'd invited over for a play date.

Following a reprimand from me for being selfish, she'd responded, "I'm not being selfish. I just don't think it's wise to let my dolls, Grace and Patience, associate with people like that." After being told she was being rude, behaving discourteously, and showing an appalling lack of both "grace" *and* "patience", she'd finally relented. I realized Wendy had learned a valuable lesson that day when I saw the two sisters walking out to their foster mother's car about an hour later. They each wore a bright smile and carried one of Wendy's dolls in their arms. I could have sworn I saw Patience wink at me as her new owner hugged the doll to her tiny chest.

I could not have been any prouder of my daughter at that moment. And, yet, somehow my pride in her had grown tenfold in all the years that followed. My watery eyes studied her now as she studied the chosen wedding gown in the mirror.

Wendy completed one more full rotation. She then turned around, with her hands on her hips. "You know, the notion of hiring a wedding planner is not such a bad idea. It would take a load off my shoulders, for sure. Are you certain you want to take on that expense though?"

"Absolutely."

"Don't forget it might take away some of your enjoyment in helping me with the wedding."

Are you kidding me? I almost asked, but caught myself just in time. "It will be worth the sacrifice, I'm sure."

"Thanks, Mom. I sure do love you."

"I love you more, sweetheart." I picked up the stack of wedding gowns still waiting to be tried on and rehung them on the rack. "What do you say we make like eggs and scramble?"

Wendy's loud groan at my cheesy remark was her only response. So I added, "There's a quaint little coffee shop on the corner called The Dunkin' Hole, and I could use a cup of espresso. Sound good to you?"

"You bet! Let's make like Siamese twins and split."

I chuckled at her corny joke, which is more than she'd done for mine. "Good. You go pay for your lovely dress while I hang up these other gowns so we can make like an exorcist and get the hell out of here."

Wendy giggled this time. "Gotta admit. I liked that one. Say, were you serious when you said a few more pounds wouldn't hurt me?"

"Of course, honey. You no longer look gaunt in the face, but you're still a bit on the scrawny side. Why do you ask?"

"When we walked by that coffee shop earlier, they had scrumptious-looking cinnamon rolls advertised on a sign in their window. I could sorely use a little comfort food right now."

"You and me both," I said cheerfully.

After Wendy purchased the wedding gown, she turned to me and said, "Ready to make like that check I just wrote and bounce?"

Laughing, the two of us practically skipped out of the bridal shop. We walked down the sidewalk arm-in-arm to the front door of a small, family-owned coffee and pastries cafe. I needed a shot of caffeine even more than I'd thought. I enjoyed a cup of their advertised flavor of the day—a robust Guatemalan espresso.

Since I didn't want my energy level to ebb during our hour-long drive home to the Alexandria Inn in Rockdale, I indulged in two refills. Wendy, who was subdued and introspective, nursed a cup of hot lemongrass tea. I was sure she had a lot on her mind, so I didn't badger her with questions or annoy her with mindless chatter. Instead, I mused about where I'd find an experienced wedding planner willing to take on the job at such a late date.

FOUR

The Alexandria Inn in the small town of Rockdale, Missouri, was a historic antebellum mansion Stone and I had restored ourselves a couple of years prior. I had sold my home in Shawnee, Kansas and moved in with him for both convenience and a desire to spend as much time with him as I could. We opened the inn as a bed and breakfast soon after the renovations were complete. The business had flourished since the day of its conception.

Although a murder occurred in the inn on its opening night, and then again a few months later—both of which crimes I helped solve—the lodging establishment's occupancy rate continued to increase. I'd hazard to guess the inn's tragic history had actually enhanced its fascination among guests. It was the same type of intrigue that drew throngs of adrenalin-junkies to cemeteries that had a reputation of being haunted.

The Alexandria Inn had become a popular venue for weddings, receptions, parties, reunions, and bar mitzvahs. A local winery had even held a wine-tasting event there the previous month. With the lovely gazebo, flower gardens, plenty of shaded picnic tables, a large, accessible chef's kitchen, and lodging accommodations available right on the premises, our property became a hot spot for local celebrations of all types. Stone had recently added four full-hookup RV sites on the property to allow even more guests to stay on the premises. He'd had the inspiration after becoming acquainted with full-time RV'ers, Rip and Rapella Ripple, from south Texas.

Stone and I were content to reside in our owner's suite at the inn. Living there had been very convenient and had come in handy many times. It allowed us to be even more accommodating in our desire to be excellent hosts, especially when it came to special events.

But the next wedding to be held at the inn was personal. My only child was going to marry the man of her dreams. Andy, a well-built, dark-haired, blue-eyed man was not only eye-candy, with a heart as soft as a melted Milky Way bar, but also a wonderful young fellow I'd be proud to call my son-in-law. I wanted their wedding to be everything Wendy had ever dreamed it would be. I vowed to do whatever it took to make her dreams come true, starting with the hiring of a wedding planner to take the pressure off of me. Oops, sorry. I meant her.

Wendy and I agreed that the one thing we couldn't delay was sending out the invitations. After Wendy had purchased the gown at the Hitching Post and we'd stopped at The Dunkin' Hole, we'd checked out the available wedding invitations and guest books at another shop in Shawnee. By the time we finished selecting a matching set, it was time for me to drive her home and return to the inn to prepare supper for our guests. The Masseys would be heading home the following morning, but the Clevengers had extended their reservations for another three days.

When I arrived back at the inn, I sorted through the mail, responded to a couple of reservation requests via email, and put fresh water in a vase full of carnations and snapdragons in the parlor. I then prepared the chicken enchiladas and *sopa de fideo* for our guests and, as usual, made enough extra food to suffice for our own supper, as well.

After putting the main dish into the oven to cook for forty-five minutes, I went upstairs to take a bath and change into a fresh outfit. While soaking in the jetted tub, I contemplated who might know of a good—and reasonable—wedding planner I could hire, even though the wedding date was barely a month away.

Wendy had been extremely busy at the morgue the last few months and, until early July, business at the inn had been incredibly hectic as well. Planning the wedding had somehow ended up on the back burner, where it had been left to simmer until suddenly we realized there was no more time to waste. We had little more than four weeks to get all our ducks in a row. At the time, those pesky little quackers were running amok all over the place.

With the wedding looming so close on the horizon, finding any planner willing to take on the challenge would not be easy, much less finding one worth his or her salt. On one hand, I was relieved that Wendy had approved of my idea. On the other, I wondered if it might turn out be a decision I'd live to regret.

Lest I be judged too harshly, let me explain that a great deal of my reluctance to be in charge of planning my daughter's wedding is that I feel totally inept in the wedding-planning department. Like clothing fashions, wedding protocol and trends frequently change. Several weeks earlier, Wendy had reminded me we needed to get the "save the date" magnets mailed out. I had failed to send out reminder magnets for both of my weddings, and, yet the ceremonies took place as planned. But now? Without a "save the date" card or magnet, or some other reminder, you simply cannot expect people to show up for the most important day of your life. According to Wendy, she couldn't forego such a modern, but terribly critical, practice.

The fact I'd initially had no idea what she was talking about scared me. I didn't want to forget some detail of great significance to my daughter only because I was unaware of its necessity. Don't even get me started on how out-of-date I felt when Wendy asked me if I had any clever ideas for their wedding hashtag. *Where does one go to buy a wedding hashtag?* I'd almost asked. Instead, I looked at her as if she'd asked me if I had any clever ideas on how to prove that the universe is based on the string theory.

"Hashtag?" I asked.

"Yeah. Good Lord, Mom. You are so last century." I just looked at her in silence. There was no denying I hadn't kept up with technology the way many folks my age had. Wendy shook her head as she continued. "You know that pound symbol you use before a tweet to identify the topic? Well, family and friends can use our wedding hashtag on Instagram and Twitter to do things like get wedding updates, view the invitation, and view all the photos from our big day. Guests can use the hashtag on their posts to include their photos in the mix."

"Oh." Her explanation did nothing to eliminate my confusion about the necessity for a wedding hashtag, but I didn't want to appear any more like a dinosaur in my daughter's eyes than I already did. "Sorry. I don't tweet."

"That pretty much went without saying."

"Did Andy have any ideas for the wedding hashtag?" I asked. Admittedly, I was going on a fishing expedition, and it netted the results I'd expected.

"He doesn't have a clue about hashtags either. As you know, Andy still uses a flip phone. So, like you, he doesn't understand how crucial it is to have the perfect wedding hashtag."

How did I pull off two weddings with nary a hashtag? Thinking about Wendy's angry words during that trying day of wedding gown shopping, I asked myself, *Wonder how she'd feel about #brideglobzillawedshand-somerancher?* I decided Wendy wouldn't find the humor in my teasing, so I kept my trap shut.

I was also reminded I was behind the times when Wendy said earlier in the summer, "I have Maeve's 'reveal party' to attend tomorrow." When she'd explained it was a get-together to reveal the gender of Maeve's baby, I thought she meant the party was to take place in the obstetrician's office as he or she performed the ultrasound that would determine if the little bugger had anything protruding from between his or her legs. Our own reveal party didn't happen until moments after Wendy entered the world, and we discovered she wouldn't be named Wendell, after all. And that, in a nutshell, explains why I felt so woefully inadequate to plan a wedding in this day and age.

While bathing, I thought about Deborah and Yvonne Custovio. The two ladies appeared to be polar opposites in both looks and personalities. Being in their mid-to-late thirties, never married, and shameless gossipmongers were the only similarities the two sisters seemed to share. People around town often referred to them as the "spinster sisters". I hated the term and didn't think either sister deserved that sort of derogatory characterization.

Deborah, the elder of the two, was tall, had long hair so blond it was almost white and looked older than her actual age. Deb—as most people called her— had been hired to fill Bertha Duckwor-thy's position as head librarian at the local library. I'd been temporarily filling the position in the interim. Deb was the shy, mild-mannered sister with a Type B personality, while her younger sister, Yvonne, was a live-wire. An outgoing socialite, this flamboyant, love-them-and-leave-them sort of gal was most definitely a Type A indi-vidual. Yvonne stood no more than five feet tall and wore her dark brown hair in a short style that must have taken a pound of liquid cement to get the spikes on top to stand straight up like proud Marines in formation. In contrast to her sister, Yvonne looked like she shouldn't be able to buy a beer without being carded.

While Deborah was rumored to be asexual, Yvonne was anything but. Yvonne was a cosmetologist at the salon I patronized, and she had worked there for over a decade. I'd been hearing about her sexual escapades for a couple of years, but felt certain most of the stories were exaggerated, or even downright lies fabricated to entertain her clients while she styled their hair. It was as if Yvonne believed she had a naughty reputation to maintain. Regardless of whether the stories were true or not, listening to them made having your hair wrapped in foil or tugged through tiny holes in a plastic cap to be highlighted a more interesting experience.

As I absentmindedly shaved my legs in the bathtub, it suddenly occurred to me that if there was a good wedding planner in the vicinity, Yvonne Custovio would likely know about them. After all, if you're anything like me, you open up like nobody's business while your hairstylist is rolling your hair or wrapping tin foil around clumps of it to dab with her paint brush. I become an open book the second I plant my behind in a hair salon's swiveling chair. I'm not typically a gossiper, but it's nearly impossible not to dive right into the middle of an active rumor mill when you're surrounded by gossipy, often exceedingly judgmental, women in a hair salon. It can be quite eye-opening at times. How else would I have discovered that Howie Clamm, who'd routinely pitched a copy of the *Rockdale Gazette* into our bushes every morning until the newspaper went totally digital last year, had begun the transition process of becoming Holly Clamm? I hoped Holly had a better arm than Howie had, even though instead of pitching newspapers into bushes, Holly was now pitching story ideas in the *Rockdale Gazette's* editorial department.

Despite the fact I'd just had my hair trimmed early in the week, I made a mental note to return to the beauty salon the following day. Yvonne would be the person most likely to know the answers to my local wedding planner questions. There was nothing intrinsically wrong with nonchalantly chatting up one's hairstylist while she trimmed your hair.

I had a busy schedule planned for the following day but figured the hair appointment wouldn't take long. After all, my hair couldn't have grown more than a millimeter since Monday. And hopefully, Yvonne, who'd been off that day to have a suspicious mole looked at by a local dermatologist, wouldn't discover I'd just had it cut by their part-time stylist, Kerri.

I relaxed as I leaned back against the back of the bathtub, closing my eyes while I soaked. I had lit several candles and added a heaping fistful of lavender bath salts to enhance the calming effects of my bath. I felt a sense of serenity as I languished in the soothing warm water.

Suddenly, as if the scented water had turned ice cold between one breath and the next, I opened my eyes and struggled to catch my breath. It was as though a voice spoke to me from beyond. I swore I heard an ethereal presence whisper the words, "You need to help Wendy pick out the perfect wedding cake from among the sixty-seven choices."

The nightmarish sensation of hearing a voice from beyond jerked me awake instantly. I was relieved to discover I'd been so relaxed I'd drifted off to sleep—which is not always a good idea when you're lying in a tub of water. I took several deep, calming breaths and reminded myself I'd found a way out of the madness.

With a hired professional to plan the wedding, my overwhelming worry about forgetting critical details would be eliminated. I'm a bit ashamed to admit this, but I'd truly almost rather slice my wrists with a cake knife than help pick out the cake it was purchased to slice.

Earlier I'd told myself I'd just have to do my best to avoid the reception cutlery until the kids' wedding day was behind us because I might be tempted to utilize one of the plastic, silver-colored knives to saw away at my radial artery in order to put myself out of my misery. Now my only concern was that my decision to hire a professional would be a sound one.

Something told me hiring a wedding planner might turn out to be a bigger basket of toil, time, and trouble than helping Wendy plan the event myself. I'd learned the hard way it was important to pay careful attention to a fleeting notion like that, yet once again I chose to ignore it. Unfortunately, I'd soon discover I really hadn't spared myself as much of the toil, time, and trouble as I'd been aiming to. Instead, I'd only taken on the responsibility of babysitting the individual I was paying to relieve me of those three things.

FIVE

"Thank you, Yvonne, for working me into your schedule. I'm in desperate need of a trim and didn't want to put it off any longer."

"Are you sure you want your hair even shorter?" Yvonne wore a dubious expression. "It's already pretty short. If I trim much more of it off, you'll look like you just enlisted in the Marine Corps. And if you don't like it that short, it'll be months before it grows back out. In fact, Kerri expressed some concern about its length after you had her cut it on Monday."

Oh crap! I thought. For one thing, I hadn't anticipated that Kerri would tell Yvonne about my Monday appointment. Secondly, and even more distressing, I'd forgotten about what I'd look like if I had my hair trimmed even shorter. Wendy and Andy's wedding was a month away. Wendy would kill me if I went home looking like a fresh recruit on the first day of boot camp.

After I'd gotten home from the salon on Monday, I'd convinced myself the style looked attractive on me as I'd studied myself in the mirror. But it wasn't a reassuring sign that Kerri and Yvonne had later discussed it between themselves. I'd likely deluded myself into thinking the new cut looked good when it actually looked anything but.

I swallowed hard and thought even harder before adopting a "silly me" expression. "Oh, I'm sorry. Did I say I wanted a trim? I must have had a brain fart. I meant I'd like to have it highlighted. Kerri's a wonderful stylist, but you know exactly how I like it, so I felt more comfortable waiting to have you do it."

"Oh, all right. Let's go wash it first then." Yvonne's voice had an impatient tone to it, and I soon discovered why she appeared troubled. "When I worked you in this morning, I'd thought this would be a ten-minute appointment, but now it's obviously going to take a lot longer than I'd planned. My next appointment is not going to be happy about having to wait. And if she somehow discovered I slept with her boyfriend last night, she'll already be a tad on the bitchy side when she gets here."

I didn't know how to respond to that comment, so I didn't. I remained silent as Yvonne hastily draped a towel around my neck and covered the bulk of my clothing with a plastic cape. I followed her as she nearly sprinted to the wash basin. It occurred to me that getting a highlight would actually give me more time to talk with her, but in her current mood, she wasn't likely to want to waste any precious time chatting about a wedding planner.

I'd have to draw as much information out of her as I could without upsetting her further. Upsetting someone who's about to color your hair is almost as risky as pissing off a surgeon who was about to perform exploratory surgery on your sedated body. I'd have to go about my pursuit for information judiciously. It would have been a good plan had I not screwed up the execution of it.

As Yvonne tested the water with her hand, waiting for it to warm up sufficiently, I tried to engage her in friendly conversation. "I'll bet you know a lot about almost every woman in town."

And slept with most of their significant others, as well, I could have added, had I not cared about how horrendous I'd look when I walked out the salon's front door. On the other hand, considering how much Yvonne bragged about her sexual exploits, she might have considered the remark a compliment.

Yvonne turned off the water, unable to make out what I was saying over the sound of it running. She rolled her eyes dramatically, sighed heavily, and asked, "What?"

"Oh, I'm sorry. I was just talking to myself."

She looked at me as if she'd rather be washing the hair of a rabid coyote. "Well, stop it!"

I nodded and closed my pie-hole tightly. Getting a list of highly respected and recommended local wedding planners out of her was going to be an even bigger challenge than I'd anticipated, if she consented to speak with me at all. She was usually much friendlier than this. I knew I'd probably have to see about getting a new stylist.

I had debated searching the Internet for a wedding planner, but was hesitant to choose one based on nothing more than online reviews. You couldn't always trust them, after all. Any given wedding planner could undoubtedly rely on their mother, aunts, sisters, and closest friends for five-star online reviews, regardless of their true and honest opinions. Surely a best friend would not post a review that read, "She planned my entire wedding for free because I was her maid-of-honor, so I really can't complain about all the mistakes that popped up throughout the ceremony and the chaotic reception that followed."

Back at Yvonne's station, I remained mum. I felt uncomfortable when she stared at me for several long seconds. Finally, she shrugged and asked, "Well, are you going to give me some kind of clue about what color you want?"

"Oh, sorry. Just the usual, please."

"The usual? Seriously? I've done a hundred dye jobs since I gave you your last highlight. I forgot my own address when I was filling out forms at the dermatology office on Monday, so don't expect me to remember what color you like your highlights to be."

"Oh, yes, of course." *Wow! Somebody needs a nap. Or perhaps a better prognosis on that unsightly mole on their neck,* I wanted to say. But, of course, I didn't. Instead, I apologized again. "I'm sorry. Why don't you just surprise me? I just need something to cover up any gray strands that are starting to sneak into my natural brown hair, and I trust your judgment."

"Natural?" Yvonne laughed. "Okay, if you say so."

"I do say so." I knew I sounded defiant, but so far I hadn't found much reason to be congenial. I'd almost convinced myself not to utter another word. In fact, I was about to stand up and walk out of the salon, when Yvonne's demeanor turned on a dime. I was caught off-guard when she said, "I'm so sorry. I've had a bad day, and shouldn't be taking it out on you."

Why? Did your next client's boyfriend give you the clap? I was tempted to respond. But, once again, I resisted the impulse and apologized. "I'm sorry for——"

"Nonsense." Yvonne patted my shoulder and smiled at me with what passed for a sincere expression of remorse. "It's I who needs to apologize for being such a grouch this morning. I've had a difficult couple of days. In fact, I had a terrible argument with my sister this morning, and I'm still smarting from some of the comments she made. Deb wasn't happy about having to give me a lift to work, and as usual, I was the recipient of a long, drawn-out lecture. Deb thinks that because I'm her little sister, she has the right to tell me how to live my life."

"Oh." I hoped Yvonne wasn't expecting an elaborate response. I was sorry if her car was having mechanical issues and that her sister had—justifiably, no doubt—reprimanded her for her reckless life-style, but I didn't think I should have to bear the brunt of her misfortune.

When Yvonne realized I was not going to jump to her defense, she immediately changed the topic and adopted a new bubbly demeanor. "So, tell me, Lexie. How's your day been so far? I have a highlight color that will be striking on you, one that will make this pixie cut even cuter. Have you got any plans for this evening? It'd be a shame not to take your lovely new 'do' out on the town tonight."

Suddenly, Miss Congeniality had morphed into Chatty Cathy. Her about-face had been sudden and unexpected, but I was delighted to see her become more amiable. I didn't want to waste the opportunity, in case her good mood faded away as quickly as disappearing ink, so I plunged right in.

"No, no plans. I've been busy planning my daughter's wedding."

"Wendy?"

"Yes."

"Kerri put highlights in her hair last week. I used to do Wendy's hair, but all of a sudden she got a burr up her——" Yvonne stopped mid-sentence, and began awkwardly combing through her drawer for a pair of scissors.

"You were saying?" I asked. I knew Wendy had switched over to Kerri several months earlier, but never asked why. I did, however, think she should have found a new stylist at an entirely different salon so she wouldn't feel uncomfortable every time she came in and sat at her new girl's station while Yvonne worked just yards away. When Yvonne ignored my prompt to finish her comment, I asked, "A burr up her what?"

"I was just saying that Wendy will look gorgeous on her big day. I don't know if Kerri's much to brag about in the sack, but she does give a very good dye job."

I found her suggestive turn of phrase distasteful but not surprising. Rather than respond to it, I changed the topic back to the wedding. "So, anyway, I'm helping Wendy plan the ceremony and it's had me running around like a headless hen. That's why I was talking to myself, you see, and appeared so scatterbrained about why I came in here today."

"Ah, yes. I can only imagine. Better you than me, is all I can say." She laughed in an agreeable fashion, before asking, "When's the wedding? I'm certain I asked Wendy, but I've forgotten."

Where's a "save the date" magnet when you need one? I thought. I told Yvonne the date and explained how little we'd actually accomplished so far. The dress had been purchased and the invitations and guest book were ordered. That was pretty much the total number of tasks we'd been able to mark off our list, which left something in the neighborhood of six-hundred and twelve more decisions that'd have to be made in the next four weeks. "Oh, and of course the 'save the date' magnets were mailed out a couple of weeks ago. That was a new one on me, I have to say. I'm really not sure how we'll be able to get everything done in time."

Yvonne had cocked an eyebrow when I indicated I was unfamiliar with the magnets that were intended to help guests remember the day of the wedding. I guess it wasn't just the roots beginning to rear their ugly grey heads that showed my age. She said, "Hmm… maybe you should see about getting someone to help."

"Hey! That sounds like a great idea." I acted like her suggestion of hiring someone to assist with the wedding planning had never even occurred to me.

"I overheard Wendy speaking about her fiancé with Kerri. How do you feel about him?" Yvonne asked.

"Andy's wonderful. I couldn't have picked a better husband for my daughter, or son-in-law for myself. He's my husband's nephew, as a matter of fact."

"Yes, she said as much. I've never met her fiancé, but I hope he's nothing like a few of his friends."

"Yes, well, Andy's a great guy." In my future son-in-law's defense, I felt compelled to add, "I don't know many of his friends, but I do know the guys in his wedding party are wonderful. I've never met his best man, Bubba Slippknott, but I have met Gunnar Wilde, who's dating Wendy's best friend, Mattie Hill."

"Isn't Gunnar that short dude who owns the Wilde Horse Ranch in Atchison?"

"Yeah, that's the fellow. His ranch is adjacent to Andy's. Gunnar and Andy both raise cattle, but Gunnar's passion is the wild horses he's adopted over the years out of Wyoming. Mattie told me he owned seventeen at last count, and two mares were due to produce foals at any time. Fascinating, huh?"

I paused for a response from Yvonne, but she clearly didn't share the wild-horse passion. So I continued with my story. "Gunnar's not much taller than my five feet, three inches and Mattie's barely five feet tall in heels, so they make a really cute couple. Andy's other groomsman, Wyatt Johnston, is a detective. He's a cherished friend of mine and one of the finest men you could ever meet."

Yvonne looked as if she'd just been told she was being fired for stealing a bobby pin from the salon. She scowled and said, "If you say so."

"Oh, do you know Wyatt?"

"You could say that." Yvonne's response was ambiguous and hinted at a former relationship with the man. Naturally, I wanted to know all the juicy details of any past interaction she'd had with Wyatt. I waited for her to expound on her remark.

After an uncomfortable length of silence, I realized an explanation would never come. I cleared my throat. It was time to segue back to the reason I came to the salon in the first place. "So, anyway, let's go back to your wonderful suggestion. You wouldn't happen to know of a reputable wedding planner, would you?"

Yvonne took a long time to mull over my question. It was as if she were giving considerable thought whether she should recommend someone to me or not. I began to think she wasn't going to reply at all, when she finally said, "Well, I do know of one in the area you could probably get, even on such short notice. Lariat's very efficient, if nothing else."

"If nothing else?" I didn't like the sound of her last three words. "So, you say she's efficient, but is she any good?"

"Lariat's a guy. His name is Lariat Jones, and he lives in Atchison."

"As do the future bride and groom, which would be convenient and a factor to consider. Do you think he's someone I can trust to handle Wendy's wedding and make it everything she wants it to be, even though we haven't allowed him a lot of time to arrange things?"

"Oh, yeah. Of course. Lariat knows his stuff, if you can keep him focused on the job at hand, anyway." Suddenly, Yvonne looked lost in thought, as if her mind was a hundred miles away. When she noticed I was waiting on the edge of my rotating chair for her to continue, she said, "I'm certain your daughter, um——"

"Wendy." I filled the name in for Yvonne when she appeared to lose her train of thought.

"I'm certain Wendy would be satisfied enough with him."

Oh, swell. I could hardly wait to tell Wendy I'd located a wedding planner I'd been assured would "satisfy her enough" *if* she could keep him focused on the job at hand. I nodded woodenly. Yvonne almost seemed to be trying to convince herself and not me of the wedding planner's prowess. But I didn't have any other wedding planner knocking on my door, begging to coordinate a rehearsal, rehearsal dinner, wedding ceremony and reception, all in a matter of a few weeks.

I decided it wouldn't hurt to check Lariat Jones out. If I wasn't happy with what he had to offer, I wasn't obligated to hire him. It's not like I was apt to see Yvonne again, so I'd probably never have to explain why I pooh-poohed her suggestion if I didn't think the wedding planner she suggested would work out. Unlike my daughter's new stylist, mine would be employed at an entirely different location. Perhaps I'd try out the new hair salon on Maple Street. After musing about that for a few moments, I turned my attention back to Yvonne.

"So, his name is Lariat, huh? Sounds really masculine. It's the perfect name for a cowboy, for example. But maybe not so much for a wedding planner. Does Lariat, by chance, do any bull-riding when he's not busy picking out the perfect flowers for a centerpiece?" I asked Yvonne in a joking manner.

"He's more of a hog-rider than a bull-rider." I can't describe the tone of Yvonne's response. It was a mixture of humor, sarcasm, and bitterness. I badly wanted to ask her to elaborate on her response, but I didn't want to seem like I was prying into her personal life. I swallowed my inquisitiveness and instead asked if she happened to have the man's contact information.

"Yeah, I have his number in my phone."

"Good," I said. "It sounds like he might be ideal, Yvonne. Is Lariat a friend of yours?"

"No, not exactly."

That's what I'd hoped to hear. If she and Lariat Jones were friends, she might have mentioned his name out of loyalty. I'd feel more confident if they were simply acquaintances, and Yvonne's suggestion was based solely on the man's professional capabilities.

"Lariat's more of a recent regret of mine than he is a friend. I gave the man a ride and seriously wish I hadn't."

"I see." I didn't "see" at all. I resisted the urge to meddle because I wasn't sure I wanted to hear Yvonne explain what kind of ride she'd given the man. I wrote down Lariat Jones' name and number, which Yvonne recited from the list of contacts in her cell phone. I then thanked her for working me into her busy schedule and recommending a wedding planner.

After Yvonne finished highlighting and styling my hair, I took a deep breath and looked into the mirror. The color of Pepto Bismol reflected back at me, causing me to gasp out loud. I had to ask myself what I was thinking when I asked Yvonne to surprise me. *I did say "surprise" and not "shock", didn't I?* "Oh, my! It's a little too pink, don't you think?"

"I think it's perfect and makes you look young and hip. You'll look like the bride's sister, rather than her mother. In fact, you'll probably be the prettiest woman at the wedding." Then, as an apparent afterthought, she added, "Other than the bride, of course."

I was too shocked to speak. I had to wonder again what caused Wendy to switch hair stylists. Were the passionate pink highlights in my hair the result of a disagreement Yvonne had had with my daughter? Or, more likely, were they the result of my self-declared friendship with Wyatt Johnston? Yvonne had clearly taken offense when I said Wyatt was one of the finest men I'd ever met. *Can I trust her recommendation for a wedding planner?* I had to wonder.

That was just one of the questions whirring through my mind as Yvonne removed the gown from around my neck. Without another word, I nodded and walked toward the front counter to fork over hard-earned money for the coloring catastrophe of my new "do". I didn't want to "do". I wanted to "undo" and vowed to wash out the color when I arrived home, even if I had to wash it twenty-seven times before supper. All I can say is that, despite Yvonne's reputation of being highly provocative and shamelessly promiscuous, she most certainly did not "give a good dye job".

I could imagine Yvonne speed-dialing Kerri the moment I left the salon, expressing her amusement about how I now looked even more comical than I had on Monday.

34

As I waited at the beauty salon counter to pay, Yvonne summoned her next client to her station. A frumpy, bottom-heavy woman shoved a crochet hook and a ball of yarn into her over-sized handbag. She wore a shawl draped around her neck identical to the one my grandmother used to wear, even though the day was hot and steamy. Before she stood up, the woman extracted a crumpled, and clearly already used, tissue from her pocket and blew her nose loudly several times. It sounded like a gaggle of geese had invaded the building. *Honk, honk, honk.*

I hated to admit it, but assuming there was any truth to Yvonne's remark about sleeping with her next customer's boyfriend, I could almost give the man a pass for choosing to spend the evening with Yvonne instead.

I paid the tab, including a ridiculously exorbitant tip for Yvonne, and exited the salon. I couldn't decide whether to rush home and wash my hair however many times it took to "unpink" it, or drive to the "Think Pink" shop in St. Joseph that catered to breast cancer patients and look for an attractive wig to wear to Wendy's wedding. Instead of doing either, I decided to indulge in two or three cups of espresso and embrace the caffeine high.

I headed for the coffee shop three doors down, ignoring the compulsion to glance at my reflection in the store windows I passed. When I reached Java Joe's, I couldn't help but see my reflection in the front door. My hair looked so horrendous, I decided against a caffeine fix. I turned around and sprinted for my car. I couldn't risk running into someone I knew in the coffee shop. I prayed the entire way home that no one would be at the inn when I arrived.

When I entered the huge mansion through a door leading into the kitchen, I came face-to-face with inn guest, Ginny Clevenger. She swallowed hard before saying, "Oh, how nice. You've had your hair colored."

"It looks absurd, doesn't it?" I asked.

"No, well, er, maybe just, um, perhaps a bit." Mrs. Clevenger stumbled over her words, clearly too kind a lady to be up-front with me. She hesitated a second. "However, if you're unhappy with it, I might be able to help. I spent most of my working life as a hair stylist, and happen to have just the stuff I'd need to strip that pink out of your hair."

"Oh, thank God. And you, too, of course." The relief in my voice was evident. I wasn't in the mood to be teased about my hair, even if it was all in good fun. "Do you happen to know if Stone's home?"

Ginny read my expression perfectly. "He's not. In fact, Stone asked me to tell you he was going to the ranch to help his nephew unload a new tractor. Or something like that."

"Oh, good." I let out a sigh of relief.

Ginny smiled. "Don't worry. We'll have your hair back to normal in a jiff, and Stone will be none the wiser. In fact, he might actually love your new look when I'm finished with you. By taking off a few of these tufts of hair on your temples that seem to have a mind of their own, I think we can make this a very attractive style. Would that be okay with you?"

"Oh, goodness. Yes! It's more than okay with me." I thanked her again. After she'd finishing un-pinking my hair, I looked in the mirror and nearly wept. The kind lady had not only stripped the pink color from my hair, but also added very attractive blond highlights and snipped off just enough stray strands to make the style look reserved, yet stylish. Although it may not be saying a heck of a lot, I thought my hair looked better than it ever had.

I could have kissed Ginny Clevenger. In fact, I did kiss her. I gave her an appreciative peck on the cheek as I thanked her profusely for saving me the embarrassment of a pink hairstyle. Sometimes plain old dumb luck is better than good planning, I realized, as I headed to the kitchen to begin supper preparations.

It should come as no surprise that I put an extra chocolate mint on Ginny's pillow that night.

SIX

When Lariat Jones arrived at the inn, I suddenly understood Yvonne's remark that he was more of a hog-rider than a bull-rider. The wedding planner rolled in on a Harley Davidson. Despite Missouri's helmet law, he had nothing but a do-rag to protect his skull in the event of an accident. And speaking of skulls, there was a large skull and crossbones on his black t-shirt. The shirt was paired with jeans that looked as if they hadn't been washed since Bernie Madoff made off with a lot of people's life savings, and they had more holes in them than O.J. Simpson's alibi. And, to be clear, they were not the fashionable type of holes that doubled the price of a pair of jeans, but rather the type caused by overuse.

"Can I help you?" I asked when he first came to the door. I thought he might have stopped for directions, or to make a reservation for family who planned to visit. I also considered the possibility he might have dropped by to try to scam me into paying him to asphalt our driveway. The expression on my face as I'd stared as his do-rag prompted Lariat to snatch it off his head and shove it in his rear pocket. I instantly wished he'd left it in place because his hair was even more disturbing.

"I'm Lariat Jones. You asked me to stop by."

"Oh." Suddenly unable to speak, I felt as if I'd been winded by blunt force trauma to the bread basket. Finally, after giving myself a chance to recover, I asked, "Do you mean the Lariat Jones who works as a wedding planner?"

"No, the Lariat Jones who delivers big-ass checks for Ed McMahon. Of course, I'm the wedding planner. How many people named Lariat Jones did you ask to stop by this morning?"

"Oh. I'm sorry. I just didn't expect…" Embarrassed, I stopped talking, not wanting to cause myself further humiliation. I stepped back as Lariat strode in, looked around the room, and whistled.

"Sweet." He said as he gave me a wink. "Nice digs."

"Thanks. Come on in." My response was a little sarcastic as he was already as "in" as he was going to get. I had expected a guy who looked more like an accountant, an English teacher, or even a gay stripper. What I hadn't expected was a man who looked to be in his early thirties with pumpkin-colored hair that stood straight up like a field of corn stalks. He sported seven piercings on his face alone, and more tattoos than you could count on an abacus, especially if, like me, you have no idea how to use one. The teardrop inked below his right eye clashed with his smile, making him appear to be having mixed emotions.

"Good afternoon. I'm Lexie Starr," I finally said. "It's nice to meet you, Mr. Jones."

"Yeah, man. You too."

Yeah, man? Is it too early in this job interview to let him down easy? I decided it probably was since I'd done nothing but introduce myself so far.

"As you're probably aware, I'm looking for someone to help with my daughter Wendy's wedding. I'd like—"

"Wendy Starr?" The look on his face indicated he was already having second thoughts about the two of us working together, which irritated me. I was having second thoughts too, but wanted it to be my decision, not his.

"Yes. Why do you ask?"

"She's marrying Andy Van Patten, isn't she? And there's a cop named Wyatt in the wedding party, right?"

"Yes. Is that a problem?" I asked.

"Well, no, not really. Besides, I need the job. There's more month than money this summer, it seems."

I was befuddled. I didn't know what to think about Lariat's remark about Wyatt. I did wonder if Yvonne's issue with the detective had anything to do with Lariat's, but I wasn't going to inquire. As I pointed Lariat toward the door, I said, "Perhaps it'd be best if you leave."

"Whatcha talking about, Ms. Starr? I said I'd do the job, even with so little time to get all the details worked out."

"Well, I…"

"Who else ya gonna get, if not me?"

His last question hit me like a second punch to the gut. The man was right. If I sent him away, I'd likely be turning down the only wedding planner available on such short notice. "I'm sorry, Mr. Jones. But I get the distinct impression you have a problem with a member of the wedding party. I don't know why, and I don't particularly care, but it makes me reluctant to hire you in case you have a bone to pick with the detective."

"Trust me, ma'am. I have no bones. Well, no bones to pick with the cop, anyway. I barely know Wyatt and just met him recently. Admittedly, it was not under great circumstances, so I'd just like to have as little interaction with him as possible."

"Is there a warrant out for your arrest, or something of that nature?" I asked. I definitely didn't want to get involved with a wanted felon.

"No, nothing like that. I have no legal issues. My rap sheet has nothing more than a drunk and disorderly charge from a little misunderstanding about a fire at a downtown bar awhile back. Let's just say the detective and I experienced a difference of opinion a few nights back, and I don't want to throw a match on a pool of gasoline, if you know what I mean. Trust me, it will not interfere with planning your daughter's wedding."

His explanation and assurance it wouldn't affect his work did nothing to ease my mind. But like he'd said, who was I going to get if not him? "All right. I doubt you'll have any interaction with Wyatt. He's just a groomsman, after all. But to be perfectly honest, I'm still a bit torn. I have to say, sir, you're not exactly what I expected. You look more like, um, a rock star than a wedding planner."

Okay, I'll admit that wasn't exactly honest. I could tell by Lariat's expression he was keenly aware I was not being straight-up with him. I'm certain he was wondering about my intentions, as was I.

"A rock star? Really?" Lariat's tone was more sarcastic than inquisitive.

I didn't trust my own voice, so I merely nodded in response.

I know the old adage about honesty being the best policy, and deceitfulness was never a good idea. But telling a guy straight to his face that he looked more like a brain-dead drug addict who'd just climbed out from under a bridge than he did someone in his chosen vocation isn't exactly a stellar idea, either.

"Okay. Enough pleasantries," Lariat said. "Let's get down to business."

Exactly what is your idea of a pleasantry? I wanted to ask. But time really was of the essence, so I plunged right in with the interview.

"Can you give me an idea of the cost and what is included in your package?" I asked.

He gave me another wink and replied, "Basically, the same as any other guy's package, except for a piercing on my—"

"Whoa! I can do without the inappropriate humor." I couldn't believe what he'd been about to say. No wonder Yvonne seemed apprehensive about recommending this fellow, even though the sexual innuendos she often spouted weren't much better. "Let's keep this strictly professional, Mr. Jones."

"All right. I'm sorry. I thought a little levity would lighten the mood, with you feeling so discomfited, and all."

"Um, well…" I didn't think "discomfited" was the best description for how I felt. Flabbergasted was better. Horrified was even more accurate. However, the fact that words like "discomfited" and "levity" dripped off this anomaly's tongue like honey encouraged me. I'd been surprised he could use either word correctly in a sentence, and was relieved he wasn't operating on a pitifully low supply of brain cells, as I'd first feared.

I reminded myself that you couldn't judge a book by its cover any more than you could judge a wedding planner by the silver hoop dangling from his nose. It reminded me of the nose rings Andy used on his cattle ranch to keep calves from trying to suckle. I looked away from Lariat's nose piercing and forced myself to take a couple of deep breaths in order to relax.

"Are you okay, lady? You seemed kind of uptight when I arrived this morning, and even more discombobulated now."

"Discombobulated? Well, I suppose I did feel somewhat unsettled earlier, but that's beside the point." If he thought I was uptight when I first laid eyes on him, I wondered what he'd think now that I was as uneasy as a flamingo with a shellfish allergy. "So, tell me about your rates and what is included in the price. I also want to hear about your qualifications as a wedding planner."

Lariat went on to explain his vast experience and reasonable rates. Before I could request to see references, he handed me a list of names and phone numbers of previous clients. Glancing at the sheet, I recognized a couple of the people on the list. I couldn't help but be impressed. One had even held their nuptials in our gazebo a few months prior. As far as I could recall, it had been a pleasant and well-organized affair. Even so, I'd have opted to interview other people for the job if not for the fact there was probably not another wedding planner between Rockdale and the Pacific Ocean who'd take on the challenge of planning a wedding scheduled to take place in just under a month.

Reluctantly, I said, "Okay. I'm satisfied with your rates, experience, and references. You've got the job. I hope you won't let me down."

"Yeah. Me neither."

"Me neither" did not exactly lessen my anxiety, but I chose to ignore the feeling in my gut. My gut, which had never misled me before, was telling me I should show the man to the door with a sincere, "Thanks, but no thanks!"

Once again my mouth did not get the memo. Instead, that mouth, which had gotten me into more tight spots than I can count, asked, "So, Mr. Jones, when can we get started?"

SEVEN

W endy and I were to meet with Lariat Jones at his office in Atchison the Wednesday after I signed the contract, which allowed him to handle much of the detail work in the planning of Wendy and Andy's wedding ceremony.

Wendy called at the last minute to inform me a local meth lab had tragically exploded and filled her autopsy lab with three new customers. The enthusiasm in her voice was unsettling. I couldn't tell if she was excited about having three new bodies to carve up like Butterball turkeys, or just happy she wouldn't have to attend the meeting with Lariat Jones. Though neither option filled me with joy, I hoped it was the latter.

On that sweltering morning in mid-July, I drove Ladybug, my yellow and black Volkswagen Bug, to Lariat's office after cleaning up the kitchen following breakfast. The only guests remaining at the inn were the Clevengers. Our next reservations were not due to arrive for several days, so I wasn't under any pressure to return home soon.

Shortly after my arrival at 103 Massachusetts Street, Lariat invited me into his tiny, rather dingy, office at the end of a tiny, even dingier, row of small mom-and-pop businesses in an older commercial area of Atchison, Kansas. The underwhelming level of dingi-ness surrounding Lariat's shop made me question, yet again, my wisdom in hiring him.

I rapped on the door, and Lariat invited me into his tiny office. After being somewhat appalled by the appearance of the shop's exterior, I was surprised the interior exuded an almost sterile aura. The cleanliness of Lariat's workspace was impressive. I extended my hand to the shop's proprietor. Instead of clasping it in a handshake, as expected, he pulled me into a quick embrace and kissed the side of my cheek as if I was a favorite aunt he hadn't seen in several years. I could smell booze on his breath, which immediately unnerved me. He offered me a cup of sassafras tea.

"I hope you like it hot, like I do."

I shrugged and took a cautious sip, wondering if the tea had been laced with rum or another form of alcohol. I was delighted to find it hadn't been spiked, and was surprised by how much the warmth of the tea enhanced its surprisingly delicious flavor. "Um, I do. I've only had cold sassafras tea in the past, although now I believe I prefer it hot. Thank you for enlightening me, Mr. Jones."

"Call me Lariat, please. Mr. Jones makes me sound like I should be a sixty-year-old CPA instead of a thirty-five-year-old free-lancer."

We chuckled at his remark, and it was then I noticed the man was actually quite handsome if you looked past the bright orange, spiked hair, multiple facial piercings, and disturbing tats, which I'll admit was a lot to look past. His smile was contagious, and he had an introspective air about him I found attractive. In other words, the guy who had turned me off at first glance was beginning to grow on me, kind of like moss grows on the north side of a tree.

"Just out of curiosity, Lariat, does your job description as a free-lancer include other services besides planning weddings?" His self-description of "free-lancer" had made me wonder if wedding plan-ning was merely one of his skill sets.

"You could say that." His cryptic response piqued my interest, but Lariat didn't elaborate. Instead, he steered away from the topic. "At the moment, your daughter's wedding is the only thing on my schedule, and we need to get cracking. We need to shake and bake while the oven's still hot if we're going to pull this wedding off without a hitch."

"I like the sound of that. Let's get cracking!"

Without thinking, I took a big gulp of the tea, which I had forgotten was piping hot, having taken barely a tiny sip of it previously. I spat most of the scalding liquid onto the Saltillo-tiled floor. Then I nearly gagged on what little I'd swallowed, which had chosen to take the road less traveled and ended up going down the wrong pipe. While I choked and hacked for a good three minutes, Lariat wiped the tea off the floor with a sweatshirt he'd had draped over the back of his chair. Then, as if he thought I had an Italian meatball lodged in my throat, he pounded me on the back five or six times until I motioned for him to stop. When I hadn't coughed for a full three seconds, he asked, "You okay?"

I nodded and responded with three or four more violent coughs, which only served to prove to the man I was anything but okay. Lariat stood by with a helpless expression and breathed a sigh of relief when at last I had expelled all the tea from my windpipe.

"Sorry, Lexie," he said. "I should have warned you to be careful. Are you alright now?"

I nodded, with tears streaming down my face, because I couldn't get any words out. Finally, I was able to clear my throat enough to speak. Embarrassed, I offered an apology for the mess. "I should have tested the tea before gulping it down as if I was on the verge of dying from dehydration."

Lariat waved off my apology as he opened a notebook. We spent the next two-and-a-half hours discussing a slew of specifics: number of invited guests, refreshments for the reception, and potential venues for a rehearsal dinner. He took detailed notes of numerous other critical aspects he'd need to know before he began planning Wendy and Andy's wedding.

The longer we engaged in conversation, the less I fixated on the wedding planner's unique appearance and apparent drinking problem, and the more I appreciated the man's meticulous attention to detail. He took copious notes and listened carefully to everything I said. He suggested ingenious ideas and made well-thought-out recommendations. I felt my anxiety ebb as we deliberated over necessary aspects of the ceremony and the party that would ensue at the completion of the vow exchange.

As Lariat refilled our tea cups for the second time, I noticed him pour something into his own cup while merely adding a pack of sweetener to mine. As far as I could detect, he liked to add a small amount of something like gin or rum to tone down the tea's natural flavor of root beer. After a little consideration, I decided he was free to add anything he wanted to his drink, be it honey, whiskey—or even turpentine, for that matter—as long as he didn't slip anything into mine without my knowledge.

For the next twenty minutes, Lariat made several phone calls while I scribbled a few notes in a little notebook I always carried with me. During a particularly frustrating exchange he had with a cake decorator named Chena Steward, Lariat walked over to a loudly humming, apartment-sized refrigerator that looked older than me, opened its squeaky door, and withdrew a bottle of Miller Lite. After a long swill that nearly rendered the bottle a dead soldier, he appeared calmer and better able to deal with Ms. Steward.

Despite the fact he now worked for me, I didn't feel as if I could insist he didn't drink on the job. After all, it wasn't as if he was employed as an air traffic controller or a neurosurgeon. In fact, I'd later realize it seemed as if the more intoxicated the man became, the better he functioned.

After he ended the call, Lariat removed another bottle of Miller Lite from the fridge. "Want a beer?"

"No thanks. Water would be nice if you have any."

Lariat reached back in the fridge and withdrew a bottle of water along with a brown paper bag. From the bag, he removed two wrapped sandwiches and several napkins, which he placed on the table in front of me. "Hope you like egg salad sandwiches."

"I love them, Lariat. But you didn't have to supply a lunch for me."

"No big deal. There's a deli a couple of doors down and I figured we'd get hungry after working for a while."

"Well, thank you very much. That was so thoughtful of you." I wasn't just spouting platitudes, either. I was touched by the guy's thoughtful actions, as they were totally unexpected. The sandwich looked delicious. Besides, I'd had nothing for breakfast other than my customary overdose of coffee. Unfortunately, the egg salad mixture was bitter and smelled as if it was on the wrong side of its expiration date. I wondered if he'd picked the sandwiches up at the deli that morning or two weeks earlier, but thought it would be rude to complain. I forced down one half of the sandwich and then wrapped up the other. "I'm going to save the rest for later this afternoon, or maybe have it for a light supper."

"Yeah. Good idea. I'll probably have the sandwich I picked up for Wendy as my supper."

Lariat polished off both halves of his sandwich and washed them down with yet another bottle of beer. He was feeling no pain by the time I departed. Apparently, his taste buds had been rendered useless by alcohol. Otherwise, I don't know how he'd be able to choke down an entire sandwich of such questionable freshness if his was as god-awful as mine had been.

I was a bit concerned about his alcohol consumption, although quite satisfied with the amount of work we'd accomplished and the sheer number of details we'd worked out in a little over three hours.

Before leaving, we agreed to meet up again at the Alexandria Inn on Friday morning. I made a mental note to have something on hand to serve him for lunch on Friday. Something much fresher, of course.

Although I didn't know it at the time, the meeting on Friday would be an eye-opening experience that would leave me once again doubting my decision to hire Lariat Jones.

I felt nauseated and light-headed that evening. At first I feared I was coming down with something. I didn't have the luxury of spare time to nurse a cold or the flu. I was relieved when I began to feel better by bedtime. Even though I realized it was probably the rancid sandwich that had upset my stomach, the thought crossed my mind that maybe Lariat Jones actually *had* slipped something into my tea when I wasn't looking. After all, it wasn't until he was refilling our cups for the second time that I observed him adding something to his. *Did that punk slip me a Mickey? And, if so, why?*

Having led a very sheltered life, I didn't know exactly what a "Mickey" was. However, from watching my share of movies and television shows, I knew slipping one to someone was a horrible thing to do. I also knew if Lariat Jones had sneaked something into my drink, the two of us were going to have words, and none of them were apt to be very pleasant. A few might even be of the four-letter variety!

Then I would be forced to fire him, despite the fact I would be left without a professional to help plan a wedding scheduled to occur in just three-and-a-half weeks.

As I slipped into bed that evening, I prayed. *Oh, Lord, please let the queasy feeling I had earlier be nothing more than something I ate—like half of the rancid sandwich—that didn't set well with me.* I would have settled for lactose intolerance at the moment since I did treat myself to a small vanilla ice cream cone on the way home from Lariat's office. I knew I didn't need the extra calories, but I desperately needed something to drown out the nasty taste the egg salad sandwich had left in my mouth.

EIGHT

W hen Friday morning dawned, I was feeling nervous and out of sorts. I snapped at Stone several times for no good reason, and felt compelled to apologize for taking my edginess out on him. Lariat Jones was due at the inn at ten, and I debated on how to approach the subject of whether or not he had added anything to my sassafras tea when we'd met on Wednesday. Stone had volunteered to deal with "the boy" himself, but I thought it was my responsibility.

At two minutes 'til ten, I heard Lariat's motorcycle pull up our long circular driveway. The fellow was prompt. I had to give him that much. I let him in through the door leading into the kitchen. He hung a black leather jacket on the inside knob of the door. The jacket had to be ungodly hot to wear in late July, but at least it would prevent the core of his body from road rash in the event of an accident.

"No helmet?" I asked.

"Nah. Don't need one."

"Oh, lucky you. Your skull must be lined with titanium. As you probably realize, they call people like you 'organ donors' and the world *does* need a lot of those. So I guess all's well that ends well."

Lariat looked at me as if I'd just asked him to go fling himself in front of a speeding bus. I felt obliged to clarify my remark. "Not that I'd want anything to happen to you. I'm just saying you should wear a helmet if you value your life. Not to mention, it is the law in Missouri. I'd at least like to keep you alive for the next month."

Clearly, my lame attempt at humor didn't make Lariat feel any better, which was evident by his next response. "Most of my route here is in Kansas, where there's no helmet law. I feel confident in rolling the dice on the few miles I travel in Missouri."

"Well, yes, but," I began. Before I could explain that although he might only be rolling the dice on a ticket for a few miles, he was rolling the dice on losing his life the entire trip, he interrupted.

"I'll try my best not to get splattered across I-29 until after August twenty-fifth. Okay?"

"Um, yes. You know I was just kidding, don't you?" As Lariat stared at me without responding, my hands turned clammy. I decided to forget about the helmet and get right to a conversation about the sassafras tea. The best way to do that was to dive right into it. "Before we get started, there's something we need to discuss."

"Sure," said Lariat. "But before I forget to ask, did you feel okay Wednesday evening?"

"As a matter of fact, no, I felt a bit..." I paused, knowing my tone sounded accusatory, but I couldn't let go of the idea he'd drugged me.

"Nauseated?" He finished my sentence when I hesitated. After I nodded, he said, "I figured as much. I was sicker than a dog that night. I'm not certain, but I think we might have gotten food poisoning from the egg salad sandwiches. I've heard eggs can go bad and make you ill. Now that I know you got sick, too, I'm going to bring it to the deli's attention. I'm so sorry I poisoned you. It wasn't intentional."

"You didn't poison me, Lariat. Apparently, a bad egg did. Literally. There's no way you could've known the sandwiches had already gone south when you purchased them." I didn't tell him the sour taste had been the reason I didn't eat the other half of my sandwich. In fact, I discarded it the moment I walked into the inn that afternoon.

Now my relief was two-fold. On one hand, I was happy I wouldn't have to fire my wedding planner; on the other, I was glad I didn't consume the entire toxic sandwich. It sounded as if Lariat had suffered a lot more from food poisoning than I had. I wasn't surprised, given the fact that he'd eaten a whole sandwich at lunchtime and mentioned he would eat the sandwich he'd purchased for Wendy for supper that evening.

"Well, again, I'm sorry it happened. So what did you want to discuss before we got busy?"

"Oh, that. Well. I. Just. Wanted." I spoke as if each word was a full sentence as I stalled to come up with a response. I certainly couldn't say, "I wanted to ask if you slipped me a Mickey." Finally, it hit me. I had a perfectly good response. "I wanted to let you know that once again Wendy's tied up this morning."

"Oh, so your daughter's into *that* kind of stuff." Lariat's reply was spoken in the form of a statement rather than a question. His expression remained deadpan as his sexual innuendo flew right over my head. My blank face must have made that apparent, as Lariat went on to explain. "You said she got 'tied up' and I thought…"

"Oh. Ha! Ha!" I said sarcastically. "I get it now. Not funny. Actually, she's busy at the county morgue because another victim of the meth-lab explosion a couple of days ago has died."

Though most of the time Lariat behaved like a perfect gentleman, his occasional inappropriate comments made me uncomfortable. I managed to set aside that disturbing feeling as we delved into our work. At lunchtime, I served pastrami on rye sandwiches. I drank a cup of coffee and offered Lariat one of Stone's Boulevard Pale Ale beers, which was brewed not far from Rockdale in Kansas City, Missouri. He enjoyed the first one so much, he helped himself to the last two beers in the fridge, as well. I wasn't concerned, as I didn't think three beers would incapacitate the slightly larger than average-sized man.

Later, I discovered he'd brought his own flasks of liquid refreshment to the meeting. Three of them, to be exact. He sipped on one after another until all three were empty.

Surprisingly, we accomplished a lot. We discussed everything from the color of the plastic cake plates to whether or not we wanted to rent a porta potty to put near the garden area where the wedding would take place. Even though delighted with the progress we were making, the thought crossed my mind that I was forking over good money to free me from even having to think about decisions of this sort. Yet here I was, deciding whether or not to place a crap shack within spitting distance of the refreshments.

"I think Wendy and Andy would prefer to have their guests use the restroom just inside the rear door of the inn. It's not that far of a walk. Besides, there's just something icky about having a tacky toilet next to the cake table," I said. Lariat agreed.

I looked over the growing list of questions I needed to ask the bride and groom. There were decisions I didn't feel were mine to make: whether to toast their union with champagne or sparkling water, whether the couple wanted to recite their own vows or not, and if they wanted to feed the guests a meal or wedding cake and punch at the reception.

They'd also need to choose who they wanted to stand at the guest book and gift table to make sure a fistful of congratulatory cards containing cash and checks didn't go missing—naturally under the guise of making sure all of the attendees remembered to sign the guest book.

The blank pages in my notebook were filling up fast. I had a list of questions I needed to ask Wendy, and another list of tasks to complete per Lariat's recommendations. I also had a third list of items that needed to be ordered or purchased. One more list and I was going to need to make a list of my lists so I could keep them all straight. Although I'd hoped all the meandering ducks would become the wedding planner's responsibility when I hired him, I didn't want them all running amok again just when they seemed to be under control. Just keeping Lariat on the right path was challenging enough.

I was happy we'd been making great progress that day, and was about to compliment Lariat on his proficiency. As I opened my mouth to speak, he suddenly slid off the seat of his chair and crumpled to the floor. He was clearly too inebriated to continue working. I let out an exasperated sigh before getting up to help Lariat back into his chair.

I didn't have the patience to deal with Mr. Jones if he was going to get drunk every time we collaborated. There'd be no more of this nonsense if I had anything to do with it. "From now on, I expect you to refrain from drinking on the job. We have a limited budget and a restricted time schedule. We don't have the luxury of wasting precious time because you are too blitzed to think straight. So, no more alcohol while working on this wedding."

"What?" Lariat looked as if he'd just woken up in the middle of a colonoscopy. "Awe you sewious, lady? I is not blizzed. I mean blitzed. I has just got me a little buzz on, that's all."

"Then I'd hate to see you totally trashed." Lariat stared at me with glazed eyes as I reprimanded him. "None-the-less, no drinking on the job or working while intoxicated. Understood? I'm concerned about you driving your motorcycle home."

"I'll be fine. Besides, I don't dwink and dwive," Lariat said as he removed the keys from his pocket and headed for the door.

"What do you mean you don't drink and drive? Are you planning to walk your motorcycle home?"

"Don't be widiculous. Like I told ya, I don't dwink and dwive. I only dwink at stop signs. Never while dwiving."

"What? Lariat, that's absurd! Give me your keys right now!"

Lariat stared at me silently, as if the proverbial cat was holding his tongue hostage with a pair of needle-nose pliers. I shook my head, and continued. "Drinking only when you're stopped at a stop sign does not make you a safe driver or any less inebriated. It only takes one miscalculation to cause a tragic accident. I won't have that on my conscience, and I don't think you want the death of an innocent bystander on your conscience, either."

Before he could object, I snatched the key ring out of his hand and shoved them in the front pocket of my jeans.

"Hey, whatcha doing?"

"Keeping you alive. I'll arrange for an Uber driver to take you home. You can collect your bike tomorrow."

He grumbled and squabbled with me and finally came to the conclusion I wasn't going to budge. "All's wight, fine."

"I'll pick you up in the morning on our way to meet the cake decorator. We'll retrieve your bike afterward."

Before he could object to my decision, he leaned his head back and passed out colder than a turkey thawing out in the kitchen sink. Five minutes later, it took three of us—Stone, the Uber driver, and me—to physically load Lariat into the backseat of the driver's Nissan Xterra. We basically had to stuff him in the car the way one would stuff dressing into the aforementioned turkey. By the time we returned to the kitchen, Stone was madder than a rabid raccoon.

"That drunken bum's the best professional planner you could find to organize the kids' wedding?"

"Yes. He was. Unfortunately, drunken bum or not, Lariat's the *only* one I could find. By the time we thought about hiring one, it was too late to get any of the other local wedding planners. The rest of them were already booked." My last remark was only an assumption on my part, but Stone had no way of knowing I hadn't placed a call to every wedding planner in northwestern Missouri.

"It's no surprise this clown was still available. He wasn't booked like the rest of them for good reason."

Stone shook his head and walked out of the kitchen. I'd known it wasn't a good idea to ask for Stone's assistance in getting Lariat into the Xterra, but he was the only other person in the inn at the time. I also knew Stone was right about Lariat, who was probably more trouble than he was worth. Still, I felt a little ticked off that I'd been chastised for hiring him. I looked out the window just in time to see the Uber driver wave at me and start his engine.

What in the world have I gotten myself into? I wondered as I watched the Xterra pull away with my wedding planner sprawled across the back seat. *If nothing else,* I told myself, *at least Lariat's not as apt to become an organ donor today as he would've been had I not confiscated the keys to his Harley.*

NINE

"Oh, no. Seriously?" I asked. I was disappointed the next morning to learn I'd be on my own again that day. I was beginning to think Wendy disliked the idea of planning a wedding even more than I did.

"Yes. It's one of those migraines I get occasionally."

Wendy had awakened with a blinding headache. She had been prone to migraines since her teenage years. More often than not, they were triggered by stressful periods in her life. She apologized, and I assured her I didn't mind working alone with the wedding planner.

"All that matters is that you rest and let that migraine subside as quickly as possible. I know how agonizing they can be. I can handle this by myself as long as you trust me to make decisions regarding the wedding cake and flowers. Those are the two things Lariat and I planned to tackle today."

"Of course I trust your judgment. And Mom? Thanks so much for all your help."

"My pleasure, sweetheart. Now go rest." I didn't want to alarm her by telling her I'd likely be cutting Lariat Jones loose that morning, opting to take on full responsibility of the wedding planning myself. After all, Wendy was already suffering from an overabundance of nervous tension and it seemed as if I'd had to be present for every tedious decision anyway, despite the good money I was paying for a wedding planner. Oh, well. At least I had peace of mind knowing no critical element would be overlooked. I guess you could say I wanted Wendy and Andy to get hitched without a hitch.

As I had a penchant for getting lost in shopping mall parking lots, I followed the driving instructions from the portable GPS device Wendy had given me the previous Christmas to use in Ladybug. She'd said I was the only person she knew who routinely circled a roundabout a minimum of three times before figuring out which exit to take. As I drove, I practiced the speech I planned to give Lariat Jones when I reached his home. I had every intention of explaining to him that after careful deliberation, I'd decided to settle up for the hours he'd worked to date, including a reasonable "severance bonus", and then we would go our separate ways. I'd be kind, but resolute.

Not certain if the address Mr. Jones had given me would lead to a homeless shelter, an apartment above a biker bar, or even a vacant lot, I knew instinctively it would not be a modest home in a well-established neighborhood, or a two-bedroom unit in a newly-developed condo complex.

His office had been in a run-down part of town; small and scarcely furnished, but clean as a new pin and adequate-enough in size to serve its purpose. I couldn't know for sure, but had a gut feeling the man depended on the income from this job to make ends meet, or at least support his beer habit.

Did Lariat have a family to support, young mouths to feed? Without knowing if he had any children, I worried about them and the role model they had to look up to. Did these children I envisioned depend on my contract with Lariat for their next meal? Lord, I hoped not.

I took a slow, deep breath and I realized I had let my imagination run wild when it should have been locked up tightly in an invisible, but secure, cage somewhere. I concentrated on following the GPS's directions to block out further unwanted thoughts.

I made a determined decision not to let a sense of bleeding-heart compassion interfere with my plans to sever ties with Lariat. Wendy might trust my judgment, but she'd never forgive me if I allowed anyone to screw up the most important day of her life. Of that, I *was* certain.

As I neared the location Lariat had written on a post-it note, my hands trembled and my breathing quickened. I wondered what I'd do if the GPS led me to a large cardboard box under a rarely traversed railroad bridge on the outskirts of town, and announced, "You have reached your destination."

Don't get me wrong. My heart went out to individuals in situations like that. My parents instilled in me a sense of compassion, and I routinely donated to homeless shelters, food pantries, and other underprivileged causes. In fact, the previous Christmas I sponsored a young family whose breadwinner had been deployed to Afghanistan. It's just that I knew myself well enough to know I could never fire a guy who obviously needed every dime I paid him.

My only other option would be to keep on driving. I could hightail it back to the safety of my home and "break up" with Lariat by text, the way many young people ended relationships in this day and age. I'd mail Lariat a very generous check for services already rendered and finish planning the wedding on my own using whatever assistance Wendy could give me.

Imagine my surprise when I pulled my car to the curb in front of 1022 Nassau Drive, a posh-looking, newly constructed mansion. Even as I walked to the stately entrance and rang the bell, I considered the possibility that I'd been given the wrong address. A gentleman in a three-piece suit opened the door of the impressive home. By his attire, I assumed he was a butler. The very idea Lariat could afford hired help threw me for a loop.

"Can I help you?" His piercing blue eyes were unwavering and he instantly reminded me of Rutger Hauer in his role as a psychopathic killer in the movie *The Hitcher*.

"Um, yes. I'm looking for Lariat. Lariat Jones? He gave me this address." The man silently stared at me for several long moments.

"Sorry, ma'am. You have the wrong address. Wait, isn't he that fellow who butchers cattle and deer?" I noticed the well-built man had yet to blink since opening the door.

"Uh, I don't know. I don't think so. The man I'm looking for is a wedding planner."

"Yes, I think he does that, too. I believe you'll find him at 2210 Nassau Drive, but I could be mistaken."

"Hmm. Why would he give me the wrong address?" It was meant to be a rhetorical question, but the man, who was apparently the homeowner, answered it anyway.

"Perhaps Mr. Jones suffers from dyslexia."

Or an alcohol addiction. "Perhaps."

"Why don't you come inside? We'll look up his address on my computer."

I followed him into the home's foyer as if he were the Pied Piper, rather than an intense-looking stranger whose demeanor gave me the willies. It hadn't occurred to me I could look up the address on my cell phone. Why, I'll never know.

I scrutinized the framed paintings lining the walls as I followed him down a long, very wide, and dimly lit hallway. To my dismay, the paintings were horrifying. One depicted a naked woman lashed to the trunk of a large tree with far-reaching roots that ran across the surface of the ground. Surrounding the terrified woman was a pack of salivating creatures I can only describe as centaurs, except that their lower halves looked more canine than equine. Draped around the woman's neck was a serpent with its fangs bared, ready to strike. And if that hadn't been chilling enough, the lady's heart was exposed, dripping blood down her abdomen. Egad!

When the man looked over his shoulder and caught me staring at a watercolor portraying bestiality between a man and a mythological-looking unicorn, he stopped, "Oh, I see you're admiring my art work. Every painting is an original created by yours truly. That one happens to be my personal favorite."

Holy crap! Because I couldn't bring myself to say I wasn't "admiring" his paintings by any stretch of the imagination, nor could I force myself to call it "art" work, I merely responded, "Your style is quite unusual."

"Yes?" By the inquiring tone in his voice, I could tell he was waiting for me to expound on my reaction to his work. So I obliged him.

"Bizarre, actually, and a bit unsettling."

"Good. That's my goal." The look he shot me made my blood run colder than glacier runoff. It was a self-satisfied smirk. "I strive to be inimitable and entice people to reflect."

Reflect? Reflect on what? The darkest imaginable side of humanity? I wanted to ask, but I was already uncomfortable enough. Instead I replied, "Your paintings are definitely one of a kind."

Just then the man, without taking his eyes off me, reached to his right and opened the door to a room more dimly lit than the hall-way. In fact, the only source of light in the room could be traced to a single flickering candle. In a freakishly peculiar voice, he said, "Join me in my studio for a few minutes, and I'll show you where I get my inspiration."

If a representative from the Guinness World Records company had timed me with a stopwatch at that moment, my name would be listed in the next edition of their publication for the fastest land-speed time ever recorded by a woman. I fled down the hall, out the front door—which he'd locked behind us—descended the porch stairs (touching only two of the seven steps), jumped in my car and drove six blocks down Nassau Drive in the time it'd take most folks to say, "No, thank you. I'd rather eat a dozen chocolate-covered tarantulas than spend another second in this ghastly place."

When I reached the sixteen-hundred block of Nassau Drive, I pulled over to catch my breath and regain at least some measure of composure. As one might expect, my vision had been glued to the rear-view mirror the entire six blocks. I feared the creepy dude would chase me down, determined to show me where his spine-chilling inspiration came from. Any squirrel with bad timing that chose to cross the street as I raced down Nassau Drive was road kill

waiting to happen. Fortunately, no squirrel or any other living crea-
ture crossed my path during my wild ride.

I knew I shouldn't have let the man scare the crap out of me the
way he did. After all, I didn't carry my Pink Lady—a pink-handled
.380 caliber pistol—in my fanny pack for no reason. I had qualified
for a conceal-and-carry permit the previous year and routinely
carried the Sig Sauer P238 for self-protection. God knows I'd never
be able to shoot another human being, no matter how dangerous or
despicable he was. Had the man threatened me in any way, I'd have
had to hope he wouldn't decide to roll the dice and do something to
make me actually have to fire it, because I'm not sure I could have.

TEN

W hen my heart rate slowed to the point I didn't feel as if I were on the verge of cardiac arrest, I pulled out into the driving lane and drove another half-dozen blocks west. I hoped the freaky artist had given me the right address for Lariat. Despite my shaken state, I noticed with each passing block, the neighborhoods became increasingly dismal looking.

When I reached the 2200 block of Nassau Drive, which consisted predominantly of older mobile homes, I found the trailer located at 2210. It appeared to be one of the newer ones on the block, albeit still manufactured well before electric slide-outs were the norm. His eight-by-forty-foot park-model travel trailer had a wooden sign in front which had *LBJ Wedding Planning, Shoe Repair, and Meat Processing, Inc.* carved into it. Apparently, Lariat worked out of his home at times, or at least used his minuscule front yard to advertise his various businesses.

His home wasn't an oversized mansion like the one twelve blocks east of it, but it wasn't a gigantic Frigidaire box, either. Rather, it was a cute, well-maintained home on wheels that sat in the middle of a small, equally well-manicured lot. The raised flower beds flanking the walkway to his front porch were immaculate and contained some of the most colorful plants I'd ever seen.

I hesitantly knocked on the door, still a bit flustered from my earlier encounter. When no one responded, I knocked harder. "Hello? Mr. Jones? Is anybody home?" After a lengthy pause, I heard rustling inside.

Finally, a scratchy voice shouted impatiently, "Give me a minute!"

It was roughly five minute later before he opened the door of his trailer. He wore the same outfit he'd had on when he'd been stuffed like an overloaded suitcase into the Uber driver's backseat the previous afternoon. "Oh, yeah. Hey! How ya doing?"

"Um, fine, Mr. Jones. More importantly, how are you doing this morning? You look a little rough around the edges. Do you recall we arranged to meet the cake decorator and florist today before you blacked out?"

"Um, yes. Of course." Lariat looked confused. I wasn't sure he even remembered who I was, much less what plans we'd made the previous day.

"Did I wake you?"

Lariat surprised me by leaning forward and placing a quick peck on my cheek. His breath reeked of alcohol. If the blue-eyed creep at the last house had done that, and I'd somehow been able to grow big enough *cojones* to utilize my Pink Lady, he might have ended up becoming Wendy's next customer in the county morgue.

Lariat apologized. "Sorry, my alarm clock must be broken. Do you mind stepping inside while I get some coffee? Gotta get rid of the cobwebs, you know. Probably need to put some clean clothes on, too."

And gargle a little mouthwash, I wanted to add.

For several reasons, I wanted to tell him I'd wait on the porch, or better yet, recite my spiel about cutting ties with him and skedaddle out of the sketchy-looking neighborhood. Unfortunately, my need for a caffeine fix rose to the occasion. Though I'd made a mistake and put myself in danger by blindly entering the artist's home, I didn't think that would be the case with Lariat. I did have the gun as a last resort, I reminded myself. "Do you happen to have an extra cup of joe for me? I could use a boost of energy myself."

For a bachelor, Lariat seemed to be very particular about his surroundings, but his fastidiousness was clearly not driven by an obsessive-compulsive disorder. Someone with OCD would not have allowed a blood-stained apron to be haphazardly draped across the picnic table outside. The table, stained with several dried-up pools of blood, sat next to a shed that looked to be decades younger than the trailer.

You'd think that observation would have factored into my questionable decision to come inside for a cup of coffee. But I pushed my uneasiness aside. I attributed the bloody apron to the fact Lariat apparently butchered farm and game animals in his spare time. According to the weird dude who lived a few blocks down Nassau Drive and the sign in Lariat's front yard, Mr. Jones also resoled shoes when he wasn't busy doing something else from the odd mixture of tricks in his bag.

Lariat assured me he had plenty of coffee, and I followed him into a neat and tidy living room area. The kitchen looked spotless, as well. The trailer was simply furnished, but it was sanitary and well-kept, which I considered much more important.

I sipped the tepid, but aromatic, brew while sitting on a booth-styled bench at his kitchen table. "Lariat, I'm a little confused by the sign out front."

"Confused? Why?"

"Well," I began nervously, "I don't understand the name of your business."

"What's to not understand?" he asked. "Oh, LBJ. The 'B' stands for Bernard, my middle name."

He had totally misread my befuddlement. "That's nice, but it's the part about the shoe repair and meat processing that baffles me."

Lariat's complacent expression was part arrogance and part amusement. "Those are just a couple of the services I offer. I also prepare income taxes in the spring and I've been known to tat a doily or two on occasion, as well. You didn't think I was a one-trick pony, did you?"

The tatting shuttle I'd noticed on his kitchen counter convinced me the man wasn't joking. I'd originally thought it was the pendant from a necklace. Unable to come up with a response, I merely shook my head. Lariat's bag of tricks had just become even odder. It seemed like a strange combination, but it stood to reason that the more services he had to offer, the more money he was apt to bring in. At that point, nothing about this eccentric individual would surprise me. He could tell me he'd played the lead part in the local production of *Annie Get Your Gun* and I wouldn't be totally taken aback.

"By the way, you wrote down the wrong address, and the oddball who lives at 1022 Nassau Drive scared the living daylights out of me." I held the post-it note up so he could see the incorrect address he'd given to me.

"Oh. Sorry about that. I must have had a bigger buzz on than I realized."

"Buzz on? Seriously? Buzz on?" I repeated. "You were stinking blitzed! Remember? That's why I had to drive here to begin with. Your bike is at my house because I took the keys from you. And it's fortunate for you that I did, because a couple of minutes later, you passed out cold."

"Oh. Well, that must be why I don't remember driving home or where I parked my bike."

"Like it or not, Mr. Jones, I have a problem with that. We discussed your drinking last night, but I'm sure you don't remember the conversation."

Lariat's blank stare convinced me I'd been correct. I tried not to make eye contact with him as I mentally prepared to explain why I'd decided to opt out of our agreement to have him plan my daughter's wedding. It suddenly crossed my mind that firing him probably would have been a better topic to bring up *before* I entered the man's home.

I was a nervous wreck as I attempted to broach the subject, certain I wore my anxiety like a fur coat.

After studying me for a few seconds, Lariat asked, "Are you aware that you drink entirely too much?"

"*I* drink too much?" My mouth dropped open as if there was a dentist leaning over me trying to extract an abscessed molar. "Did *you* just accuse *me* of drinking too much?"

"Yes. Although I'd prefer to think of it more as an observation than an accusation. That much caffeine can't be good for you. I can tell by how uptight and cranky you are this morning that you've already had way too much coffee. I think you should forego the rest of that cup so we can knuckle down and get to work."

"Um. Okay." I looked down into my half-empty coffee cup like a kid who'd had his hand slapped for reaching into a cookie jar half-an-hour before suppertime. I'd actually been about to ask if I could top off my cup, but now I felt obligated to pour what was left in it down the drain. I felt like a heroin addict who'd just had the syringe yanked out of his vein before the drug had been injected.

Lariat excused himself and walked down the hallway to a bedroom at the rear of the mobile home. After he'd ambled off, I gulped down a couple more quaffs of coffee. And then a couple more. When I realized the cup was nearly empty, I got up and walked to the Mr. Coffee machine on the counter. I refilled the cup to about where it'd been when Lariat has exited the room. He returned to the kitchen looking quite spiffy just as I sat back down.

"I told the cake decorator, Chena Steward, we'd be at her shop by ten," he said. "That gives us less than twenty minutes to get there. I despise tardiness, so we'd best be getting on our way. It's a fifteen-minute walk from here."

In the blink of an eye, Lariat had morphed from a hung-over bum into a proficient businessman. The same coffee that Lariat seemed to think had made me an uptight grumpster had cleared the cobwebs from his head and transformed his personality. His sudden and unexpected professional demeanor had me questioning the wisdom of firing him.

So, rather than begin my well-practiced "I'm sorry, but I have to let you go" speech, I said, "Sorry if I've been a little crabby this morning. We can take my car to Ms. Steward's shop if you'd rather not walk."

"If it's all the same with you, I'd prefer to walk." Lariat gave me the once-over as he spoke, which made me both uncomfortable and self-conscious. I was also disappointed I couldn't guzzle the coffee I'd just poured into my cup without feeling humiliated by Lariat's reproachful glare. Grouchy or not, I could have used a little more caffeine in my system. After the heart-stopping *Fear Factor* episode I'd just experienced a mile down Nassau Drive, I felt as if I was still a quart low. I set my half-full cup in the kitchen sink and stood up after Lariat added, "I think the exercise would be beneficial for both of us."

Not sure whether or not to be offended by his remark, I instinctively reached down and tugged on my shirt, trying to pull it down over my thighs as much as possible. I'd gained seven or eight pounds since my marriage to Stone, and I hadn't exactly looked like Twiggy before our vows. Okay, to be perfectly honest, it was more like ten or eleven pounds. But who's counting?

Lariat's remark brought to mind one of the things I loved most about my husband. He carried an extra twenty or so pounds on his frame. For adequate insulation, he maintained. And, as many women may agree, chunkiness absolutely loves company.

"Not that you need the exercise, by any means," Lariat added, having noticed my instinctive reaction to his comment. "I know a lot of ladies my age who'd kill to have your figure."

How could I have ever even considered canceling my contract with this man? Granted, he had a bad drinking habit. But who was I to throw stones? My consumption of coffee would likely kill me years before his consumption of alcohol did him in. Not only had he showed concern about my own dangerous drinking habit, which I'll admit is a full-fledged caffeine addiction, but he possessed loads of charm and charisma.

Okay, "loads of charm and charisma" might be pushing it. But the man seemed oblivious to the extra baggage on my frame—which had congregated primarily in my caboose region—and for that, he gets extra credit.

"Walking would be my preference, too. Let's get on our way, Mr. Jones. We have an appointment to keep, and we don't want to keep Ms. Steward waiting."

"It's Lariat. Remember? I'm a relatively young freelancer, not an accountant on the brink of retirement."

"As you wish. Let's quit standing around blathering, Lariat, and hit the bricks."

ELEVEN

"Good morning, darling," Chena Steward greeted Lariat the moment we walked through the door of her bakery. Lariat responded with a quick embrace and had to stand on his tiptoes to land a peck on Chena's cheek. She was a tall, thin woman in her early thirties with short, jet black hair. It must've taken a lot of time and hair gel to make her hair look as wild and unruly as it did. The style made "bed head" look tame, and it was surprisingly attractive on her. If I had tried to pull off the same hairstyle, I'd have Stone calling me "Minnie" or asking if I'd stuck my finger in a light socket.

I could detect pock marks on the woman's face, despite the thick layer of makeup. Chena had apparently suffered from severe acne as a teenager. Lariat mentioned on the walk over that the former All-Collegiate basketball star had played power forward for the Kansas State Lady Wildcats during her three-year stint in college. She'd dropped out after her junior year and gone on to study at the Kearney Culinary Academy, fifty miles southeast of her hometown of Atchison.

Like Rockdale, Atchison was a small town and pretty much everyone who lived there knew everyone else. This was especially true for people whose occupations brought them together frequently: for instance, a habitual criminal and a bails bondsman, a celebrity and a plastic surgeon, or a wedding planner and a cake decorator. With that in mind, it wasn't surprising Lariat and Chena were well-acquainted.

Men can sometimes be pretty ignorant when it comes to a woman's emotions, and Lariat was a prime example. The longing in Ms. Steward's eyes and her demeanor indicated she clearly wanted to form a closer, more intimate bond with Lariat Jones. Lariat, on the other hand, didn't seem to have a clue about the depth of her desire. His hug and peck on her cheek were given out of habit, I was sure. He probably kissed the cheek of every woman he interacted with, from his dental hygienist to the lady who bagged his groceries at the local supermarket. As a matter of fact, he had greeted me the same way less than a half-hour earlier, and I was under no delusions he harbored any romantic feelings for me, despite the sexual innuendos that dripped off his tongue like excess saliva.

Chena still wore a love-struck look on her face when Lariat introduced her to me. "Chena, this is my client, Lexie Starr. We're here about the Van Patten nuptials on August twenty-fifth. As we discussed over the phone, we don't have a lot of time to sit on our thumbs, so we'd like to get the wedding cake ordered this morning."

"Van Patten, as in Andy Van Patten?" Chena asked.

"Yes. That's the one." I replied with pride, even though she'd addressed Lariat when she asked the question. Curious, I asked, "Do you know Andy?"

"Not personally. One of his groomsmen, Gunnar Wilde, is my ex-fiancé. As I'm sure you know, Andy owns the ranch next to Gunnar's. Gunnar, incidentally, broke off our engagement after Andy introduced him to Mattie Hill, who I believe is also in the wedding party."

"Yes. She's my daughter's maid of honor and her closest friend."

"Really?" she asked. "How interesting."

I didn't know what else to say. I hadn't liked the expression on Chena's face as she'd spoken. However, considering the difference in height between this former basketball star and Gunnar Wilde, I had to think his new girlfriend, Mattie Hill, was a much better match for him. Gunnar barely surpassed my height by a couple of inches, and I felt like "Jeff" to Chena's "Mutt" as I stood next to her. Even though Chena probably only viewed Lariat as potential rebound material, I felt as though she and him would make a better pair than she and Gunnar. *If you think you can use Lariat to make your ex jealous, Chena, you have another think coming,* I thought. *Gunnar is totally smitten with Mattie. He thinks of you as a dodged bullet.*

I mused silently as Lariat chatted with the cake decorator. Since moving to Atchison over a year ago, Andy had been renovating the old farm house on the cattle ranch he'd purchased. Working on the house and taking care of the livestock filled most of his waking hours, so he'd made few new friends in the area.

After becoming acquainted with Gunnar, Andy had introduced his new neighbor to Wendy's best friend, Mattie Hill, and the two couples had gone out on a double-date. Gunnar and Mattie had clicked immediately, and were growing closer with each passing day.

Wendy had chosen a co-worker, Sara Short, as her second bridesmaid. Sara was employed at the county morgue as a forensic scientist, and she and Wendy had bonded over their work since Wendy's recent appointment as the county's head medical examiner. When Andy had needed a groomsman to offset Sara, he'd asked Gunnar to fill the position. Sara and Gunnar, Bubba and Mattie, and Wyatt Johnston and Veronica Prescott rounded out the designated wedding party. In my unbiased opinion, a finer group of individuals would be difficult to find.

As my daughter's best friend, Mattie was almost like a second daughter to me. She spent as much time at the inn as Wendy. Understandably, wherever Mattie went, so went her current boyfriend. Gunnar had made it clear to me during an exchange one day over coffee that he'd felt blessed when he met Mattie and couldn't break it off with his previous girlfriend fast enough, whom he'd never mentioned by name. Referencing the old *Roadrunner* cartoons, his actual words were, "I felt like the roadrunner who'd barely missed being crushed to death by an oversized anvil falling from the sky." This was not something I wanted to share with

Gunnar's former fiancé, however, so after Chena begrudgingly mentioned Gunnar's new relationship with Mattie again, I simply replied, "I'm so sorry about your broken engagement."

"Oh, yeah. I'm sure you are."

Chena glared at me while tugging on her left ear lobe. I suddenly felt very uncomfortable with the idea of her being involved in any way with Wendy and Andy's impending union. "Maybe it'd be best if we didn't…"

Lariat turned and glared at me. He excused us for a moment and whispered to me, "Do you have another cake decorator in mind who isn't already booked solid for the entire month of August?"

"Well, no, but—"

"Neither do I. I assure you that, despite her connection to a member of the wedding party, Chena will do an exceptional job on the cake and you won't be disappointed. There's no reason she and Gunnar will even have to cross paths. Don't let something like this screw up a beautiful wedding."

I consented, knowing his assertion was no doubt correct. We rejoined Chena and I said, "Okay, let's get down to business."

"All right." Chena motioned us toward a couple of chairs positioned in front of her desk. She pulled a price list from the top drawer. "As you can see, the base price is five-hundred dollars for a three-tiered, single-flavored basic wedding cake."

"Five-hundred dollars?" I asked. Even though I knew I was comparing apples to oranges when it came to wedding cakes, I thought back to the sixty dollars I'd paid in total for two sheet cakes, chocolate and yellow crème, when I married Stone. Granted, I'd purchased them from Pete's Pantry, our local grocery store, and there were no fancy designs or decorations on them whatsoever. However, our guests had gobbled them down just as much as they would have the five-hundred dollar cake Chena Steward proposed to deliver.

"Yes, five-hundred dollars. Is that a problem?"

"Um, no, but what do you mean by 'base price'?"

Chena frowned and crossed her arms over her chest. "This is not a one-size-fits-all type of business, ma'am."

"Yes, I understand that, but—"

Chena sighed. "Five hundred covers the basic three-tiered cake. There's an additional fee if you want a premium flavor, such as red velvet. Fondant is costlier than the classic butter cream icing. Hand-piped lacy designs are more expensive than decorating the cake with ribbons or flowers. There is a set charge for delivery, set-up, utensils, and so forth. And, understandably, there's a fee for expedited services if the cake is ordered less than thirty days before the event. Since there are only twenty-six days until the wedding, that fee will be added to the base price."

"Naturally," I replied dryly. "And the fee for 'expedited services'?"

"Only an extra hundred dollars."

Only an extra hundred? I wanted to ask if she normally began baking a wedding cake a full month prior to the ceremony, but knew I couldn't pull it off without sounding sarcastic, which of course is exactly the way I'd have meant it. Lariat had warned me Chena Steward was not the cheapest baker in town, but was the only one we'd be able to hire at such a late date. I didn't want to disappoint my daughter, so I held my tongue and replied as pleasantly as I could. "Yes. I understand."

"One-hundred dollars for expedited services is actually quite reasonable," Chena said defensively. My incredulous expression had clearly given my true feelings away. Again, Chena pulled on her left ear lobe as she spoke.

"I see. So am I to understand that your justification for charging an 'expedited services' fee is that you need to begin preparing this cake immediately, even though the ceremony is still twenty-six days away?"

I'd tried to remain congenial, but my tongue had a mind of its own. Her defensive reaction had rubbed me the wrong way and caused me to feel defensive, as well—about *her* unwarranted defensiveness. Suddenly, I completely understood Gunnar's falling-anvil remark.

"Of course not! That's not the point!" Chena tugged on that poor ear lobe again, which appeared to hang quite a bit lower than the right one from all of the stretching it endured. In anger, she repeated herself. "That's not the point!"

"Just out of curiosity then, what *is* the point? Twenty-six days seems like plenty of notice to prepare a wedding cake that isn't needed until August twenty-fifth."

Chena snarled as she spat out her response. "I do have to purchase the necessary ingredients and decorating paraphernalia in advance, you know."

I swore I saw spittle shoot from her mouth and land on my shirt sleeve. I instinctively swiped my sleeve against my denim jeans and tried not to gag. I'd have to remember to toss the shirt directly into the washing machine when I returned home.

I looked up and spoke as calmly and collectively as I could. "Wal-Mart is open 24/7. Jot down a list of the items you need and I'll pick them up and deliver them to you this afternoon. That way, you'll have twenty-five days left over from your allotted time for last-minute shopping."

Lariat suddenly looked up from his feet, which he'd been staring at throughout our heated exchange. His eyes were wide, as if just noticing his right shoe was from a different pair than his left. I could tell he was afraid a cat fight was about to break out right in front of him. I had no intention of engaging in a physical confrontation with anyone, but I also wasn't going to let some too-tall, two-bit cake decorator take advantage of me. I felt confident Lariat would defend me should Chena decide to slam dunk me into the oversized trash can next to her display counter.

I couldn't shake the feeling Chena was being vindictive because Wendy's maid of honor had snatched Gunnar, Chena's ex-fiancé, out from under her pitchfork. It fleetingly crossed my mind that Chena might feel compelled to tamper with the cake batter in order to exact revenge. The rest of the wedding guests who might partake of the cake would just be considered unfortunate, but necessary, collateral damage. I shook the silly notion from my mind.

I looked squarely at Lariat. "Perhaps it would be best if we looked into other options before we make our decision."

The wedding planner spoke in a voice so low I had to lean in toward him to hear what he had to say. "Like I already told you, she's our *only* option. Trust me, if I had another, I'd have considered it first. For that matter, if I had enough space to personally take on a cake-decorating business, I would. But as you saw this morning, I don't have the luxury of a chef's kitchen."

I shrugged my shoulders and shook my head. I *did* have a chef's kitchen. Could I take a cake-decorating class and attempt to make the wedding cake myself? No, I couldn't. I routinely left bread in the toaster until it was black as tar and smoldering. I couldn't be trusted with something as important as a wedding cake. Wendy would be horrified if I even suggested baking the cake myself. "Oh, all right. Guess we have no choice but to bite the bullet on this one."

I had been skeptical of Chena Steward from the moment I'd laid eyes on her. Her ghostly white complexion reminded me of a vampire that couldn't tolerate sunshine, and her rail-thin body looked as if she had never eaten one bite of cake, or anything else that contained more than a gram of sugar. I'd always found it hard to trust extremely skinny bakers, cooks, or chefs. In my opinion, hiring an ultra-thin baker is akin to investing your life savings with an investment broker who'd just declared bankruptcy for the third time. Of course, that could just be my jealousy talking.

Lariat turned his attention from me, whom he'd clearly deduced was a lost cause, to the cake decorator. "Chena, is the expedited service fee really necessary? I can't imagine you'd want to lose a potential client or get a reputation of gouging customers."

Chena let out a dramatic sigh and looked toward the ceiling in absolute silence. She appeared to be asking the powers-that-be for enough patience to deal with the difficult customer in front of her. "Oh, all right. I'd hate to pass this opportunity up. Therefore, I'll forego the last-minute fee this once since it *is* only a few days over the thirty-day cut-off period."

That's mighty big of you, I wanted to say. Instead, knowing this woman was our only option short of me taking cake-decorating lessons, I uttered, "Thanks. I appreciate the kind gesture. The kids are operating on a limited budget for this event, so I'd like to—"

Without letting me finish my remark, Chena asked, "Do you have any idea what the average cost of a wedding is these days?"

"Um, well, no. Can't say that I have that statistic on the tip of my tongue." I didn't say so out loud, but I would have wagered that fact *would* be on the tip of Stone's tongue had he been there. He would've surely read or heard the statistic somewhere and, like everything else, stored the information into the steel trap of his brain.

"The average cost of a wedding is upwards of thirty-three thousand dollars." Chena gave the answer with a self-righteous smirk.

"Holy crap! Thirty-three thousand? For a wedding? Seriously? That's plum ridiculous. The average cost of my two weddings came closer to twelve hundred!" I exclaimed in shock.

Once again, I knew I shouldn't compare apples to oranges. My first wedding occurred back in the dark ages and was hardly elaborate even by 1985 standards. The second took place on Stone's property with a handful of our closest family and friends present. I'd worn an attractive but simple dress, and had only my daughter and Andy standing up for us. A simple reception followed the exchange of vows. It had been an inexpensive, but beautiful, affair.

"Those weddings must have been real dandies," Chena replied after a derisive laugh. I didn't appreciate her sarcasm, but was unable to come up with a fitting retort.

"Okay, ladies. There's no time for chasing rainbows." Lariat seized the moment and clapped his hands, lest the pause in our contentious discussion was short-lived. "Let's decide what kind of cake we want for Wendy and Andy's reception and get it ordered so we can make our eleven-o'clock appointment with the florist."

Chena and I both nodded in reluctant agreement as we stared into each other's eyes, not wanting to be the first one to blink or look away. This was not the auspicious beginning I'd been hoping for. Finally, I took the high road and lowered my gaze.

"Okay, fine," I said. "We'd like a simple triple-layer, white cake with minimal frills and extras. Pretty, but not elaborate. Like I said, we are trying to keep costs down as much as possible so Andy doesn't have to get a second mortgage on his cattle ranch to finance their wedding."

"Okay, then. That's good. That's very good, Ms. Starr," Lariat said in an obvious attempt to calm me. He had correctly sensed that my last remark was a jab at Chena's prices. Before the cake decorator had a chance to reply, he pointed to the form attached to the clipboard in front of her. "Did you get that? Maybe you should write it down before you forget."

With a huff, Chena said, "She's chosen to order a plain white cake for the most important day of her daughter's life. Who could forget that? Trust me, I won't forget."

Lariat grabbed my arm before I could poke Chena Steward in the eye with one of the sample cake knives laid out on the bakery's front counter. He briskly steered me toward the door, and, over his shoulder, said, "I'll get with you later on the price."

There had to be tiny puffs of smoke floating out of my ears as we exited the bakery shop. I was surprised Lariat didn't mention it because I could distinctly feel the heat blistering my eardrums. Perhaps he had noticed but decided not to stoke the still smoldering embers.

As we made our way down the sidewalk toward Lily's-in-Bloom Floral Shop, located three blocks down the street, I wondered if Chena had taken her frustration out on her left ear lobe. She reminded me of a woman who could have been a defendant in the Salem witch trials, and I felt certain she was already visualizing in her mind the voodoo doll she was going to create in my likeness.

Later that evening, I turned on my computer and researched the cost of wedding cakes. Having never ordered a wedding cake from a professional decorator before, I thought Chena Steward's prices were outlandish, way beyond what one would expect to pay. I soon discovered her prices were no more than the average going rate for a three-tiered decorated cake. I felt a momentary sense of embarrassment for the way I'd behaved in the woman's shop. I wrote my behavior off as an overreaction to sticker shock and vowed to restrain myself from responding like that in the future. I'd just have to learn to accept the high cost of getting hitched in this day and age and pray I'd never have to help plan another wedding again in my lifetime.

If for some reason, Wendy and Andy's marriage did not last until death they did part, or my own death—whichever came first—I'd do my damnedest to steer Wendy toward joining a convent. With her beautiful face, ideal height and slender physique, she'd look stunning in an all-black habit.

TWELVE

When Lariat and I arrived at Lily's-in-Bloom Floral Shop a few minutes later, we were surprised to find Wendy chatting with the owner, Lily Franks.

"I feel bad," she said, "for piling so much of the responsibility on your shoulders, Mom, so I decided to meet you guys here."

"I'm so glad you could join us, honey." I was touched by Wendy's concern. When asked if she felt better, she assured us her headache had abated.

Lariat's hangover had completely worn off too and he stood motionless beside me with a blank expression. I had to introduce myself to the floral shop owner because Lariat seemed tongue-tied. Lily's lovely aquamarine eyes seemed to sparkle as we shook hands.

Lily was slightly on the plump side, but so was I, so I'm in no position to throw shade on anyone with a weight problem, not that I would have anyway. I actually would have felt more confidence in the cake decorator if Chena had Lily's figure instead of that of a runway model. Lily's tiny ears were delicate, nearly translucent, and only served to make her long, narrow nose appear more prominent. She was short in stature and had the tiniest feet I've ever seen on a grown woman. I was amazed she could stand upright without wobbling. Her wrist sported a tattoo of a lily, for which I complimented her.

"I thought it was appropriate," she replied. "Certainly more appropriate than the Minnie Mouse tattoo at the base of my spine."

"A Minnie Mouse tramp stamp?" Wendy asked. I was afraid Lily would be offended by the remark, but she just laughed.

"I told you it was inappropriate, didn't I?"

"Oh, you'd be surprised by some of the off-the-wall tattoos I see while performing autopsies. A few of them are in locations most folks would never think to have a tat inked."

"I can only imagine." The florist shuddered dramatically. "But kudos to you for being appointed to the medical examiner position after Uncle Nate retired."

"I thought I recognized you," Wendy said. "Weren't you at your uncle's retirement party?"

The two ladies continued their exchange while Lariat and I sat quietly by. I was pleased to find Lily so personable and easy to work with. Where the cake decorator had been cold and calculating, Lily was warm and friendly. More importantly, her creations were stunning and her rates seemed reasonable, or at least compared to the arrangement I'd purchased online recently for a great-uncle's funeral. She and Wendy had clicked immediately, which warmed my heart.

I turned to Lariat, who seemed to be in a stupor. "What all do we need to order?"

"Beats me."

"Do you have any suggestions or ideas?" Wendy asked Lariat.

He merely shook his head slowly, like it weighed more than the rest of his body parts combined. The only thing he'd managed to do since stepping into the floral shop was kiss the shop owner on both cheeks—his standard greeting when it came to women.

It suddenly became clear to me. Not only was Lariat completely sober, he was also completely unable to function as a wedding planner without some measure of alcohol coursing through his veins. The man couldn't make a simple decision or form a complete sentence, and I knew it was because his usual "buzz" had worn off. With a very limited time to get everything arranged, I realized I needed to get some alcohol into Mr. Jones. And I needed to do it quickly.

"Lariat, do you happen to have any liquor in your bag?" My tone was anything but cordial.

"Unfortunately not. I usually never leave home without my friends, Jim, Jack, and Johnnie, but my flasks are in my saddle bags on my bike, which I seem to have misplaced. Why do you ask?"

"You are about as productive as a dead slug this morning." I couldn't believe I was ticked off that my wedding planner was sober. "And, once again, your Harley is at the Alexandria Inn."

"It is? How'd it get there?" Lariat asked.

I shook my head in exasperation. Thankfully, having dealt with Lariat on numerous occasions, Lily recognized the problem instantly. She gazed at Lariat as she spoke. "I have Crown Royal in my cabinet and cola in the cooler, if you'd like something to mix it with."

Lariat perked up upon hearing her words. "Thanks, Lily," he replied. "Drinking it straight up is more efficient." He grinned broadly and then gave me a questioning glance.

I nodded in response to his unasked question. "It goes against my better judgment, but go pour a little of that whiskey down your gullet quickly so we can get this traffic jam moving."

"Sure, if you insist," he replied with a grin.

I wondered then if I'd been played, but it was too late to back-track. "Don't drink too much," I pleaded as he took the half-full bottle Lily offered and headed to the exit.

"I'll be back in no time. You ladies feel free to proceed without me." Wham! The front door closed behind him.

Oh, boy! I may regret that rash decision, I thought. I wondered if he'd return to the shop or we'd seen the last of him for the day.

"What were you thinking, Mom?" Wendy asked, her voice filled with alarm.

I glanced over at my daughter. She looked as if I'd just told the man to go get trashed before he helped her plan the most important day of her life. Which, basically, is exactly what I'd done.

Stunned, Wendy added, "And who are Jim, Jack, and Johnnie?"

"That'd be Jim Beam, Jack Daniels, and Johnnie Walker," Lily said. She smiled at me as she attempted to calm my daughter, whose feathers I'd unintentionally ruffled. "I've been working with Lariat for several years now. Stone sober, he's worthless as training wheels on a stationary bike. Wet his whistle a bit, and he's brilliant."

I patted Wendy's shoulder. "Relax. It'll all work out just fine."

Fifteen minutes later, Lariat waltzed back in with a nearly empty whiskey bottle and all his pistons pumping. Now that his familiar buzz had returned, he appeared as sharp and efficient as ever. It took less than thirty minutes to pick out the floral necessities. Wendy was decisive about what type of flowers she wanted: white orchids, a contrasting red flower, and baby's breath used as a filler. She quietly scanned through a catalog to select the perfect red blossom to set off the centerpieces for the tables. The boutonnieres and bouquets would be miniature versions.

"Look at this one, Mom. It's beautiful, and it's called the palm of Christ. Isn't that just perfect?"

Before I could agree, Lily asked, "Are you sure you want that in your wedding arrangements?"

"Absolutely!" Wendy nodded, and added, "Why not?"

"Well, it's just that the palm of Christ—" Lily began. She then shrugged, and said, "Oh, never mind. It shouldn't present a problem. It is rather expensive though."

"That's okay." Wendy's response didn't surprise me. When she decides on what she wants, she never hesitates to spend a little more to get it.

"All right. If you're positive." Lily waited for Wendy to confirm before notating the choice on the order form.

For some reason, the florist seemed tentative about including the pretty red flowers in the arrangements. Perhaps the flower's scent was not overly pleasant, or the flower was difficult to come by. Whatever the reason, Lily's demeanor was curious. However, seeing how pleased Wendy appeared with her selections, I shook off my feeling of uncertainty.

Wendy had chosen a simple, but classy, arrangement. I was glad she'd been able to join us after all, as I would have picked a more elaborate assortment that Wendy might have considered outlandishly gaudy.

Lariat guided Wendy as she made her selections. He advised her against using the same table centerpieces for both the rehearsal dinner and the reception. "The fresh flower arrangements will be perfect for the rehearsal dinner, but it'd be a waste of money to use them for the outdoor reception. In the heat of summer, they'd keel over faster than someone suffering from heat stroke. I have some beautiful silk arrangements that will match your theme perfectly. I'd be happy to lend them to you for the reception at no cost."

Lariat brought up photos on his phone and showed the silk arrangements to Wendy. She nodded and whispered something to him I couldn't make out. Then turning to me, she gave a thumbs-up gesture, accompanied by an ear-to-ear smile. The two seemed totally *simpatico*, but then they were nearly the same age and didn't have a twenty-year age gap like Lariat and I did. Wendy even offered to give him a ride to the inn to collect his Harley after she'd completed her selections, which was a relief to me. I was pleased she seemed happy with the wedding planner I'd hired, not that there were other options available if she wasn't.

If the rest of the wedding planning progresses as smoothly as ordering the floral arrangements, we'll soon be sitting back, chilling like a bottle of champagne, until the big day arrives. That thought reminded me that we needed to add "purchase Dom Perignon" to our list of things to do. When asked, Wendy had indicated the celebratory champagne was not a corner she wanted to cut. "Anything short of Dom Perignon," she'd said, "would cheapen the traditional toast."

Naturally, Lariat had agreed. His opinion about substituting sparkling water for champagne was, "Why not just toast with lemonade as if you were hosting a first-grader's birthday party?"

I also needed to ask my best friend, Sheila Davidson, if she'd supply some of her infamous spiked punch for the refreshments table. It was potent enough to warrant a warning label, but delightfully delicious, and would hopefully decrease the consumption of the expensive champagne.

Why did it seem as if every time I crossed a task off, I added two more to the list?

THIRTEEN

I watched Lariat and Wendy work in perfect harmony with Lily Franks as they finalized the floral selections at the Lily's-in-Bloom Floral Shop. For the first time, I had complete confidence that the wedding, along with all of its components, would proceed flawlessly. I poured myself a cup of coffee from a Keurig machine on the shop's counter. I sat back on a tasteful couch, arranged in the corner of the room with a matching chair and modern accent table. On the table was a stack of magazines, including the latest *People* magazine and several issues of *Birds and Blooms*. I sipped the fresh brew, content and relaxed. When I felt a tap on my shoulder, it scared the bejesus out of me. I abruptly lurched forward and coffee splashed out of my cup and onto my white blouse.

"Oh, no! I'm so sorry, ma'am. I didn't mean to startle you," exclaimed a petite young lady.

She placed her hands over her mouth like Macaulay Culkin had in the *Home Alone* movie. Her short blonde, purple-streaked hairstyle would have looked ridiculous on someone my age, but was actually quite cute on the young lady whose irises were so black, they were nearly indiscernible from her pupils. She grabbed a towel off the counter and began to swipe at the fresh coffee stains. All she accomplished was to smear the stains and make it less likely I'd ever be able to "Shout" them out.

"That's quite all right, my dear. I shouldn't have been daydreaming. Hand me the towel and I'll go rinse this shirt in the restroom." I noticed a fresh, ugly scar on her wrist as she turned the towel over to me.

The young lady apologized again before pointing the way to the ladies' room. "The restroom's across from the big cooler where we store our floral arrangements and fresh flowers."

When I returned from the washroom, the young woman introduced herself as Raven Kostaki. She'd just moved to the area from the east coast and felt fortunate to have landed the job as Lily's assistant. She'd taken a three-month lease on a studio apartment, hoping to find more permanent housing in Rockdale in the interim.

Lily looked over, clearly growing impatient with Raven's lollygagging, and said, "Raven, could you fetch Ms. Starr a bottle of water out of the cooler?"

I hadn't requested another beverage, so was certain Lily had sent her away with a specific purpose in mind. After the young assistant left the room, Lily told me about her new hire. "I could tell Raven was in a bad way when she applied for the job."

"Does that explain the scar on her wrist?" I asked.

"Yes. Sadly, it's the result of an attempted suicide that occurred right before she moved here. My former assistant had recently quit due to a complicated pregnancy, and I was in desperate need of filling the vacancy. I thought Raven could use a break, so I hired her. Raven's been a godsend, too. She's got a good eye for creating exquisite floral arrangements. Now if I can only get her to focus on the tasks at hand rather than her recent troubles."

As I listened to Lily, I noticed a letter sticking out of the satchel Raven had left on the table in front of me. A sudden feeling I can't explain compelled me to snap a photo of it with my phone. Before Lily could explain what those recent troubles were, Raven returned to the room with a cold bottle of water for me.

"Thank you. What made you decide to move to the Midwest?" I asked Raven.

"Bad breakup, mostly." With a forlorn expression, Raven looked down at the red welt on her wrist.

"Oh, I'm sorry to hear that." I gave Raven a rueful smile. As was my nature, I felt obliged to cheer her up. "I think you'll find Rockdale a charming place to live. A beautiful woman like you will have no trouble finding suitable male companionship around here. I've recently read that men outnumber women nearly two to one in this town. With those kinds of odds, I'm sure you'll find the one who was meant for you."

I'd read no such thing, but short of contacting every citizen in Rockdale and recording their gender, I figured Raven would never realize I was only trying to build up her confidence. Unless she had an "in" with the census department, of course. She seemed to be an individual whose self-esteem was in desperate need of bolstering, and with Lariat and Lily now assisting Wendy, I had the luxury of time to donate to the cause.

I might as well have used that time finding a cure for cancer or solving the world peace conundrum. Instead of being encouraged, Raven dissolved into a puddle of tears. As a bonus, I'd annoyed Lily while upsetting Raven.

Lily glanced over to see what the fuss was all about. She then looked at me as if I'd deliberately broken a pact we'd just agreed upon. I realized then her purpose in sending Raven from the room to fetch water for me was to get me on board with her mission to get her new young assistant's head into the flower game, and off her distressing love life. Lily sounded perturbed when she scolded her new assistant. "Raven, what are you still doing out here? I thought I told you twenty minutes ago to get those six delivery orders ready to ship out. You clock out in just over an hour, and those flowers are hardly going to arrange themselves, are they?"

I thought Lily's remarks were a bit harsh. After all, her assistant was clearly overwrought. Then again, I wasn't the one paying Raven an hourly wage to complete necessary tasks, either. I flashed Lily an apologetic smile and grasped Raven's trembling hand.

"It will all work out, honey," I said to her. "Trust me. You'll look back one day and wonder why you'd ever been so upset about this breakup. For now, you should probably get back to work. It'll take your mind off of your woes."

Raven glanced at me in disgust and yanked her hand away as if she'd just learned I'd been handling nuclear waste before entering the shop. I'd truly been trying to soothe her, not distress her. I guess I'll never understand how dramatic this millennial generation can be. It often seems as if every little setback is the end of the world for them. Perhaps I was just as expressive when I was Raven's age, but the sun had risen and set enough times by now that I'd forgotten those long-ago emotions.

While Raven sobbed in the back room, Wendy, Lariat, and Lily finished up their business. I watched as Wendy wrote a check to Lily as a deposit on her flower order. I was sorry I'd upset Lily's assistant, but glad to mark another task off our to-do list. It wouldn't be long before we had the entire wedding-planning chore behind us. Then, I'd be able to kick back and relax, enjoy my daughter's wedding, and happily wave goodbye to the blissful newlyweds as they left for their honeymoon in Cozumel.

Or so I hoped.

FOURTEEN

The next morning, I sat on the front porch of the inn, sipping coffee from my Tervis tumbler, while waiting for Wendy to pick me up. She had made an appointment to have her hair trimmed and asked if I'd like to tag along. I was overjoyed because, after all, what mother doesn't like knowing her daughter enjoys her company?

Even so, had I realized her appointment was with Yvonne Custovio, I might have conjured up a migraine, or a chore I desperately needed to get done that morning.

"We need to hurry," Wendy said as soon as I slid into the passenger seat a few minutes later. "Yvonne gets so pissed when her clients are late."

"Yvonne? I thought you switched over to Kerri?"

"I did. But Kerri's on vacation, so I ended up with Yvonne instead."

"Why don't you try the new salon on Maple Street? They might have a stylist you like better."

"Oh, I really don't mind the way Yvonne does my hair. Truthfully, I just get tired of hearing about all of her sexual escapades, half of which I think are fabricated to entertain her clients. I don't find them all that entertaining."

"Nor do I, dear. That's why I'm switching over to the new salon next time I have my hair done."

"Really?" Wendy asked as we pulled into the salon's parking lot, which was only a few blocks from the inn. "That's kind of a shame. I know you've been going to Yvonne in recent months, and I think your hair looks better now than ever. I swear, you look like you and I could be sisters. No one would believe you're my mother!"

I didn't know if Wendy was just flattering me or honestly thought my new style made me look younger. Either way, my new style had nothing to do with Yvonne and I thanked my lucky stars again that Ginny Clevenger had chosen the Alexandria Inn to stay at during her recent vacation.

Upon exiting the hair salon forty minutes later, Wendy and I decided to stop at the same coffee shop I'd been too embarrassed to be seen in the previous week after Yvonne had "pinkened" my hair. Wendy seemed a little out of sorts. I asked her about her mood change once we'd gotten our coffee and found a table.

"Yvonne was acting really odd today. Barely said ten words to me the entire time, when normally she rarely stops to take a breath. I think the only thing she said was, 'Working your mother into my schedule last week was a waste of my time and her money'. I didn't know what she was talking about, so I didn't respond. Do you have any idea what's gotten into her?"

"I have no idea, honey. I wouldn't worry about it, though. Probably just PMSing or something. Or maybe she just hasn't had a good roll in the hay for several days!"

"Mom!" Wendy laughed with a snort. "I can't believe you said that."

I had hoped saying something outrageous would take her mind off her inquiry, and it worked. I chuckled along with Wendy until she forgot she'd even asked me a question. I didn't particularly want to go into detail about my recent hair appointment with Yvonne, and had to wonder if Wendy would have said the same nice things about my new hairstyle if it was still glow-in-the-dark pink.

Even though Ginny Clevenger had kindly washed the color out of my hair as soon as I'd returned home, I couldn't imagine why Yvonne would hold my aversion to pink hair against Wendy. But then, I didn't know what had transpired between them to cause Wendy to switch over to Yvonne's co-worker, either, although I'd guess there was more to it than the fact Wendy had just become tired of Yvonne's outlandish stories. I decided it was better not to dwell on hair. Instead, I said, "Last week when I told Yvonne who all was in your wedding party, she seemed to have an issue with Wyatt. Do you know if the two ever dated?"

"No, I don't. Like you, I've only known the two of them a couple of years, but I can't ever imagine them as a couple. Can you?" Wendy asked with a guffaw. "I'd think Wyatt would sooner bite the head off a rattlesnake than go out with Yvonne. He stopped her for speeding in a school zone a while back, and she basically offered up her body to get out of a ticket—a very expensive one, at that. Didn't work though, and she's contacted him several times since with offers to meet him for lunch somewhere so they could get to know each other better."

"Fat chance of that." Even as I spoke, I wondered why Wendy never passed on juicy information like that to her mother. Did she not realize that inquiring minds want to know?

"Exactly. Wyatt is totally devoted to Veronica. Even if he wasn't, he doesn't care for brazen women like Yvonne. She's sniffing up the wrong tree, for sure."

As Wendy spoke, I realized she'd used the perfect cliché, even if she hadn't used it correctly. Detective Johnston was actually built like a tree—a mighty oak, to be more precise—and as handsome a man as you'd likely find in all of Rockdale. Wyatt was six feet, six inches of pure muscle and sex appeal.

But the sun rose and set on Veronica Prescott as far as Wyatt was concerned. He'd reconnected with his old classmate when her father had been murdered in the Alexandria Inn on its opening night. I'd not only helped nail her father's killer, but had also helped Veronica find her soul mate in our good friend, Wyatt. I asked Wendy, "Do you think Yvonne's angry that she can't charm the pants off the sexy detective?"

"Wouldn't be surprised," Wendy said. "Oh, well. Whatever floats her boat. It doesn't matter to me. So, how do you think my hair looks? Not too short?"

"No, not at all. It's perfect, honey. You look absolutely beautiful. But then, you always look beautiful to me." We spent the better part of the next hour chatting about Wendy's upcoming wedding while I drained three cups of coffee and Wendy polished off two. When I began to signal to the waitress for an additional refill, Wendy grabbed my arm and shook her head. That was the sign I'd had enough.

"Your hands are already fluttering like butterfly wings," Wendy cautioned. "Hey! I haven't told you about the three autopsies I performed after the meth lab explosion yet, have I?"

I pretended to listen to Wendy's grisly lecture about the dissection of severely burned cadavers and responded with a nod whenever it seemed appropriate, but I couldn't get Yvonne's attitude toward Wendy that afternoon out of my mind. Just because Yvonne had been ticketed for speeding by a member of Wendy's wedding party didn't seem like a good enough reason to give my daughter the cold shoulder. The fact I'd decided pink hair wasn't my style and washed it out didn't seem significant enough to be a sore spot, either. In my opinion, vivid pink hair should be legally banned once an individual reached half-a-century in age, which for me was a ship that had left the harbor just over a year ago.

Eventually the tale of three charred bodies reached its conclusion and our conversation changed from one topic to another, with Wendy doing most of the talking. I pondered the situation with Yvonne while trying to appear interested in Wendy's babbling.

So it seems Wyatt gave Yvonne a speeding ticket. Big deal. Who doesn't get one of those on occasion? Just last week, Stone had been stopped by the highway patrol on his way to Kansas City and issued a warning. Could there be something else—something more earth-shattering—bothering Yvonne that I'm not privy to? And if so, is there some way I can find out what that "something" is? I don't know why I even care, but for some reason, I do.

As I tuned back in to Wendy's ramblings, I realized she'd reverted back to her original topic and had delved into the middle of a gory, but incredibly thorough description of the recent autopsy of a prominent Rockdale citizen. My stomach fluttered in time to the sudden palsy my hands had developed as she explained the difference between the Virchow technique, where the cadaver's organs are removed individually, and the Rokitansky technique, where they're removed as a connected group. Incidentally, Wendy prefers to take them out one by one so she can examine each of them in greater detail. I excused myself to go inside and use the coffee shop's restroom, but upon returning, Wendy picked right back up where she'd left off. So much for hoping she'd lose her train of thought and decide to talk about something more pleasant.

Wendy had always been particularly fascinated with the reconstitution of bodies following an examination. As I squirmed in my chair on the outside patio of Java Joe's, she described in morbid detail how she lines the inside of the abdomen with cotton wool and places any dissected organs in bags to prevent leakage before returning them to the body.

"How nice, dear," I said, trying not to upchuck the coffee I'd drunk all over my gruesome offspring. I prayed this was not the kind of subject Wendy considered "pillow talk", or Andy Van Patten might one day be second-guessing his decision to spend the rest of his life with my daughter.

FIFTEEN

"Of course you're welcome to join me for a cup of coffee, Wyatt." I held the back door open for the strapping gentleman to come into the kitchen. "I just unwrapped some raspberry scones."

"I know. I smelled them from over on Sycamore Street." We laughed as we took seats at the table. The detective sat in what we lovingly referred to as "Wyatt's chair". He preferred to have his back against the wall. Literally, in this case. It was the cop in him, he'd told us.

"I'm glad you stopped by this morning. I went to the hair salon with Wendy yesterday and her stylist, Yvonne Custovio, acted very strangely the whole time we were there."

Wyatt groaned at the sound of her name. "Has she ever *not* acted strangely? I am truly beginning to wish when I clocked her exceeding the speed limit again, I'd turned off my radar gun and let her keep right on going."

"Again?" I asked. "Oh, my goodness. Yvonne could have killed someone."

"Exactly! That's why I *couldn't* let her keep right on going."

I was just getting ready to ask if he'd known her prior to the speeding-ticket incident, but I didn't have to. He launched right into an explanation about their previous relationship without being prompted.

"Yvonne was in the same graduating class as Veronica and me. During our senior year, Yvonne and I went on a few dates before I asked her to be my prom date. She was up for prom queen, and I was on the docket for king. She had visions of us both being crowned prom royalty and running off into the sunset to grow old together." Wyatt paused for a second, looking at the ring finger on his left hand, which was bare. He seemed to be imagining a wedding ring on that finger, and I had to wonder if he was beginning to visualize a life as Veronica's husband. They'd been dating even longer than Wendy and Andy, and he seemed totally enamored with her.

"And?" I prompted, when he remained silent. "Were you crowned prom queen and king?"

"Not exactly." After a moment of reflection, he continued. "Well, I was crowned king, but Yvonne lost out. Veronica was crowned queen and, as they say, the rest is history."

"Veronica? Oh, goodness. No kidding?" My mouth hung open in surprise. "And neither you nor Veronica has ever thought to mention that to me?"

"Truthfully, Lexie, I've never thought it was all that important, or even worth mentioning. It seems a lifetime ago, and we've outgrown those silly little high school traditions."

"I'm surprised Wendy didn't know about it." I was not to be deterred.

"Oh, I'm sure Veronica has mentioned the prom royalty stuff, but I doubt she told Wendy I took Yvonne as my date but left the dance with Veronica."

"Wyatt!" I shook my finger at him. "That wasn't very nice."

"I know." Wyatt hung his head in embarrassment. "It's not something either Veronica or I are proud of. In fact, now that I think about it, I doubt Veronica mentioned anything at all to Wendy about the prom. "

That explained why Veronica had not shared the story with Wendy, who in turn would have hopefully shared it with me. But it seemed like a ridiculous reason for Yvonne Custovio to still harbor a grudge against Wyatt.

"So what happened next?" I asked, as I refilled both coffee cups. Wyatt snatched a second scone before responding. He was a bottomless pit when it came to eating.

"I started dating Veronica. We only dated a short while, though, before she dumped me for the football quarterback, Johnny Kirkpatrick, who led our team to the state championship that year."

"Sounds like one of those 'karma' things to me." I winked at Wyatt to let him know I was teasing. "I do recall you saying the two of you had briefly dated in high school. I'm sorry Veronica dumped you for the football star back then, but in the end things turned out pretty darn well for you two."

Wyatt smiled. "Yep. In the long run, I ended up with her and Johnny didn't. Incidentally, Johnny ended up with Cedric Clemmons, who played trombone in the marching band. Johnny and Cedric have been happily married since Missouri legalized same-sex marriages back in 2015. So things seem to have turned out well for Johnny. too."

Wyatt hung around another ten minutes, and we spent the time discussing the upcoming wedding. He glanced at his watch and stood to go. "I still need to get fitted for my tuxedo. I'd better get that done this afternoon."

"Yes, you'd better, or Wendy will have your head on a skewer."

"You meant a guillotine rack, didn't you?"

"Yeah, that too." We laughed and Wyatt carried his cup to the sink and rinsed it out before placing it on the top rack of the dishwasher. He was not only exceedingly good-looking, but also the ultimate gentleman. Veronica would be one lucky lady to land this fellow as her husband. I wondered what was taking so long for Wyatt to pop the question, but decided it was none of my business. Instead, I asked, "Are you familiar with Lariat Jones?"

"Lariat Jones?" Wyatt looked confused by my question. "Sure. Lariat processed a white-tail buck I shot a couple of years ago. Of course that was before I promised Veronica I'd stop hunting, and also before I arrested Lariat on a drunk and disorderly charge when he tried to burn down that sleazy bar on Elm Street one night. Oh, and when I ticketed Yvonne not long ago, he was in the vehicle with her, drunk as a skunk."

"Yikes!" I said. "And here I hired him to plan Wendy and Andy's wedding, knowing he had a drinking problem. So far he seems to be handling everything pretty well. But, still…"

"I wouldn't worry, Lexie. He may have it in for me, but I'm sure he'll do a satisfactory enough job."

There it was again—a "satisfactory enough job". I swallowed hard. "Please don't tell Wendy about the drunk and disorderly charge, or that you think Lariat will do a 'satisfactory enough job'. I'm having to keep him liquored up just so he can function as the wedding planner."

"Sure thing." Wyatt nodded as if he understood my plight perfectly. He then leaned down, kissed my cheek, grabbed one last scone for the road, and was out the back door in a flash.

I needed another shot of caffeine before I met up with Lariat at the caterer's house, but a case of acute arrhythmia from the coffee wouldn't help matters any. Nor would a chastisement from Lariat about my caffeine addiction. Therefore, I decided to forego that fourth cup and follow Wyatt out the back door to get in my car and head downtown. With any luck at all, the visit to the caterer would go as smoothly as the trip to the floral shop the previous day had gone.

SIXTEEN

I planned to meet Lariat at the caterer's house, and told Wendy there was no reason she had to take time off from work to go with me. She'd already mentioned a bad car wreck on I-29 that had left two new bodies on ice at the county morgue where her lab was located. I knew without a doubt I'd soon hear every sickening detail about the victims' fatal injuries.

I had hired Georgia Piney in the past to cater several events, including Wendy's thirtieth birthday party just over a year ago, and had been very satisfied with both the food and her service. I had no qualms about hiring her to cater the wedding. When I arrived, Lariat's Harley sat parked in Georgia's driveway, and I was surprised to find the two sitting at her kitchen table, laughing and drinking wine out of red Solo cups.

I slid into an empty chair and accepted Georgia's offer of a cup of wine. After all, I figured, if I couldn't beat them, I might as well join them. The wine was a red pinot noir. I seldom drank wine, but when I did, I preferred a dry white, like a Riesling or Chardonnay. But, as with coffee, I don't tend to be very picky and will pretty much drink anything anyone sets in front of me.

I'd only planned on nursing the one serving of wine, but while chatting amicably with Georgia and Lariat, I consumed more than I should have. Not nearly as much as Lariat did, however. In his case, cup after cup went down like a chubby kid on a seesaw. It took only minutes to agree on a menu and a price, and the three of us spent the next hour working our way through three-and-a-half bottles of wine while discussing everything from whether chili should be made with or without beans, to Georgia's twin daughters, to the great discount Pete's Pantry offered on three-ply toilet paper in that week's grocery advertisement.

By the time we decided to leave, Lariat wasn't the only one with a buzz on. I was so tipsy, I was afraid to drive myself home. The last thing I wanted was to end up in the emergency room following a car accident or, worse yet, to occupy a third icy tray in Wendy's lab. Most importantly, I never wanted to get someone else injured or killed because of my own stupidity. There was nothing more irresponsible than driving while under the influence of a mind-altering substance.

Stone had gone fishing with our next-door neighbor that morning, so I called Wendy at work. I explained the situation and asked if she'd mind driving over to the Piney's on her lunch break and escorting me and the wedding planner back to the inn.

"Damn!" Wendy exclaimed. "You didn't tell me there'd be wine at the meeting with the caterer. I might have called in sick if I'd known that. You know I never turn my nose up at free wine."

"I know you better than that," I replied, in a slurry mess no doubt. "You'd never call in sick to work unless it was an extreme emergency. Especially when you've got two fresh ones in your lab. Besides, if you had joined us this morning, none of the three of us would be able to drive legally right now."

"No, probably not. I have the Uber app on my phone. Don't you?" Wendy asked. "Not that I want you to call for a ride. I don't mind coming to get you guys, but it's handy to have when you're in a pinch. I'll be clocking out for lunch in about five minutes, and can grab a sandwich on the way. I'll grab you and Lariat each one, too. Maybe it'll absorb some of that alcohol."

"Yes, thank you. I do have the Uber app and actually use it on occasion. However, I'd be too embarrassed to get into a stranger's car in my current condition, with an even drunker young man as my sidekick. Here's the address to put in your GPS."

After I gave Wendy the address to the Pineys' home, I turned around to tell Lariat that my daughter would be driving us home and he could collect his motorcycle later on. Lariat was fast asleep at the kitchen table. He had his forehead resting on his hands, which were splayed out flat against the glass table. I glanced at Georgia who just shrugged. I shrugged back in return.

"Nice young man," Georgia said. "Likes his wine a little too much, though."

"You think?"

SEVENTEEN

W endy, Lariat, and I sat on a bench outside the little photography studio on Main Street called Frozen in Time. The name was fitting for the gallery that highlighted the photography skills of the shop's owner, Annie Frieze. Through her storefront window, I could see most of the framed photos on display were of nature and wildlife, along with an occasional still life. According to Lariat, Ms. Frieze also photographed weddings, reunions, and took senior photos for the Rockdale High School. He informed us Annie wouldn't be easy to book due to her hectic schedule, but that he'd muster up all the charm he had to win her over. He'd said, "She's the best photographer in the area, and worth the extra effort before we have to settle for someone else."

I smelled whiskey on Lariat's breath when Wendy and I first arrived to find him already sprawled out on the outdoor bench. When I cocked an eyebrow at him, he responded, "Hair of the dog."

I silently prayed that dog wouldn't come to bite us in the you-know-what, but knew Lariat tended to be at his best and most charming when he had his buzz on.

We had arranged to meet the gallery's proprietor at ten o'clock.

At ten twenty-five, she had still not arrived to open up her shop. We were gathering up our things to leave when Annie Frieze pulled up to the curb in what seemed like a block-long vintage Lincoln Town Car.

"Greetings, folks!" Annie exclaimed as she hopped out of her car. A black woman in her mid-to-late thirties, she had a lithe body and a full afro. She also had a uniquely shaped nose that reminded me of Barbara Streisand and, like the ultra-talented singer, Annie was a beautiful woman. She sprinted around her car and extended her hand in greeting. "Sorry, I'm late. On my way here, I drove past a field of wild turkeys and just had to stop and snap a few photos."

"Of course," I said, grasping her outstretched hand in a friendly handshake. "No problem, whatsoever, Ms. Frieze."

"That's quite all right," Wendy chimed in politely, without offering her own hand to the photographer. Then the tone of her voice turned to ice. "Who could resist a flock of turkeys? Besides, it's not like we have anything else to do with our wedding just two *(oomph!)*—"

With Lariat on one side of her, and me on the other, Wendy got an elbow jabbed into both sides of her ribs. I whispered, "Wendy! She's not only the best, but possibly the only, photographer we might be able to get to shoot your wedding on such short notice. For goodness' sakes, don't antagonize her."

Lariat merely gazed at Wendy in dismay before returning Annie's greeting. As I'd expected, he walked over and kissed her on both cheeks. I'd been prepared to kiss an entirely different cheek of hers if that's what it took to book her for Wendy and Andy's upcoming nuptials.

Despite Wendy's rudeness, I was puzzled by the hateful look Annie gave Wendy. From Wendy's expression, I sensed she was trying to place where she'd seen Annie in the past. I asked the photographer, "Have you two met before?"

"You could say that," Annie replied dryly. "I was a contestant in the annual Buchanan County Photography contest last fall, and your daughter had been chosen to be one of the judges."

"Oh," Wendy said quietly. "Now I remember where I'd seen you before."

"Oh, how nice," I said, still not sure how such a distinction had earned Wendy a look of loathing from Ms. Frieze. "I remember that. An elderly gentleman from Easton won the grand prize of twenty-thousand dollars."

"Twenty-five thousand, to be exact. Mr. Critton's grand prize entry, for which Wendy cast the deciding vote, was a still-life photograph of a pair of old tattered boots." Annie could not have sounded any more disgusted or in a higher state of disbelief. To emphasize her incredulity, she repeated herself. "A pair of old tattered work boots! And I'd swear the old man took the photo with an antique instamatic camera from the eighties."

"I see." I didn't see at all. *Why would Annie be upset with my daughter because some elderly gentleman decided to take a grainy picture of his boots?* I wondered. I didn't have to wonder long, however.

"My entry, which took second place to the old man's damned dirty boots, was an action shot of a pack of coyotes taking down a white-tail doe in the middle of a colorful meadow on a misty Autumn morning."

"Sounds like you captured an incredible shot." I truly admired anyone willing to wait patiently at the edge of a meadow, colorful and misty or not, for an action shot such as the one Annie described. I could sit in the woods surrounded by salt licks for four months and never have a deer appear, much less have it be followed into the woods by a pack of salivating coyotes hunting for their supper. I was forever amazed, and occasionally horrified, by the amazing footage shown on the Animal Plant channel. I often wondered how in the world someone had been able to capture such intricate events in nature such as a mongoose outsmarting a cobra, or a group of elephants rescuing a baby from the jaws of a crocodile. I also occasionally wondered what would persuade a person to stake himself out in such close of proximity of a cobra or a crocodile in the first place. Still, I was impressed by people who were willing to risk personal injury to capture such images. Unfortunately, Wendy didn't appear to have inherited my love and appreciation for nature.

"Yes, I did get an incredible—" Annie began.

"And gruesome," Wendy interjected.

"—photograph." Annie finished her remark as if Wendy had never interrupted her.

I was in complete agreement with Wendy, but still a little shocked at her appraisal of Annie's subject matter. After all, Wendy was a woman who enjoyed every aspect of dissecting human beings in order to figure out what caused them to give up the ghost. What's more, Wendy seemed to enjoy even more the reciting of the autopsies to her resigned mother.

I listened as Annie continued her tirade. "According to your daughter, my depiction of Mother Nature's food chain in action was not as captivating as a pair of scuffed-up old boots."

"I'm sure Wendy was highly impressed with the quality of your—" I tried to calm the turbulent waters, hoping my daughter wouldn't make any further antagonistic comments, but Wendy was not to be silenced.

"Mr. Critton's boots told a story of a hard-working immigrant who, against all odds, raised a family and realized the American dream." Wendy explained her justification for deciding to cast her vote in favor of the man who took home the hefty grand prize.

"Are you trying to tell me my photo didn't tell a story?" An incensed Annie nearly snarled as she added, "Tell that to the poor deer."

"That's just it, Ms. Frieze. I, along with several other judges, found your photo to be emotionally disturbing. I realize that being able to move people with nothing but a photograph is a good thing, but I couldn't in good conscience vote for it. Mr. Critton had managed to capture a moving photo as well, with nothing more than a black-and-white photo of the shoes he'd worn as a potato farmer."

"Yada, yada, yada," Annie said sarcastically, using a phrase made famous by the popular *Seinfield* series. "Good for him."

Trying to smooth Annie's ruffled feathers, I said, "It sounds like Mr. Critton probably needed the monetary reward more than an ultra-successful photographer like yourself. Besides, Annie, I'm sure the prize for second place was impressive, too."

"I won a turkey."

"A turkey?" I swallowed hard. Not so impressive, after all. "Well, with the contest being in the fall, I'm sure that was a nice—"

"I'm a vegan."

"Oh." I was unable to come up with more than a one-word response, but still able to glare at Wendy when she laughed out loud.

Annie also leveled a glare at my daughter. "I told them to stick their damned turkey where the sun don't shine."

I glanced at Wendy, who nodded her head and confirmed Annie's statement. "Yep. That's what she told us. Which was just fine with me because I ended up taking the turkey home after she declined it. Remember that juicy Butterball we had for supper last Thanksgiving, Mom?"

Now, even a one-word response was beyond my reach. I remained silent and motionless until Annie grunted and took a menacing stride toward Wendy. Wendy took a step forward and closed the gap between herself and the photographer. The situation had suddenly gotten so tense, I could feel static electricity in the air. Before the confrontation could escalate into a sidewalk brawl, I stepped between them.

"Come on, ladies," I said. "Let's let bygones be bygones. I'm sure both photographs were deserving in their own way, and there's no sense in revisiting something that happened in the past."

"Yes. Lexie's right," Lariat agreed, looking as if he needed a shot of bourbon. *Where's Jim and Jack when you need them?* I thought. Lariat cast me an appreciative glance and continued. "Let's go inside and concentrate on the upcoming wedding."

After a lengthy pause, both women finally relented and stepped back. Without taking their eyes off each other, they moved toward the front door. Once we were inside the gallery, Annie spoke directly to Lariat, as if Wendy and I were not even in the room. "I told you numerous times, I am booked solid. I don't know how I could possibly fit another wedding into my schedule."

"I know, Annie," Lariat said. He then stopped for a few

moments and studied the photographer's face before commenting. "I swear, you look younger every time I see you. You need to give me the name of the exfoliating cream you use. It's like you literally have no pores. You're absolutely stunning this morning."

Lariat's flattery was so obviously manufactured that I wanted to gag. Wendy and I exchanged a glance that told me she found it nauseating, as well. However, when I looked at Annie, I could see she ate up Lariat's praise as if it were a hot fudge sundae. With a flicker of her eyelashes and a seductive tilt of her head, she asked, "Really? Stunning?"

"Absolutely!" Lariat exclaimed. "You look as if you've retained the best plastic surgeon in the country or found the fountain of youth hidden in your own back yard."

"Oh, my. Well, thank you. Actually, I haven't had any work done. It's *au naturale*, with a little help from a product I buy at Wal-Mart."

"I want the name of that product!" Lariat insisted.

"Me too!" I added, feigning the same level of interest Lariat had. I noticed Wendy sat silently with her arms crossed rather than joining in on Lariat's and my BS session, which kind of irritated me. It was to her benefit more than anyone else's that we win Annie over, after all. Out of pure annoyance, I said, "It wouldn't hurt you to give it a try, Wendy."

Wendy scowled at me as the photographer beamed for a full minute. Annie then opened her notebook and scrutinized her appointments. Finally, she shrugged. "I have an end-of-summer showing here at the gallery on the twenty-sixth. I suppose if I set up a couple of days in advance, I could fit the wedding in. I'd only have time to take a few group photos and the actual ceremony. I wouldn't be able to hang around for the reception or any of that nonsense."

"That'd be fine. We don't really need any photos of the nonsense following the ceremony, Annie," I said, glancing at Wendy for her consent.

Wendy blanched. "Seriously, Mother? I wouldn't classify cutting the wedding cake, making our first toast, my first dance with my husband, or tossing the wedding bouquet as nonsense."

"I'm sorry, Wendy," I said. I suddenly realized how callous I'd sounded when I'd only been doing my best to appease Annie Frieze. "I didn't mean that the way it sounded. I only meant to say that the group shots and those of the actual ceremony are the most important photographs, particularly when it comes to a professional photographer. Wyatt took some amazing photos with his new Nikon, and I'm certain he'd be happy to take as many candid shots after the ceremony as you'd like."

"Well, I suppose that'd be all right. He has taken some remarkable photos with that camera," Wendy replied.

"I'm sure he could take an award-winning photo of your wedding shoes if you'd like," Annie muttered to no one in particular. We all took the high road and ignored her.

Wendy shook her head at Annie's caustic remark. She then turned to Lariat, whose opinion she evidently valued more than mine. "What do you think?"

"I agree with your mom. That'd be an ideal solution and save you some money in the long run."

"Good point," Wendy replied.

"Are you talking about Wyatt, as in Detective Johnston?" Annie asked.

"Yes." Wendy was unmistakably perplexed by the question. "Why do you ask?"

Annie laughed, but not in a humorous way. It was more of a "you've got to be kidding" chuckle. She looked at Wendy. "You think it's safe to have the detective at the same venue as Yvonne Custovio? When she cut my hair Monday, she told me she plans to crash the wedding. Yvonne's hoping to have an opportunity to confront the police officer who caused her to lose her driver's license for a year."

"A year?" Wendy asked. "No kidding? Man, that'd be rough. I had no idea. Yvonne never mentioned losing her license."

"Hmmm," I began. "I guess that explains why Wyatt told me he'd clocked her significantly exceeding the speed limit 'again'. I only knew about the school zone infraction."

"Yes, that was a while back," Annie explained. "Then two weeks ago, he stopped her again for speeding in a construction zone—doing fifty-eight in a thirty-mile-an-hour zone—and despite her best attempts to talk him out of writing her a ticket, he did. At Yvonne's court hearing last Friday, her license was suspended because it was her third infraction in the span of six months. She thinks he targeted her intentionally after the school-zone ticket he'd written her earlier and suspects he'd been following her, hoping to catch her exceeding the speed limit."

"It doesn't sound like he'd have to follow her for very long to catch her speeding. That girl has a reputation for being hell on wheels and treats Main Street like it's the Talladega racetrack. It serves her right," Wendy said in the detective's defense. "Wyatt's just trying to keep her from killing someone. If it hadn't been Wyatt, it'd have been another police officer. I'm surprised Yvonne hasn't landed someone in my morgue already."

"True enough," Annie agreed. She smiled at Wendy for the first time since pulling her Lincoln up to the curb outside. "So what's it going to be? My fee is a flat fifteen hundred for what I've outlined on this form."

Wendy perused the form Annie handed her, nodded in agreement, and then handed it back to the photographer. "Sounds fine, I guess. Can you pencil us in? I'd be happy to leave a deposit, just as I did with Lily Franks and Chena Steward."

"You bet your sweet bippy you'll be leaving a deposit, Ms. Starr. A healthy one, as a matter of fact. You don't think I've gotten to be successful by being unconditionally trusting, do you?" Annie laughed in such a way to let Wendy know she was kidding, yet not kidding at the same time.

As my daughter rolled her eyes, I breathed a sigh of relief. Wendy withdrew the checkbook from her purse and reluctantly wrote a check for seven hundred and fifty dollars to retain the photographer. We had nearly every one of our little quackers in a row now, and would soon be able to sit back and relax until the big day arrived.

EIGHTEEN

"Come on in!" I shouted at the sound of someone rapping on the back door of the inn. It was August twenty-fourth, the day before the wedding, and I'd been running around all morning like a mouse looking for a bag of cookies to chew a hole in. I stood in the kitchen now, arranging the food Georgia Piney had just delivered for that evening's rehearsal dinner. Her barbecue brisket smelled so delicious, my mouth watered. "Door's open!"

"How did you know you weren't inviting the neighborhood axe murderer inside?"

At the sound of Sheila Davidson's voice, I turned and opened my arms to welcome my best friend with a warm embrace. I hadn't seen her in several months. I then gave her husband, Randy, a big hug. "Oh, you two are certainly a sight for sore eyes. I am so glad you arrived in time for the rehearsal this afternoon."

"We wouldn't miss it for the world. It's not every day my goddaughter gets married, you know," Sheila said. "Speaking of sore eyes, or an eye sore in this case, what's with the gaudy-looking lime-green travel trailer that pulled in behind us? There are actually sunflowers painted on both sides of it."

"Oh, good!" I clapped my hands in delight. "The Ripples have arrived."

"So that's the Rip and Rapella you've told us about? They must be every bit as eccentric as you've described them." Sheila looked out the back window to convince herself her eyes weren't playing tricks on her. I simply smiled.

Rapella once told me she'd given the travel trailer the unique paint job to give their home-on-wheels a "little personality and flair". I had to admit, thanks to Rapella, the colorful RV would definitely stand out in a crowded campground.

"Yes. Rapella's a little more eccentric than Rip," I replied. "You'll absolutely love her. If you and I could produce offspring, Rapella is exactly the kind of child we'd have."

Randy laughed. "So you're saying you and my wife's child would be a seventy-year-old woman?"

"Not exactly. But Rapella does have a nice mixture of both of our traits. She's impulsive, crafty, and daring like me, and assertive, wickedly clever, and has an abundance of diverse and useful skill sets like Sheila. I wouldn't doubt that Rapella could rewire a lamp while dangling by one hand from a bridge abutment as she's attempting to capture a killer."

"An individual with a 'nice mixture' of traits like that sounds totally terrifying to me. Remind me to steer clear of Rapella Ripple." The expression on Randy's face as he spoke was priceless and soon had all three of us cracking up. He lifted two suitcases off the floor. "Same suite as before, Lexie?"

"Absolutely. Stone and I actually named it the Davidson Suite after you two stayed here for our wedding."

"How sweet of you," Sheila said. "Randy, I'll get the box of punch ingredients out of the car while you—"

"No, honey," he replied. "I'll get the box after I put the luggage in our room. You stay here and visit with Lexie. I'm sure she can use some help getting ready for this evening."

Sheila gave Randy a quick peck on the lips and hung her purse around his neck. He groaned in response. Her purse was nearly as big and heavy as one of the suitcases. Randy listed to the left as he walked away, due to the weight of Sheila's oversized purse, and muttered, "I thought I told you to leave the kitchen sink behind."

Rapella breezed into the room, exuding a boatload of energy and enthusiasm. "Howdy folks! Long time no see, Lexie. Rip's outside chatting with Stone, who's showing him where to park the Chartreuse Caboose. We're thrilled you've added a few RV sites to the grounds."

I gave Rapella a hug and introduced her to Sheila, who was having a fit of the giggles at the name the Ripples had given their travel trailer. I told Rapella what we'd been discussing before she walked in. She look confused, as if trying to figure out how Sheila and I could produce offspring. "So, you're saying that if you two could somehow reproduce, your child would be a seventy-year-old woman?"

"I'm beginning to think Rapella's more like Randy than either of us." Sheila and I laughed heartily at Sheila's remark. Rapella just looked at us as if we were a couple of cackling old hens that needed to be crated and shipped to Tyson for processing.

A few seconds later, Clyde "Rip" Ripple walked into the room and stood beside his wife. "Sorry to inform you, ladies, but there is no one in the world like Rapella. She is most definitely one-of-a-kind."

"You are absolutely correct about that," I responded before giving him a welcoming embrace. "It's great to see you again, Rip."

"You too, Leslie."

I didn't bother to correct him, as I thought his trouble remembering names gave him an endearing quality. Rapella, however, felt differently. She put her hands on her hips and scolded her husband. "Clyde Jackson Ripple! We just went over this as we were pulling into the driveway. Her name is Lexie. Lex-E. Say it! Lex-E. Come on, Rip. Say it!"

"Okay, okay. Lex-E. That's what I meant to say." Rip flashed me an apologetic smile. "Sorry, Lexie. I promise I won't forget your name again."

"You're damned right you won't," Rapella huffed. "If we have to go over it a hundred times tonight, Rip, you are going to get it right the next time."

Stone entered the kitchen, carrying the box of punch supplies from the trunk of Sheila and Randy's car. He looked rather shocked at how many bottles of booze were in the box. "I take it this comes inside?"

After Sheila assured him it did, Stone set the heavy box down on the kitchen table. "What is Rip going to get right next time?"

"Lisa's name," Rip replied. "My bride is upset because I got it wrong the first time."

A chorus of exaggerated groans filled the kitchen.

The sun blazed in the summer sky the following morning. The big day was upon us and I felt content knowing the rehearsal the night before and the dinner that followed had went off without a snag. Wendy could not have been more delighted, which made me extremely happy. For the very first time, I felt confident I'd made a wise decision when I'd hired Lariat Jones to help plan the wedding.

Having heard the weather forecast, I became concerned about the high heat index expected for that afternoon. The groomsmen would be dressed in black tuxedos, the worst possible color for a day in the upper nineties. I felt bad knowing they'd be uncomfortable, but Wendy had insisted. It had been her decision to make, not mine, so I never debated the choice as aggressively as I probably should have.

I checked the schedule for the day. Lily and Raven would deliver the floral arrangements, bouquets, and boutonnieres at eleven o'clock, followed by Chena's cake delivery at noon. By then, Stone, Randy, and Rip would have the tables and chairs set up. Sheila and Rapella had volunteered to help Lariat with the decorations. Detective Johnston, one of the groomsmen, had offered to pitch in wherever assistance was needed. I had agreed, as long as he was dressed in his tux when the photographer arrived.

Annie planned to arrive around one o'clock to take photos of the wedding party prior to the ceremony, which was scheduled for two o'clock. Knowing Annie would leave directly after the ceremony to prepare for her gallery exhibit the following day, Wyatt agreed to capture an assortment of candid photographs with his new Nikon after the actual wedding ceremony.

Georgia would arrive between one-fifteen and one-thirty with all of the food for the reception. She'd insisted on setting up the refreshment table at the last possible moment so the shrimp rollups, and other perishable food items wouldn't spoil in the oppressive heat.

All of my ducks were in perfect alignment, lined up and performing in precision like South Korean soldiers marching in a military parade. I tried to contain the smug, self-satisfied smile that plastered itself across my face at random moments throughout the morning. I didn't want to come across as being full of myself or already soused from sampling Sheila's punch.

With all the planning, toil, and trouble I'd invested in the wedding, I wasn't expecting that anything could possibly go wrong and prevent this day from being the most memorable and wonderful day of my daughter's life. But then again, I could list a zillion and three things that had occurred in the course of my fifty-one years that I hadn't anticipated. The day *would* turn out to be memorable, at least. One out of two ain't bad.

NINETEEN

Wedding Day - August 25, 2018

"Nine-one-one. Do you have an emergency?"

"Yes, ma'am." My voice quivered uncontrollably. "We need an ambulance. Right away!"

"What is your name and the nature of your emergency?"

"My name is Lexie Starr. In the middle of my daughter's wedding, one of the groomsmen collapsed to the ground."

"Is he breathing, ma'am?"

I glanced over to watch Raven Kostaki perform chest compressions on Bubba Slippknott. "Someone's doing CPR, but he doesn't seem to be responding."

"What is your address? I'll dispatch assistance immediately. Continue administering CPR until help arrives. Does he have a pulse?" The operator's voice was calm and matter-of-fact. *Doesn't she realize this was a life-or-death situation?*

"I'm not sure." I recited the address and implored her to ask the ambulance driver to hurry. "We need them here A.S.A.P."

"Help is on the way, ma'am."

I swear I could actually hear the woman's eyes roll over the phone. But I realized she couldn't allow herself to become overly distressed every time she took an emergency call, or she'd soon develop severe hypertension.

Moments earlier, Reverend Bob Zimmerman, minister of the local Methodist Church, had asked if anyone had any objections to the union of Andy Van Patten, my husband's nephew, and Wendy, my thirty-one-year-old daughter.

"Erg, I, uh——" The six-foot-eight best man tried to speak, then took a step back and keeled over like a tree toppled by a chainsaw.

"Well, that was a rather dramatic objection," Reverend Bob, as the cleric preferred to be called, said with a chuckle.

At first everyone laughed, thinking Bubba had either fainted from the exhilaration of the moment, or was acting out a rather tasteless prank for everyone's amusement. However, it soon became apparent it was no joke, nor had Bubba merely passed out.

I studied the scene in front of me. Some wedding guests ran around like squirrels looking for nuts to bury. Others looked as if they'd been dipped in a vat of nitrogen and were frozen in time. The groom wore an expression of disbelief. He'd clearly anticipated he'd be kissing his new bride right about now instead of looking down at his best man's lifeless body.

Wyatt Johnston, our good friend and one of Rockdale's finest detectives for sixteen years, stepped around Gunnar Wilde to tend to Bubba, who lay motionless on the ground. Kneeling down, he checked his fellow groomsman for a pulse and respirations. He looked up at me and shook his head.

Like several other people, I'd been video-taping the ceremony when Bubba collapsed. As I took in the scene, my camera continued to record. Stone hushed the crowd, which collectively sounded like the buzzing of a high-voltage transformer.

"Is there a doctor in the house?" Stone shouted.

Rattled by the unexpected turn of events, I found myself mentally correcting his use of the "in the house" phrase. We were actually outdoors, gathered around the gazebo he'd built for our own nuptials the previous year. I shook my head to clear the cobwebs and quickly regained my focus. As the proud mother of the county's chief medical examiner, I replied, "Wendy. She has a medical degree."

Every eye in the crowd turned to gawk at me. I guess they couldn't wrap their heads around the idea of the medical examiner—dressed in full bridal regalia, a long veil and an even longer train—kneeling down on the ground to give the kiss of life to the best man.

"It may be heat stroke," Wendy informed the crowd, as she tossed her bouquet to the side, ripped off her veil, and rushed toward the unconscious man.

That's my girl! I wanted to shout.

From the back row, someone called out, "I'm trained in CPR!" It was the floral assistant, Raven Kostaki, who'd been seated next to the Ripples.

Oh, thank God, I said under my breath. *A grass stain on Wendy's beautiful silk gown would've been a crying shame.*

Despite the sweltering heat of the late-summer day, Raven valiantly attempted to breathe life back into Bubba. Beads of sweat had formed across her brow, and she labored without pausing to swipe it from her forehead. Andy watched in horror as he knelt beside the man who'd been his best friend since seventh grade.

Detective Johnston dropped to his knees just then to assist Raven by taking over with the chest compressions. Raven continued with the mouth-to-mouth portion of the resuscitation efforts. Wendy was standing nearby in order to step in if either Wyatt or Raven needed to be relieved.

I clicked my camera off and studied the crowd. To the right of me stood Lariat. He looked as if nothing amiss had occurred to disrupt the ceremony, which I found odd. Chena Steward, the cake decorator, watched in horror as the floral assistant and the detective continued their administrations on Bubba. I was surprised she'd hung around for the ceremony after she'd delivered the wedding cake.

There seemed to be multiple wedding crashers present. Yvonne and Deb Custovio weren't on the guest list, but Wendy could have given an oral invitation at her last hair appointment when Yvonne highlighted her hair. Although as dissimilar as a goldfish and a bucket of coal, the sisters were kind of a package deal. Neither was encumbered with a spouse, and the two were often seen together at both public and private events.

Raven wasn't on the guest list, either, but as a representative of Lily's-in-Bloom Floral Shop, she'd helped distribute the flower arrangements and hand out the bouquets and boutonnieres to the wedding party. It'd been ninety-five degrees when the ceremony started and had only become hotter from that point on. In such heat, the floral bouquets the wedding party were adorned with would need to be stored in the refrigerator quickly after the completion of the ceremony, or they'd wilt faster than lettuce with bacon grease poured on top of it. Lariat had warned us not to have fresh flower arrangements at the outdoor reception for just that reason. But whether it was to help me store the floral bouquets afterward, or not, I was thankful Raven had stayed. The young lady hadn't hesitated to jump in to try and save the best man's life.

Lily Franks had stopped by for a few minutes prior to the ceremony, but had understandably hastened to get back to her shop to wait on customers. It's probably just as well, as she and Yvonne were dressed all in black as if they were attending a funeral rather than a wedding. They had on identical black blazers, which Lily removed as soon as she spotted Yvonne's matching attire. Before Lily scurried off, I had assured her that the flowers she'd provided were just as fresh and colorful as we'd hoped they'd be.

Sirens could soon be heard approaching from the west. Stone hurried out to meet the first responders and motioned for them to drive around back to the garden area. No more than thirty seconds later, an emergency medical technician ripped open Bubba's shirt and placed a defibrillation pad on each side of his chest. I briefly wondered what the penalty would be when the ruined shirt was returned to the tuxedo rental shop. Looking back, this was a clear indication I was in a state of shock and not utilizing enough of the brain cells I had at my disposal.

Ker-thump! Bubba's torso jumped off the ground in reaction to the electrical jolt, but it was to no avail. *Ker-thump! Ker-thump!*

It seemed to take a dozen attempts to restore Bubba's pulse, though it was probably more like four or five. I'd been too flustered to keep track. When the technician finally gave a thumbs-up, the overwhelming relief in the crowd was palpable.

An oxygen mask was strapped to Bubba's face, and he was lifted onto a gurney. He'd yet to open his eyes, but was now at least taking shallow breaths. The EMT's loaded the gurney into the back of the waiting ambulance. Once inside, a technician hastily reached for the defibrillator machine. *Has Bubba coded again?* I fretted.

Reverend Bob climbed into the ambulance, telling the driver he'd like to accompany Mr. Slippknott to the hospital. He wanted to be on hand to provide spiritual guidance to the family who'd surely gather in masses around the patient's bedside. The doors closed and, with sirens blaring, the ambulance sped off before anyone could inform the Reverend that Bubba had traveled from South Carolina to participate in the wedding and had no family in Rockdale. I prayed the cleric's presence wouldn't be needed to administer last rites rather than the spiritual guidance he'd hoped to provide.

I turned to Stone, who was standing beside me wearing an expression of helplessness. "Bubba passed out before Wendy and Andy were pronounced man and wife. How are we going to finish the ceremony?"

I don't know if he was trying to lighten the mood, or was in a similar state of mind as I, but Stone bellowed out, "Is there another preacher in the house?"

A communal gasp arose from the onlookers as Andy kissed his fiancé goodbye and raced to his pickup truck, determined to follow the ambulance. I'm certain he thought someone should be on hand to answer questions and be an advocate for Bubba once he arrived at the trauma center. I was in complete accordance and relieved he'd chosen to tail the ambulance to the hospital in St. Joseph.

The stunned bride-to-be looked on in obvious distress. Wendy hollered out to her husband-to-be, even though he was probably seven or eight blocks from the inn at that point. "You can't just leave me here! How are we going to get married now?"

In normal situations, Stone was always kind and thoughtful. But this was not a normal situation. And as Bubba's godfather, Stone's emotions were no doubt in turmoil. I'm sure he didn't mean to be hurtful or insensitive when he shouted, "Is there another groom in the house?"

With no disrespect intended, all but a few wedding guests, who were still in a state of disbelief, thought Stone's question was hysterical. Even I laughed out loud without thinking, for which I blame Sheila's punch. I stopped abruptly when I noticed Wendy had dissolved into tears. Stone apologized profusely as I tried my best to calm my daughter. My comforting words did nothing to soothe her. I didn't tell her, or Stone, I'd overheard an EMT tell the ambulance driver the chances of Bubba surviving whatever had felled him like a giant sequoia did not look promising.

We were standing behind a table of strategically placed wedding items: bowls of butter mints and salted mixed nuts, bottles of Dom Perignon and monogrammed wine glasses, and a horrid-looking but ridiculously expensive three-tiered cake. The iced monstrosity looked as if its expiration date had passed several days prior to its delivery.

I wasn't thinking straight when I tried another tactic to take Wendy's mind off the tragic event that had just wreaked havoc on her wedding day. "Honey, I see no reason why you and Andy can't still spend next week celebrating your relationship at the resort in Cozumel. After all, it's already paid for."

"Celebrating our relationship?" Wendy cried out hysterically. "I want to be celebrating our marriage."

Before I could stop her, Wendy picked up a crystal wine glass full of Sheila's spiked punch and slammed it down on the table. I breathed a sigh of relief when the goblet withstood the impact. The few drops of punch that had fallen on the cake could only improve it, as far as I was concerned, but scattered shards of glass would have rendered the pathetic cake useless before the guests had been given an opportunity to partake of it.

Wendy's brash reaction appeared to startle the wedding guests. They stood in silence, staring at Wendy and me, clearly waiting to be told what was expected of them now that the groom, best man, and officiating cleric had vacated the premises.

In a sniveling voice, Wendy asked, "What should we do now, Mom?"

When no better option came to mind, I spread my arms out and drew the guests' attention to the lop-sided concoction on the table. I smiled and exclaimed, "Let them eat cake!"

A number of things then occurred simultaneously: Stone raced to his truck to follow Andy to the hospital, a blubbering Wendy sprinted to the back door of the bed and breakfast Stone and I owned and operated, an estimated eighty-five guests scurried to the table to feast on Sheila's spiked punch, champagne, and wedding cake, and Raven Kostaki fell to the ground for no apparent reason.

As Detective Johnston rushed to Raven's side, I thought back to the day I'd promised Wendy that her wedding day would be one she'd never forget. At the time, I had no way of knowing how prophetically accurate that vow would turn out to be. Instead of a cherished memory filled with love and happiness, her special day grew worse with each passing moment. It had transformed from a marriage celebration to absolute mayhem in the blink of an eye.

Not knowing what else to do, I turned to go after Wendy. As I passed through the crowd, I heard Hazel Hallberg whisper to Orpha White, "Reckon them two sickly kids had already taken a bite of this butt-ugly cake?"

Orpha shrugged at the notion of a tainted wedding cake and, after a brief contemplative pause, both ladies shoved another forkful of it into their mouths. Although I believed Hazel's cutting remark had been made in jest, I had to wonder if one of the old biddies might not be the next to topple over like a Bradford pear tree in a Midwestern tornado.

I raced after Wendy, who'd retreated to the inn in distress as the sirens from the ambulance faded into the distance. As I neared the back door of the inn leading into the kitchen, I prayed that Andy's best friend had already regained full consciousness and was back to his normal joking, light-hearted self. I couldn't help but mull over the fact that two young and seemingly healthy adults had suffered similar fainting spells within minutes of each other.

Raven, who'd performed CPR on Bubba, had been the person in the closest proximity to him after he'd stopped breathing. Just moments after discontinuing CPR on him to let the medics take over, she had collapsed to the ground in much the same manner as the man she had worked so hard to revive. Raven now seemed to be in stable condition, even though she was about to be transported by a second ambulance to the same hospital as Bubba for further observation.

Did Bubba suffer from a heat stroke, as Wendy suggested? Was Raven subsequently overtaken by a combination of the oppressive August weather and the fatigue she likely felt from her resuscitation efforts? Was it merely a terrible coincidence or were the two events somehow related?

These questions filtered through my mind as I entered the kitchen. Unbeknownst to me, I'd soon be trying to connect the dots of the mystifying incident, despite my promise to Stone to never again involve myself in a police matter. There'd be a distinction this time, however. The police department would never even realize an investigation was due. If not for Sheila and me, they never *would* have known something was wrong regarding Bubba's sudden health crisis. Like the medical staff at the local hospital, they'd have chocked it up to a fluke occurrence brought on by the heat of the day and several other contributing factors.

Bubba deserved justice and, if he ever regained consciousness, he deserved to know what had caused him to pass out, stop breathing, and eventually slip into a coma. Fortunately, Sheila and I were on our toes, and would strive to bring the truth to light. On the flip side, that wouldn't happen until after we both nearly lost our own lives.

TWENTY

I found an inconsolable Wendy in the kitchen of the Alexandria Inn, where she'd sought refuge after bolting from her thwarted wedding ceremony. I'd be glad when she and Andy were officially married. If nothing else, maybe my daughter's erratic behavior would return to normal. For the last few weeks, Wendy had been deliriously happy one moment and deep in despair the next. Her roller-coaster emotions were giving me motion sickness. I'd have understood if her current state of despondency was based solely on concern for Bubba and Raven, but it was of a more self-centered nature.

"Come on, honey. It's probably not as bad as it seems right now." *"Probably", being the operative word,* I wanted to add. I stroked her back as she sobbed into her hands. "I'm sure Bubba will pull through, and we'll all be gathered together in the garden soon to watch you and Andy exchange vows."

It became clear that Wendy had sucked in too much air as she tried to respond. "But, (hiccup) Mom, we already exchanged vows. It was the wedding (hiccup) rings we never got to exchange. So Reverend Bob never had the chance to pronounce us man and (hiccup) wife."

"You know, it's quite likely that the pronouncement of a couple as man and wife is not necessary to make your marriage official. Maybe those technicalities aren't as significant as you think."

Wendy's weeping stopped on a dime. She straightened her shoulders and clenched her fists. By the look on her face, you'd have thought I'd just informed her the blemish on her forehead stood out like a beacon in the night in every single photo taken before the ceremony. For most rational people, that piece of information would be totally irrelevant. To Wendy, however, it would be akin to a large asteroid hitting the earth and killing off two-thirds of the world's population.

"Oh my God, Mom. How can you—"

Before I could clarify my remarks, Wendy collapsed in a new round of hysterical bawling. I'd about had enough of her overly dramatic and childish behavior. If she didn't calm down soon, I was going to have to slap my daughter on what should have been her wedding day. "Oh, for goodness sakes, Wendy. Snap out of it. You're acting like a self-absorbed drama queen. Frankly, dear, the only thing you should be concerned about right now is the well-being of Andy's best friend and Raven, who also had to be transported to the hospital. For all we know, Bubba might have already passed or is on the verge of it. Don't you think that's a little more important at the moment than having to delay the official certification of your marriage? Have you been a coroner for so long that you've lost complete sensitivity to the plight and welfare of others?"

Wendy's tanned complexion paled, which is remarkable considering the tan had been sprayed on at a salon. "I'm actually classified as a medical examiner, but you are so right. What's wrong with me? I've only been thinking about myself. Andy will be devastated if Bubba dies. And Raven, too? I didn't even realize she'd...oh, my. I'm so sorry. I've been acting so self-absorbed. I guess I'm just..."

"Stressed out?" I supplied when Wendy couldn't seem to come up with the proper adjective. "It's normal to be on edge in a situation like this, dear. Let's put the wedding ceremony on the shelf right now and concentrate on Bubba and Raven. Okay?"

"Absolutely!" With that Wendy fled the room as if someone had just whacked a hornet's nest above her with a baseball bat. In what seemed like mere seconds, she returned to the room in blue jeans and a silky blue-and-white striped blouse. "Why are you still sitting there? We need to get to the hospital to see if there's anything we can do."

The fact that my daughter was back to her normal, thoughtful self was the only bright spot in what currently was a very bleak situation. My hands trembled as I rushed upstairs and hurriedly changed into an outfit similar to the one Wendy now wore.

Wendy waited impatiently at the door as I descended the staircase. "Let's go!"

I nearly tripped over my own feet in my haste. We scurried out to the garden area, where most of the guests still lingered. I informed everyone that the ceremony would be rescheduled due to the unexpected circumstances, and they'd receive an email or text when the new date had been established. A few in the crowd looked disappointed on hearing my announcement. Did they truly think we intended for them to wait for Bubba and Raven to return from the hospital, and that the ceremony would continue as though nothing had happened?

During my announcement, I glanced over at Lariat, who looked as if he'd just seen a stripper in a thong and pasties pop out of the wedding cake. I was unnerved by the delighted expression on his face. Delight was unbefitting the situation.

Was he, for some unknown reason, pleased that the ceremony had been interrupted? Could he already be adding up the money he was apt to make to plan a second attempt at a wedding? Or, more likely, were the numerous gulps I'd seen him take from a flask he'd been toting around in his coat jacket beginning to kick in? He hadn't shied away from the spiked punch bowl, either. Lariat was a high-functioning alcoholic. He more than likely had a buzz on, as he was in the habit of calling his drunken stupors.

Although the peculiar dude was adept at planning and multi-tasking, he'd been an odd duck since day one, I told myself. *So whatever's going on in Lariat's mind is neither here nor there at the moment. I've got more important fish to fry right now.*

Sheila walked over, joined by Rapella, who Stone and I had become close to after getting acquainted with her and her husband, Rip, at a Wyoming campground the previous year. Sheila asked, "Lexie, is there anything we can do while you guys are at the hospital?"

"Bless you both. Would you mind collecting the refreshments and wedding paraphernalia and putting it all in the kitchen? You can put the leftover cake on the bottom shelf of the extra fridge in the pantry, and simply stack the rest of the stuff on the table and counters for me to deal with later. For the kids' sake, I'd like to preserve as much of it as possible to keep the cost of a duplicate wedding to a minimum."

"Yes, of course. Fortunately, my secret-recipe punch has kept most of the guests from indulging in the champagne. I'll gather up the full bottles of bubbly first, so no more of them get uncorked," Sheila said.

"Good idea. I've already downed a couple of glasses of your punch. As I've told you a dozen times, it's simply amazing. I can't believe you won't share your recipe, or at least tell me what kinds of fruit juices and liquor you use. Good grief, it's not like we haven't been best friends for decades."

"Did Duke give away the secret recipe for Bush's baked beans? No. Not to anyone. Has the Coca-Cola Company shared its secret recipe to any old soda company that came along and requested it? Of course not. Their secret formula has been kept in a safe-deposit vault in an Atlanta bank for nearly a century. And my secret formula is stored right here." Sheila pointed to her temple as she spoke. Her words sounded a little slurred, and her stance was none too stable. "As you know, Lexie, it's a lot more potent than one might think. We may have to call for an Uber driver to haul some of your elderly church friends home, considering how rapidly the punch bowl is being depleted. I've already refilled it twice, and it's about to run dry for a third time. Thank goodness Randy and I are bunking here, because I might have drunk a little too much of it myself."

Just in case she hadn't, I assumed, Sheila lifted her cup to her lips and killed off what punch was left. I drained my cup, as well, because I didn't want to have it in the car as Wendy drove us to the hospital. If I spilled red punch on the upholstery of her new vehicle, there'd be hell to pay.

"I agree with Lexie," Rapella said. "It's simply delicious, Sheila. I can tell tequila, my drink of choice, is included in the recipe."

"You're correct," Sheila replied. "But that's all I'm going to tell you."

Rapella giggled and lifted her own red cup of punch as if in a toast. It was clear she'd also indulged a tad too much. She tipped her head back and downed the rest of her drink as if it were a shot of her favorite tequila. "No matter what else is in it, it makes for a fabulous combination."

"Thanks, Rapella. My spiked punch recipe is my only claim to fame. And Lexie, you and Wendy need to get going. Rapella and I will be happy to clean up here. When you get a chance, text me an update on the groomsman and the floral assistant who both took ill. I'll be certain to pass it on to the Ripples." Sheila patted Rapella on the shoulder. The simple tap nearly caused Rapella to lose her balance. That damned punch truly was more potent than one would imagine.

I assured Sheila I'd keep them both in the loop, and then hopped into the passenger seat of Wendy's car, which had just pulled up beside me. Sitting in the car with the door open, I thanked Sheila and Rapella again. "The boutonnieres and bouquets should probably go into the fridge too, if you can make room for them."

Before either of them could respond, my neck snapped back against the headrest and my door slammed shut of its own accord as Wendy stomped on the accelerator. As we raced down the highway, I said a prayer for Raven's well-being. She'd worked valiantly to save Bubba before succumbing to a fainting spell of her own. I then said another one for my daughter and me at the corner of Fourth and Walnut, when Wendy barely missed being t-boned by a passenger van full of children on their way to a church camp. A magnetic sign on the front of the van, which read "Camp Saves-a-Lot", seemed a mere six inches from my face for a split, heart-stopping second. I'm sure I looked as if I had saucers for eyes as I gazed in terror out the window at the large oncoming vehicle. The children in the van were no doubt having a merry little laugh over the near-collision and the hysterical-looking woman in the passenger seat of the car they'd nearly struck.

After my life ceased flashing before my eyes, I glanced at Wendy, who appeared unfazed. She clearly had no clue my timely prayer had just saved the two of us from a grisly demise.

I'd soon discover my final prayer during the car ride would go unanswered. Bubba would not be up and dressed, laughing about his fainting spell as he signed discharge papers. Instead, when we arrived at the Wheatfield Memorial Hospital in St. Joseph, Missouri, we learned he was comatose and clinging to life by a thin, tattered thread.

TWENTY-ONE

I had a strong premonition of impending doom the second we walked into the ICU waiting room. Andy's tuxedo jacket was folded over the back of his chair, and he was using the sleeve of his dress shirt to wipe tears from his cheeks. He was a naturally upbeat guy. I'd never seen the handsome young man upset before. The sight of him crying tugged at my heartstrings and made my own eyes fill with tears.

Stone had his arm draped across the back of Andy's chair as well, no doubt wrinkling the tuxedo jacket beyond the limited threshold of getting the damage deposit returned. When Stone noticed our presence, he looked up and shook his head. I could tell by his expression he had been unable to adequately console his nephew.

The relief on Stone's face was evident when he spotted Wendy walk into the room behind me. She rushed to Andy's side as Stone stood up and motioned for me to walk with him. "We're going to go grab some coffee, kids. We'll be right back."

Neither Andy nor Wendy appeared to hear his remark, or even notice that Stone and I were in the same time zone as they were.

They were deeply engrossed with each other. I could feel the love they shared as they gazed into each other's eyes.

"Has Bubba—" I stopped, unable to finish my question, but Stone knew what I was trying to ask.

"No. Not yet, anyway," Stone whispered. "He's still comatose, and is currently on life support. They are operating on the belief Bubba suffered severe heat stroke, between the brutal heat and humidity today, and the excitement of the moment. Supporting that assumption is the fact they've determined he was very dehydrated, possibly due to the elevated sodium level in his system."

"Can heat stroke be fatal?" I asked, not sure I wanted to hear the answer.

"Yes. It's rare, but it happens. The EMT's who delivered Bubba to the hospital had reported his body temperature was 100.5 degrees when they'd arrived on the scene to treat him, which was a lot lower than the nurse practitioner said they'd expect from a comatose heat-stroke victim. In fact, Dr. Schnuck said they would've been more convinced he'd suffered heat stroke if his temperature had been in the 104-degree range, or higher."

"If that's the case, shouldn't they be checking for other issues that might have caused this to happen?"

"They are. Just not as diligently as I'd like. They've run a few tests but nothing else has stood out as an alternative cause for his collapse. The cardiologist on the team evaluated him for a possible heart attack, perhaps caused by an undiagnosed heart valve problem or some other type of cardiac abnormality. But the EKG came back normal, as did other cardiac testing."

"Did they check into any pre-existing conditions Bubba might have?"

"With no immediate family present, they couldn't get much information. They did question Andy in depth as soon as we arrived. The two of them are as close as brothers, you know. But Andy wasn't aware of any serious medical conditions his friend might have, other than a mild case of asthma that hadn't bothered Bubba at all since high school. He also knew his buddy had undergone a complete physical exam recently for his job, and had been declared 'fit as a fiddle'."

"Clearly, not all fiddles are as fit as they appear," I said in a sad voice. "I never did understand that cliché, anyway. What does being fit have to do with a fiddle? Does a cello look at a fiddle and say, 'Look at the neck on that dude! I need to exercise more and trim down so I can look as fit as he does?'"

Without responding, Stone looked at me as if he were a bartender trying to determine whether or not to serve me another drink. Knowing I had a tendency to babble when I was on edge, he put his arm around my shoulder as we continued to walk down a long hallway. In an attempt to comfort me, he said, "Maybe it'll turn out to be nothing, honey. Just a fluke, perhaps."

I felt anything but comforted by his remark. "Yes, but often these kinds of flukes turn out to be deadly. Did they rule out a blood sugar issue?"

"The doctor told Andy that Bubba's blood sugar was ninety-four when tested in the ambulance. A perfectly normal level, he said. I heard Andy tell the physician who quizzed him that Bubba had been diagnosed as a borderline diabetic about two years ago. So he cut out sugar and, like your out-of-shape cello apparently needs to do, Bubba joined a gym. Between the dietary changes and increased exercise, he lost thirty pounds, lowered his BMI level, and dropped his average fasting blood sugar level significantly." Stone stopped speaking as he reached for his wallet.

"That's good," I replied, watching Stone dig for dollar bills as we stood in front of a canteen-style coffee machine.

After he returned his wallet to his back pocket, Stone continued. "It seems big Bubba is scared to death of needles, and the very idea of giving himself insulin injections was all the incentive he needed to make some lifestyle changes. Oh, sorry. I suppose 'scared to death' wasn't the best phrase to use."

"Good as any, I suppose. So that lumberjack-looking dude is afraid of needles, huh? Big old baby." We laughed, but only to help ease our tension. There was nothing funny about Bubba's condition.

"The combination of not knowing for certain what caused Bubba to stop breathing and being unable to question him, is making matters even more challenging for Dr. Schnuck and the rest of the medical staff," Stone said. "Even though the medical team assigned to Bubba is treating him as though he'd suffered an extreme heat stroke, it's obvious they aren't positive their presumption is correct. They're concerned there may be something else going on with Bubba they're overlooking."

"So what are they going to do now?"

"They're still running various tests and waiting for the results of a tox screen to come back. They put him on a breathing machine, of course, and aren't allowing any visitors in his room."

"Why not?"

"If Bubba were to flat-line again, they'd need all hands on deck and the patient's family and friends well out of their way within seconds. Those few seconds needed to clear the room of visitors could be the difference in life or death in a 'Code Blue' situation."

"Oh, good Lord. I guess you're right." I was sorry I'd asked. "Speaking of family, have Bubba's parents been notified? I assume they live on the east coast, as well."

"Andy said his parents were both killed in a bad car wreck when Bubba was barely out of diapers. But he does have an older sister in Arco, Idaho, named Sam, whom Andy's trying to contact."

"Arco? Why does that town sound familiar?"

"Probably because it was the first town ever to be lit by electricity generated solely by nuclear power. It was subsequently the site of the world's first, and the United States' only, fatal nuclear reactor accident. And, as you probably know, Arco was originally named Root Hog."

Stone's remark was said so matter-of-factly, I was flattered he'd think I'd actually know of any of those interesting facts, especially the original name of a town in Idaho. I could count my list of familiar Idaho towns on my right hand. Stone amazed me with all of the facts and figures he could dig out of his memory banks. I'd learned never to challenge him to a game of *Trivial Pursuit*. And fact-checking him on the Internet had nearly always proven to be a waste of time.

"Root Hog, huh? No, I don't think that is why it sounds familiar to me," I said with a smile. Then it hit me where I'd heard of the town before. "Oh, now I remember. Not long ago, while I was helping Deb Custovio get familiarized with her new position at the library one day, she told me her sister, Yvonne, who just happens to be my hairstylist, lived there years ago while attending a cosmetology school."

"Arco's a relatively small town, little more than a thousand residents, so Sam and Yvonne might be acquainted with each other. Then again, their paths may have never crossed."

"Really?" I asked. "You know the population of Arco, Idaho? I don't even know what the population of Rockdale is, and I've lived there for two years."

"Rockdale's official population is 9,889."

"You couldn't have just said 'around ten-thousand' and made me feel a little less uninformed?" I teased before returning to the subject at hand. "I assume Sam is short for Samantha?"

"Yes."

"Let's let Andy know that when he reaches Sam, he can offer her a complimentary suite at the inn for as long as necessary. Staying with us would be more convenient for her than a hotel. For one thing, it wouldn't cost her anything, and for another, she could use my vehicle whenever she wants. I'll have access to yours or Wendy's if an emergency arises."

"Good idea. I hope he can reach her soon. In the event it proves to be something other than heat exposure, she may know of something in Bubba's medical records that can be useful to the staff."

"Yes, and it would be nice for Bubba to have a close family member here for him," I said. "So her name's Samantha Slippknott, huh?"

"Uh-huh. That was her maiden name, anyway. Andy told me she prefers to be called Sam."

"That's nice, although I prefer Samantha. Makes me think of Samantha Stephens, from one of my favorite shows growing up."

"And what would that be?"

"*Bewitched,* of course." As I replied, I looked up at him and tried to twitch my nose. My attempt to imitate Elizabeth Montgomery's classic trademark move must have been comical, because it was the first time I'd seen Stone laugh all day. I was hoping that by injecting a little light-heartedness into our conversation, it'd take his mind off the reality of the situation, if only for a moment or two.

"*Bewitched?* Hmmm. I don't remember that one."

"You don't remember *Bewitched?*" I was flabbergasted. "What planet did you grow up on?"

"Several, actually. Krypton and Vulcan, to name two. For the most part, I pretended to live on the *USS Enterprise.*"

"As in *Star Trek?*"

"Yep. I imagined myself as Captain Kirk, of course."

"Of course. Somehow I never pictured you as a Trekkie." I laughed as I visualized Stone pretending to be at the helm of the starship, guiding it to "new worlds, where no man has gone before". While he was saving the universe, I was pretending to be Nancy Drew, craftily solving crimes. It's no wonder I couldn't resist getting involved in murders that hit close to home as an adult. "You know what? We should talk more. There's obviously a lot we still don't know about each other."

"And eliminate the allure of intrigue?" Stone laughed heartily this time, and then quickly scanned the area to ensure no one was watching us. "I've heard women think mysterious men are sexy. I'm afraid if you know too much about me, you wouldn't love me as much as you thought you did."

"That would never, ever happen, my dear."

Stone grew more serious as we entered the hospital's main lobby and turned down a lengthy hallway to the ICU waiting room. Halfway down the hallway, Stone stopped me to continue our conversation out of earshot of Andy and Wendy. "I wonder if Andy's been able to reach Sam yet. He couldn't even leave a message earlier because it said her mailbox was full. I'm not sure what that means, but he seemed to."

"It means her voice mail message capacity had been reached," I explained. In the rare event I knew something Stone didn't, I didn't hesitate to gloat about it. "You really need to use your cell phone more often so you can learn the lingo."

"I hate cell phones. I got along just fine for nearly half a century without one, as did everyone else my age. Now, everyone acts as if they couldn't possibly survive without one in their hand 24/7," Stone grumbled.

"I know, dear." Somehow Stone always managed to take the fun out of my knowing more about something than he did, and this was no exception. Deflated like a used airbag, I reverted to our original topic. "Andy told me Sam was married. I'm assume she changed her surname to her husband's when she married. I imagine that was a welcome relief. Her new name can't possibly be worse than Slippknott."

"You'd think not, wouldn't you?" Stone asked wryly. "Now her name is Samantha Slippknott-Sloppenbanger."

"Slippknott-Sloppenbanger? She actually hyphenated her last name? That makes for quite a mouthful."

"Is that why you chose to keep your former name, rather than be Alexandria Marie Starr-Van Patten?" Stone flashed me a warm smile. For the umpteenth time, I was amazed at how white and straight his teeth were.

"Not really. I was just too lazy to order new checks," I replied in jest.

"Yeah, right. Oh, by the way. I heard they want to keep Raven overnight for observation, even though she appears to be none the worse for wear," Stone said. "It was nice of her to step in and try to revive Bubba, wasn't it? The paramedics said she kept oxygen going to his brain until they arrived with the defibrillator. She's a hero in my book."

"Thank God for Raven and her quick thinking." I agreed that Raven's actions had been heroic. "Poor thing. I'm glad she seems to be all right. She recently moved to Rockdale and just started working for Lily Franks at the Lily's-in-Bloom Floral Shop six or seven weeks ago."

"With the recent move and all, I'm sure this is very traumatic for her. The ER doctor told me they have her on oxygen as a precaution. He said Raven exhibited some of the same symptoms as Bubba, but to a lesser degree. She did, however, present a slightly higher temperature than Bubba's, at 101.7. They suspect she experienced heat stroke or exhaustion, as well. In the unlikely event that wasn't the cause, they're trying to determine if there's some other kind of connection to both of them suddenly passing out. I don't know how it could have been anything but the heat. I felt a little overwhelmed by the mugginess this afternoon, too. I swear, in that monkey suit I had on, I could feel the sweat running down my back and forming a puddle in my dress shoes."

"I guess you're right. It *was* incredibly scorching and humid. And here I thought I was just having a hot flash." Even though I hoped everyone's assumption of the two incidents being caused by the heat of the day was correct, I couldn't get past the feeling there was something entirely different at play that had yet to come to light. But saying something like that out loud would only worry Stone. His blood pressure had dropped significantly since I'd assured him I'd never involve myself in a murder case again, after nearly losing my life a year ago while trying to track down a killer in an RV park in Cheyenne, Wyoming. With all that behind us, there was no sense in tipping over the outhouse now. The last thing I needed was for my husband to stroke out on me.

"Andy and Wendy must be beside themselves."

"Speaking of which, Lexie, we need to get back to the waiting room. After all they've been through today, the kids will probably welcome some support."

"And they'll probably welcome these cups of coffee, too."

"Even though they came out of a vending machine?" Stone asked. He was much more persnickety about coffee than I was. But then, I don't know of anyone who isn't.

"As I've always said, bad coffee is better than no coffee any day of the week."

"Yikes!" Stone exclaimed as he looked down at his coffee. "This is strong and thick enough to seal the cracks in the hospital's parking lot."

"I actually thought it was pretty tasty."

Stone shook his head and looked up toward the ceiling. "Beam me up, Scotty!"

TWENTY-TWO

The hospital released Raven a few hours later. She had arrived in the ER with a slightly elevated temperature and a perfect sodium level. Since regaining consciousness just moments after passing out at the wedding, she'd exhibited no other symptoms other than a bit of light-headedness and some minor confusion. Within an hour of arriving at the hospital, Raven's temperature had returned to normal. The temperature inside the hospital had been so cool—to prevent the growth of bacteria, no doubt—Raven was probably more in danger of suffering from hypothermia than heat stroke.

Against the doctor's recommendations, she insisted she be released. Though the medical staff wasn't fully confident that heat stroke or heat exhaustion caused her fainting spell, they couldn't find a good reason to hold her overnight. The medical team attending to her had voiced an interest in retaining her for testing purposes, but when Raven expressed concern about the limits of her health insurance coverage, the medical team relented and discharged her.

Bubba Slippknott remained comatose and his prognosis looked grim. The tox screen results came back later that day. He had tested negative to all of the toxins covered by the analysis. The head physician stated that though not all toxins were included in the standard screening, it did include the most probable poisons people have been known to ingest, accidental or otherwise. The tox screen reports did not, the doctor emphasized, rule out some of the more uncommon poisonous substances.

For the moment, all we could do was sit back and pray as we waited for his condition to either improve or, God forbid, take a turn for the worse. Most of the predictions that came from the hospital staff were not optimistic. In fact, it appeared as if their focus changed and they were now more worried about how to protect themselves from a potential malpractice lawsuit if the patient passed while under their care.

Neither Stone nor Andy had left the hospital since Bubba had been wheeled into the trauma center on a gurney. Andy had tried to reach Bubba's sister, Samantha, numerous times to no avail. He did, however, reach Sam's best friend, who claimed not to have seen her in several days. According to the friend, Sam hadn't showed up at work for the past two days. This friend, who'd been keeping an eye on Sam during her husband's deployment, had contacted the building super at Sam's apartment complex. He checked her apartment and found nothing amiss. Nor did he find his tenant.

Andy had advised Sam's friend to contact the police and she promised she would do so. He'd told her about Bubba's dire condition and explained Sam needed to get in touch with the ICU department as soon as possible. The friend recalled Sam mention once that Bubba had been deathly allergic to peanuts as a child, but thought he'd pretty much grown out of it by adulthood—or had learned to avoid them. And, as Andy had told the head physician, Bubba was mildly asthmatic, although he hadn't had an asthma attack in years.

"Though his condition may not be related to a peanut allergy, there *was* a bowl of mixed nuts on the refreshment table," I told Stone. "I recall the doctor telling us Bubba's sodium level had been elevated. I can't think of anything else on that table that was particularly salty, except maybe the shrimp rollups."

"I saw Bubba sampling the icing on the cake when he thought no one was looking." Stone chuckled at the memory, then grew serious. "There weren't any nuts in the cake or icing were there?"

"No. At least there shouldn't have been. I'm sure we'd have paid extra for them if there were."

"Andy remembers Bubba ate a handful of mixed nuts while they mingled with the guests before the ceremony began. A handful's not a lot, but the doctor said it doesn't take much to cause anaphylactic shock if someone is highly allergic to a certain substance."

"Well, maybe the few peanuts in that handful *are* what caused Bubba to pass out," I said skeptically, "but what about Raven? What are the odds she has a nut allergy, too?"

"Yeah, that's just it," Stone replied. "Dr. Schnuck said Raven claimed she had only one allergy—to penicillin. They were preparing to give her intravenous antibiotics, but nixed the idea after questioning her. They went ahead and put Bubba on them, just in case, hoping it might be helpful if he had an infection of some kind. In essence, the medical staff took the information about Bubba's childhood peanut allergy with a grain of salt."

"Maybe they shouldn't have dismissed it so hastily," I said.

"Well, obviously they didn't think it had any bearing on their patient's condition, but they assured us they weren't going to rule it out, along with any other kind of known, or undiagnosed, allergy. People can develop allergies at any time during their lifetime, Dr. Schnuck said, but the general consensus among the medical staff remained unchanged. They believe Bubba had been wound up by the excitement of the day, extremely hot from wearing a black tuxedo in the brutal sun, and ultimately overcome by heatstroke."

I thanked Stone for filling me in and left him to resume his pacing, as both he and Andy had been doing since Wendy and I first arrived at the hospital. Just then, a cluster of physicians walked in through another portal. Stone and Andy pounced on them like kittens on a bead of light from a laser pointer. They insisted Bubba be transferred to a larger hospital that was more able to deal with his illness.

Stone barked at one of the head physicians in frustration. "Why in the hell can't Bubba be life-flighted to a better-equipped trauma center, like the Mayo Clinic, where his chances of survival would be greatly enhanced?"

I wasn't sure "life-flighted" was the proper term, but neither life-flown or life-flit sounded right, either. I suppose the fact I was even ruminating over such a trivial thing showed how frazzled I felt.

"The Mayo Clinic is just over three-hundred miles as the crow flies." I could see Stone's blood pressure shooting up like a Roman candle as he spoke to the attending physician. "Bubba could be flown there in short order. If his insurance won't cover it, I'll pay for it personally."

I wasn't surprised Stone knew how far it was for a crow to fly to what was one of the most advanced medical centers in the world. I also wasn't particularly surprised when the medical staff rebuffed his suggestion. However, I'll admit I *was* slightly surprised when Stone offered to pay the cost of life-flighting Bubba to Minnesota if the young man's insurance wouldn't approve the expense. I could visualize our plans of taking an extended Mediterranean cruise that winter evaporating like morning dew on a musk melon. However, I, too, was willing to sacrifice whatever it took to make sure Bubba received the best care possible.

The medical staff didn't seem to appreciate Stone's inference that they weren't competent enough to keep the young man alive. But protecting their sensitive feelings just then was not high on my husband's priority list.

TWENTY-THREE

An hour later, Stone and I were walking up the hallway toward the parking lot. Exhausted, I knew I needed to get some sleep as much as Stone clearly did. By riding with him, Wendy's car would be available if she chose to return to the ranch before Andy. I had a hunch he'd be spending the night at the hospital to be on hand if Bubba regained consciousness.

As we rounded a corner, we came face-to-face with Sheila and Randy. I hugged them both. "Are you here to check on Bubba? I'm sorry. I should have sent you an update before now."

"No, that's not it," Sheila said. "Wendy updated us on his condition earlier."

"Then why are—"

"I brought Sheila in to be looked at," Randy cut in. I then noticed his worried expression, and that Sheila's face matched her light green eye shadow. "She's been released and we were just on our way out."

"Been released? Oh, no. What's wrong?" I asked Randy, as if Sheila was physically incapable of speaking for herself.

"She started feeling a little woozy and acting confused. I walked into your kitchen and found her placing a box full of the small bouquets and boutonnieres into the oven, and then had to help her to a chair before she lost her balance. With Bubba and Raven suddenly getting seriously ill like they did, I didn't want to take any chances on Sheila getting sick, too."

"I'm glad you didn't. This situation is getting curiouser and curiouser. How are you feeling now, Sheila?" I grasped her hands in mine. She looked worn out and wobbly. "Did the doctors determine you'd had too much exposure to the heat and humidity, as they believe Bubba and Raven did?"

"The nurse told me that was their best guess." As Sheila spoke, Randy leaned in to steady her.

"Best guess?" Stone asked. He was frustrated already without hearing the emergency room personnel were making wild-ass guesses at the cause of their patients' illnesses. "*That's* what they're paid the big bucks for? I could have come up with that conclusion without spending a single second in medical school."

I didn't want to give Stone a chance to get even more worked up. I was certain his blood pressure was already elevated to a dangerous level. So I asked, "Did they run any tests in the event it wasn't caused by the heat?"

"The lab drew blood, of course. They have a tendency to do that even if you only come in to the emergency room with a small gash that needs to be stitched up. It's clear they can really stick it to the insurance companies for blood work. According to the nurse, my vitals were normal, other than my blood pressure, which was off the charts. I'm sure just being here elevated my blood pressure. It typically goes up thirty points the second someone in a white coat walks into the room."

"Mine does that, too," Randy added.

"As does mine," I said. "I think it's called white-coat syndrome."

"Mine has been off the charts since we walked into this sorry excuse for a hospital," Stone grumbled.

"Sheila's also hypoglycemic, you know," Randy went on after giving Stone a sympathetic smile. "I found some orange juice in your fridge and had her drink a glass of it just in case her blood sugar was low. Her glucose level tested perfect in the emergency room."

I nodded at Randy. "That's good. I'll bet low blood sugar is exactly what caused her dizziness and confusion. I remember the day she passed out in the high school parking lot after it dropped too low. She had to have her jaw wired shut after hitting her mouth on the hood of her car."

"Yes, I'm sure you do remember that incidence," Sheila said in mock annoyance. "And I recall you saying you were finally going to get a much-needed vacation from my non-stop jabbering."

We all laughed. Then I asked, "Did you happen to notice if any of the food on the refreshment table tasted suspicious?"

"Randy and I stopped for brunch on our way to Rockdale, so I didn't eat anything at the wedding except for a piece of the cake."

"I didn't have a bite of anything," Randy added.

"But I *was* drinking plenty of punch—" Sheila stopped abruptly as she noticed the look on her husband's face. In a more subdued voice, she finished her statement. "To stay hydrated in the sizzling heat, of course."

"What?" He asked. At Sheila's comment, Randy cocked his head and stared at her as if he'd just learned his wife had been downing cups full of paint thinner all morning. I read his expression perfectly. Like Randy, I also wondered if Sheila had "over-sampled" her own concoction. Its reputation for being potent was well-earned.

"You don't happen to have a peanut allergy you've never told me about, do you?" I asked my friend, sparing her a grilling by her husband. I knew her well enough to know she'd rather answer my question than the one currently forming in Randy's head.

"No, of course not. When I have an eyelash out of place, I call and discuss it with you for ten minutes. Why do you ask?"

"Well, there goes the peanut-allergy theory," I murmured. After explaining what Sam's friend had told Andy on the phone, I then told the Davidsons about the baffling situation with Bubba's sister.

"Wow! That *is* worrisome. It sounds as if Sam vanished into thin air," Sheila said. "Do you think there's any chance her disappearance is connected to Bubba's health crisis?"

"Exactly my point. On one hand, it seems like a far-fetched notion. But on the other, nothing about this situation is normal. As if we didn't have enough to worry about, huh?"

"That's for sure," Sheila agreed. Randy nodded, as well.

I sensed Stone was about to chastise me for inferring something reprehensible might have happened, so I spoke quickly. "Well, I'm relieved you are feeling better. I hope you're not just putting on a brave face, as you often do when you don't want anyone to worry over you."

"Truly, I'm fine now," Sheila assured me. "In fact, I tried to talk Randy out of bringing me here, but you know what a worrywart he is."

"Love will do that to a person," Randy said defensively. "However, had I known how much punch you——"

"And rightfully so, Sheila," I said, interrupting her husband as I knew Sheila would do for me if I were in her shoes. "Did the ER docs give you any discharge instructions?"

"To stop drinking——" Randy began, his voice dripping with sarcasm. Stone began to chuckle along with Randy.

Sheila cut them both off this time and replied, "They advised me to go home and rest for the remainder of the evening, which means we'll be staying another night or two, if that's all right with you. Fortunately, I over-packed more than I normally do. I even threw in a couple of extra days' worth of clothes for Randy."

"Of course, it's fine with me. You can always use our laundry facilities if needed. I'd be delighted to have you two stay until we can have a 'do-over' of the wedding ceremony. Now that we live farther apart, I don't get to spend nearly enough time with my dearest friend."

"Well, we'll see," Randy answered. "She may feel back to her normal, lively self in the morning after her hang——"

"But——" Sheila and I butted into Randy's response simultaneously. The look Sheila gave him seemed to have a positive effect. Positive in my opinion, at least, since I would love to have more time to visit with her, and I knew she felt the same.

"Well, we don't really have anything pressing at home, and it might not be such a bad idea to kick back here for a few days. We could both use some rest and relaxation." Randy looked lovingly at his wife. It was clear his remarks about the punch had only been in jest. Then, he turned to me. "While we're here, I can help around the inn so Stone will be free to check on Bubba's progress here at the hospital."

"That would be awesome, Randy. I'd appreciate it very much."

"As would I, buddy," Stone added. "Come on. We'll walk with you guys to the parking lot. We're heading home now ourselves."

I waved to a couple of emergency room nurses who knew me by name on our way out of the hospital. Regrettably, I'd visited the ER far too many times in the last couple of years. That was one of the reasons I'd promised Stone I'd give up sticking my nose into murder cases, even though my investigations had always been of a personal nature.

An emergency room physician entered the hospital as we were exiting and greeted me. "Hey there, Lexie. Long time, no see."

"And we'd like to keep it that way, Dr. Johnson." Stone beat me to the punch at responding to the physician.

My sleuthing habits often had a tendency to make the killer intent on bringing me down permanently in order to eliminate the chance that I'd stumble across an incriminating clue. The fact I'd immediately cease to be a pain in their ass if their attempt to silence me was successful was an added bonus for them. Incidents such as those had scared me, naturally, but they'd absolutely terrified Stone.

As those thoughts flitted through my mind on the drive home, I wondered again if something more devious than heat exhaustion was behind the sudden illnesses of now three attendees of the wedding the previous afternoon. There was also the mysterious disappearance of Bubba's sister in Arco, Idaho, which was equally disturbing.

Randy's remarks were not totally off base. It was true Sheila drank more of the spiked punch than she should have, but I'd think the emergency room technicians would have said so had they thought that was what was the cause of her symptoms. Instead, they'd "guessed" she'd fallen victim to too much heat exposure. So, what were the chances of all three of them falling victim to excessive heat exposure at the same approximate time period? Coincidental? I doubted it.

Yes, it had been a hot, muggy day, which was not uncommon during the "dog days of summer" in the Midwest. It'd been just as oppressive outside for the previous two weeks, other than the one day it was overcast and rainy.

Though varied in the degree of severity, all three of the victims' symptoms seemed to be consistent with each other, which leaned toward the presumed diagnosis of heat exhaustion or heatstroke. In my opinion though, it could point toward something entirely different. All three individuals could have been exposed to some unknown hazard, which in turn brought on their sudden illness. It sounded ludicrous, but not as ludicrous as three individuals falling ill—and in such a narrow window of time because of heat exposure—on a typical summer day in Missouri.

I've always said a person should leave no stone unturned when trying to determine a logical explanation for whatever tragic event had taken place. Or, whatever crime had been committed. I knew I wouldn't rest until the reason behind these illnesses had been resolved.

I thought back to the first meeting I'd had with Lariat. I'd suspected he'd slipped something into my drink, but it turned out to be a case of mild food poisoning. Could something the caterer delivered an hour earlier have gone bad so quickly, or had the food been tainted even before its arrival? I'd always had very good experiences with Georgia Piney's Catering Services in the past, but did recall being underwhelmed with some of her online reviews. I had convinced myself that only customers of the company who'd had a bad experience would take the time to post a review. That seems to be a common scourge to what could generally be a helpful tool when researching something on the Internet. The disgruntled had a tendency to protest loudly, while the contented rejoiced silently. *If unhappy people are described as disgruntled, why are pleased folks not described as "gruntled"?* The fact I found myself wondering about such a thing was a clue I needed to chill out and clear my mind. But doing so was easier said than done.

Thinking back, the fruit and vegetable tray seemed suspect. I hadn't been satisfied with the cherry tomatoes or the strawberries. The cheese tray could have been fresher, too. It probably wasn't a great idea to have the shrimp rollups sitting out in the heat, but that was my fault, not Georgia's. I had put them out on the pre-ceremony snack table instead of storing them in the refrigerator and saving them exclusively for the reception.

Could Bubba have developed an allergy to shellfish? I should have turned on the radio right then to distract myself, because the more questions I asked, the more distraught I became. But I didn't. Instead, I continued to fret over the possibilities.

I had seen Bubba mingling around the refreshment table eating shrimp rollups with Andy and a couple of other young men. And let's face it, the six-foot-eight-inch fellow was like a bull moose that consumed food almost constantly to keep his body fueled. However, I knew for a fact Sheila didn't ingest any of the shrimp rollups. *Oh, good Lord! Maybe I should have posted a sign listing ingredients by each food item on the refreshment table.*

By the time I pulled into the Alexandria Inn's driveway, I was a royal mess. I had convinced myself it was my fault three people had fallen ill at the wedding. I also felt guilty about agreeing with Wendy that the men in the wedding party should wear black tuxes. She'd been adamant about it, saying, "I know it's not the best color to wear in the sun, but damn, men sure look hot in black tuxes!"

They had certainly looked hot, all right. Unfortunately, in more ways than one. I should have tried harder to talk her into having the groomsmen wear white, or at least a color lighter than black. My tendency to wear guilt like a cloak was beginning to weigh heavy on me.

Oh, God! If Bubba dies, could I be held responsible for his death? The murder weapon of choice being a black tuxedo. Or a blasted peanut. Or shellfish. I started wondering what kind of punishment was handed down to a defendant convicted of manslaughter for wielding a lethal shrimp rollup against her victim. I didn't know the answer to that question, but I did know I was in dire need of a caffeine boost. Unlike most folks, coffee had a calming effect on me. Or, at least it did until I was midway through my fifth cup in one setting. At that point, I became wired like a car bomb, ready to explode at the flick of a switch.

After arriving at the inn, Stone headed for the den to catch the evening news, and I headed straight for the coffee pot. I needed something to calm me down so I could think logically, rather than scare myself silly while in the midst of a panic attack.

And then it hit me like a meteorite falling at great speed from the sky. Was it even remotely possible we could be looking at an attempted murder, or murders? Was Samantha in great peril or, God forbid, already deceased? Should an armed guard be stationed outside Bubba's hospital room? Worse yet, if Bubba didn't survive his medical crisis, could we be looking at another full-fledged murder on the grounds of the Alexandria Inn? Was the inn cursed? Were customers risking their lives by merely visiting our lodging facility? Even three cups of coffee could not stop the frightening thoughts and questions from swirling through my mind. It wasn't long before I was midway through my fourth cup and could actually hear an ominous ticking sound inside my head.

To dilute all the caffeine I'd drank, I poured myself a large glass of leftover punch. The punch was so refreshing, I refilled my cup before forcing myself to get busy putting the wedding stuff away. As I did, I noticed the box of bouquets and boutonnieres. Randy must have removed the box from the oven, where he'd caught Sheila storing it away, and left it on the counter. I straightened the floral accessories in the box. Bubba's boutonniere had been crumpled, and half of the palm of Christ flower petals ripped off by the EMTs who'd arrived on the scene to revive him.

With a sense of melancholy, I held his tattered boutonniere to my nose to inhale the slightly stale fragrance of the flowers. Each boutonniere had the beautiful red blossoms that had a more bitter aroma than one would expect. I'm no flower expert, but I knew some blossoms were beautiful to look at, yet had fragrances that were less than appealing.

Trying to keep the waterworks at bay, I quickly placed the boutonniere back into the box with the others. I closed the lid and placed it in the extra fridge in the pantry. There'd been just enough room on the shelf below the half-eaten wedding cake. The cake, which wasn't very attractive to begin with, now looked like it'd been attacked by a couple of hungry crows—and I'm not referring to Hazel Hallberg and Orpha White, the ladies from my church, but to the actual birds.

My stomach growled. I hadn't had anything but a breakfast bar all day. Unable to resist, I pushed aside my earlier suspicions about the cake being tainted and pinched off a chunk, and ate it. Considering how unsightly it was, it was quite moist and tasty. I pinched off another chunk and washed it down with the last of the fruit punch in my glass. The alcohol in the drink burned my esophagus all the way down to my navel. The fact I thought I saw steam emanating from my belly button was a sign I'd consumed too much of Sheila's high-octane punch, but it didn't register at the time.

I sat the empty glass in the sink and hastily threw the nuts and shrimp rollups into the trash can, bowls and all, as if I was covertly trying to get rid of incriminating evidence. In actuality, I knew I'd never be able to use those bowls again without feeling an odd sense of remorse. Nor would I ever be able to rest until I convinced myself the tragic situation was not, in some form or fashion, no one's fault but my own.

TWENTY-FOUR

A s I soaked in the master suite's whirlpool bath later that evening, I began to feel light-headed. For a full minute, I struggled to catch my breath. Afraid I'd pass out in the tub and drown, I banged on the wall with as much strength as I could muster. Within seconds, I heard Stone racing up the stairs, calling my name frantically.

"Lexie? Lexie? Where are you?"

"In the tub." I tried to yell, but nothing came out but a hoarse whisper. Fortunately, Stone yanked open the bathroom door and knelt next to the tub. The worried expression on his face faded in and out of my vision. I felt like someone who'd smoked too much weed at a Rolling Stones concert. Not that I'd ever done such a thing, mind you.

"What's wrong, baby? Are you okay?"

He pulled the plug in the tub to let the water drain, then pulled out his phone. I heard him talking but couldn't make out the words. When I recognized the words "nine-one-one", I came out of my fog enough to tell him I didn't need medical attention. The last thing I wanted was to make another trip to the emergency room in the back of an ambulance.

"Don't call nine-one-one, honey. I am starting to feel normal again already." I was still weak, but breathing better and able to form full sentences. "I started feeling disoriented and my head began spinning. Then I had difficulty catching my breath. I truly thought I was going to pass out."

"Don't you go pulling a Whitney Houston on me," Stone said. He instantly regretted his remark. "Sorry. That wasn't funny. In fact, it wasn't humorous at all. What just happened to you was eerily similar to the symptoms exhibited by Bubba and Raven."

"And Sheila," I added.

"What in heaven's name is going on? Do you think there could be some potent, highly contagious virus going around?"

"Could be. It's certainly a possibility we should run by the medical staff tending to Bubba. I'm also wondering if something on the refreshment table is the culprit. There might be something all four of us ate, although I don't recall having a sample of anything before the wedding." Thinking back, I retraced my actions as well as I could. "Well, I did have a couple bites of the wedding cake this evening. Damn it! Now that I think about it, Sheila said she had a piece of it too before getting ill. That must be it. I'm sorry, Stone. I was really hungry."

"You certainly don't have to apologize for being hungry, honey. I was thinking about cutting off a piece of it for myself, but changed my mind after looking at it."

"No doubt. After being butchered by the wedding guests, the cake now looks as if it stepped on an I.U.D. Seriously, Stone, I'm now worried there may be a whole slew of wedding guests who have fallen ill that we're not even aware of. If it was the cake, I know there's likely dozens of affected individuals. I'm so sorry I didn't check—"

"Check what, honey? How were you to know if the cake, or something on the refreshment table, wasn't up to snuff? Relax, it's not your fault." Stone leaned over the tub and cradled me in his arms, his shirt soaking up the moisture from my wet skin. He finally released me and said, "Let's get you dried off and tucked into bed. I know you are as worn out and on edge as I am. I'm just relieved you're all right now."

Stone helped me out of the tub and handed me a towel. Standing behind me, he wrapped his arms around my towel-clad body and kissed the back of my neck. Tender moments like this made me realize how lucky I was to have found such a loving man to spend the rest of my life with.

I thought back to that silly promise I'd made to him not to get involved in any more murder cases. Why my gut was telling me that foul play had been involved in Bubba's condition, I can't begin to tell you. But the feeling was there, and it was doing a number on my gut. Or *was* it that damned cake? Now I found myself actually hoping it *was* the wedding cake. *It's awful,* I thought, *but not nearly as awful as being the result of foul play. How many wedding guests ate a slice after I foolishly shouted, "Let them eat cake!"?*

I needed to make some phone calls in the morning. I hated the thought that our guests may have contracted food poisoning at the wedding. That's not a very thoughtful way to show appreciation for their presence at the wedding and the nice gifts they'd brought for the bride and groom. I had to remind myself it wasn't my fault. I had no validated reason to believe the cake was contaminated.

The very possibility horrified me, but I needed to step up to the plate and call a few people. Hazel and Orpha came to mind. I knew for a fact they'd both gobbled down big forkfuls of the cake while criticizing its appearance. Not that their criticism wasn't right on target.

"Should we have the cake tested?" Stone asked.

"Huh?"

"Like you, I wonder if it might be the common denominator in everyone's sudden illness."

"I can hardly show up at a crime lab and ask them to test the cake as possible evidence," I replied without thinking.

"Crime lab?" Stone was clearly puzzled by my remark. "I was thinking we could take a sample to the hospital, and they might be able to see if it's tainted somehow. You know, like with salmonella, for example. Salmonella is occasionally found in eggs, which is a common ingredient in cake. Either way, that cake needs to go. Want me to call Reverend Bob over to give it last rites?"

"Wouldn't hurt." I chuckled, hoping he'd forgotten my earlier outburst. No such luck.

"What were you talking about when you mentioned taking the cake to a crime lab?" Stone asked.

"Oh, nothing. I was just babbling." I knew my voice would give me away if my demeanor, which was like that of a cornered prison escapee, hadn't already done the trick.

"Lexie, are you harboring some hare-brained idea that someone deliberately tried to hurt Bubba?" Stone asked. "And maybe Raven?"

"Don't forget Sheila. And me, perhaps." After my remarks, Stone gazed at me in silence. "That's just it, Stone. I don't believe in coincidences. As you said earlier, I think there must be a common denominator in all of this. Mine, fortunately, was short-lived. As was Sheila's. Even Raven wasn't affected to the degree Bubba was. And, yes, the common thread might be something as innocent as food poisoning. Or, even heat stroke. But what if it wasn't so innocent? What if there's a devil's pitchfork in the knife rack?"

"Huh?" Stone asked. "A what in the what?"

"You know what I mean."

"Not really. But I seriously doubt that—"

"What if there's something nefarious at play, and more and more victims are affected?" I cut Stone off, not wanting to be lectured about how ridiculous my suspicions were. Unfortunately, I'd only delayed the inevitable.

"I know how your mind works, Lexie." Stone spoke matter-of-factly, as if he were addressing a wayward child. "You automatically assume the worst, and—"

"No, I don't. I'm not assuming anything. I'm merely pointing out a viable potentiality."

Stone ignored my rebuttal. "I'll admit there's always the possibility of something unscrupulous having occurred. It's just as possible that the sun will collide with the moon tomorrow."

"You don't have to be sarcastic. I'm just worried and trying not to overlook anything. You know my motto has always been 'leave no stone unturned'." I felt as if I was defending myself in an interrogation room. "I have a right to be concerned about——"

"I'm concerned, too, Lexie. I don't want to rule out anything at this point, either, but let's not go there quite yet. I don't want to see you putting your life in danger, as you have an unhealthy habit of doing when you butt into matters of this sort."

"Hey!" I responded angrily because I was getting miffed now. It was the "butt into" part that really put a bucket of gravel in my craw. "That's not fair. I've never 'butted into' a case. Furthermore, the police have found my help very instrumental in solving a number of murder cases, and you know it."

"And your 'help' almost got you killed every single time!" Stone's voice rose and his amicable mood vanished like a mirage on the Sahara Desert. "Why do you think the doctor put me on blood pressure medicine?"

"Because you pour enough salt on your food to melt an inch-thick layer of ice off the Brooklyn Bridge. That's why!" I shouted.

If I hadn't felt a little light-headed and sick to my stomach, I would have stomped out of the room for effect. Instead, I plopped down on the edge of the bed. A tear rolled unchecked down my cheek. Stone never could stand to see me cry, and he caved in like a Florida sinkhole every single time. When he noticed the tear, he sat beside me and put his arms around me.

"I'm sorry, honey. I was out of line, and I apologize. You've been remarkably effective at solving homicide cases." Stone spoke soothingly as he caressed my back. I could tell his blood pressure was settling back down to a non-life-threatening level. "In fact, if this turns out to be an intentional assault on my godson, I promise I'll give you my blessing to butt—I mean look—into it."

Those were words I'd never thought I'd hear my husband utter, and they nearly pushed me once again to the brink of passing out. I prayed his remark would turn out to be a moot point, because I wasn't sure I had another murder investigation in me. Though his earlier comment had ticked me off, he wasn't entirely wrong that I'd nearly gotten killed in every one of my quests to hunt down a killer.

When I commit myself to something, I commit wholeheartedly. It's just my nature.

"Will you forgive me, honey?" Stone asked softly.

"How could I not? I love you more than life itself. I'm sorry, too." I kissed him as he pulled me into his embrace. "I hate it when we fight."

Stone agreed, and with a suggestive wink, he added, "But I love it when we make up."

"Rain check?" I asked. "I wouldn't want to upchuck a chunk of contaminated cake on you."

"Absolutely." He gave an understanding smile, pulled back the covers, and tucked me into bed. He kissed my forehead and said with a chuckle, "And I wouldn't want to fall asleep on you, my dear. I'll be lucky if I don't fall asleep standing up in the shower."

"Perhaps you should wait to shower until morning."

"I would if I didn't feel like I'd spent the afternoon sifting through a trash dumpster. I'll make it a quickie."

Stone walked into the bathroom for his short shower. *A cold one?* I wondered in amusement. I didn't wonder for long, however, for I was nearly asleep when he climbed into bed beside me a few minutes later, in search of some much-needed rest.

Little did I know at the time I'd soon be repeating Stone's words to him, demanding he stand by his promise and give me his blessing to look into the situation regarding Bubba's current condition.

TWENTY-FIVE

I struggled to stay asleep that night, unable to wrap my head around the fact that Bubba's life hung in the balance. I woke up on several occasions with my nightshirt clinging to my skin from excess perspiration. Just before daylight, I heard Stone ask in a sleepy voice, "You okay, honey? You're flopping like a goldfish that's jumped out of its bowl."

"Sorry. Just restless, I guess."

"Why don't you take some melatonin so you can get some shut-eye?"

Hours later, after I'd finally been able to fall asleep, I felt a warm hand on my shoulder, shaking me gently. I opened my eyes to see Stone looking down at me with obvious concern. I smiled at him, and asked, "Good morning. What time is it?"

"Almost ten."

"Oh, no. I really overslept."

"I'm sure you needed the rest. Don't worry. Everything's been taken care of. Rapella whipped up some pancakes, eggs, and bacon for everyone."

"Bless her heart. I'm so glad she and Rip are here. When did you get up?"

"Six-thirty. I've already been to the hospital and back. Bubba's condition had not changed, and there were no indications it'd change any time soon. Andy is just now on his way back to the ranch. He was worried about Wendy being alone out there in the middle of nowhere."

"Good. I know Andy's distraught, but he needs some rest, too. There's not much either one of you can do to help Bubba, especially if either of you become incapacitated due to sleep deprivation."

"That's basically what I told Andy when he insisted on staying overnight at the hospital. He stayed anyway."

"Glad you were finally able to persuade him to go home for a spell. So there have been no new updates from the medical staff whatsoever?"

"Unfortunately, no. But Sam's due in this afternoon. Hopefully, she'll have something to share about her brother's medical history that will prove to be useful."

"They finally got in touch with her?" I asked.

"Yes. Thank goodness!"

"Where had she been?"

"New Hampshire." Stone responded as if his answer would make perfect sense to me. It didn't. Why would the girl up and travel to New Hampshire without telling anyone? Stone might as well have said Samantha suddenly decided to take a shuttle up to the space station.

"What was Sam doing in New Hampshire?"

"She made an unplanned trip there to care for an elderly aunt who'd fallen and broken a hip. You see, her best friend was concerned for Sam's well-being, so she used the key she'd been given to enter Sam's apartment. She searched for a clue as to where Sam might have gone, and when she found nothing, she became alarmed. She then notified the police, who finally tracked Sam at her aunt's place. It seems Sam and Bubba's aunt lives out in the middle of nowhere and Sam can't get a signal on her phone. The elderly aunt doesn't even have Internet service, according to Sam, which she said was like camping out on the moon."

"That'd be rough, but I'm just thankful she's alive." I exhaled dramatically. My emotional reaction was not lost on my husband. "I mean, I couldn't imagine having something horrible happen to both siblings at the same time."

"Uh, yeah." He appeared dubious. I'm sure finding Sam dead had never crossed Stone's mind. I hoped he hadn't read more into my response than just relief that the young lady had been located. Unfortunately, in an attempt to explain my reaction, I'd only made Stone's skepticism amplify. "Why would you ever think she wouldn't be found alive?"

"You know I don't believe in coincidences, and I was afraid that both Samantha and Bub—" I stopped suddenly. I had no desire to argue with Stone two days in a row. When I'd mentioned to Stone the previous evening that I suspected Sam's absence may have been associated with Bubba's sudden collapse at the wedding, my comment irritated him. Therefore, I'd been reluctant to revisit my suspicions with him—or anyone else, for that matter. Well, other than with Sheila, that is. It was physically impossible for me not to share my every thought and feeling with my best friend. She had chewed the suggestion over for a minute or two and then agreed with me the situation was too absurd to rule out foul play.

"Yes. Go on."

"It's just that Samantha and Bubba—" I began, only to once again stop short of finishing my thought.

"Samantha and Bubba what?" Stone asked, clearly growing impatient.

"Um, well, I—" I struggled to come up with a response, hoping that if I stalled long enough, Stone would drop the subject. But he was persistent.

"What were you about to say about Samantha and Bubba?"

"Nothing. Other than I hope her elderly aunt's all right, but Bubba needs her more than the aunt does right now."

Stone gave me a look of doubt. I guess he knew me too well, which was not always a good thing. As my eyes grew misty, Stone relented. Rather than continue to push me, he pulled me into a hug,

"Sam will arrive at the airport a little after two today. A Lyft driver will take her straight to the hospital."

"That's great news."

Stone nodded. "I just hope she can help the medical staff determine what happened to Bubba."

"Yeah, me too." I picked my eyeglasses up off my night stand and put them on. "I need to get up, get dressed, and fix myself some toast."

"Fine, just don't burn down the inn in the process." Stone laughed, kissed me on the forehead, and stood up to leave. As he walked toward the bedroom door, he added, "The last piece of bread you toasted cost us over fifteen-hundred dollars in smoke damage repairs."

I threw my pillow, which hit the back of the door as it closed behind Stone. I could hear him chuckling all the way down the staircase.

Samantha Slippknott-Sloppenbanger was a beauty. She would put most super models to shame; tall like her brother, and slender, with wavy, strawberry-blond hair that hung almost to her waistline. After giving her a few minutes to weep at Bubba's bedside, the medical staff pulled her aside to gather his medical history.

Sam reiterated to the doctors nearly everything Andy had already told them. Bubba had been mildly asthmatic as a teenager, had been diagnosed as a borderline diabetic, and was allergic to peanuts. The only new information she had to relate was that her older brother had recently developed an acute allergy to sulfur.

"That is valuable information, ma'am," the medical staff assured Samantha. "Being allergic to sulfur doesn't necessarily mean Bubba is allergic to sulfa, otherwise known as sulfite sensitivity. Sulfa is found in many medications, including the antibiotic we've been giving your brother via his IV. So, just in case he's allergic to sulfa as well as sulfur, we will suspend the infusion so we aren't inadvertently worsening the problem. Allergies to sulfa, sulfur, and/or sulfite are surprisingly common."

We all hung around the ICU, waiting to hear if Bubba improved after the antibiotic drip had been discontinued. When Bubba's second night in the ICU drew to a close, he remained comatose, and his condition status was changed from serious to critical.

"The next twenty-four hours will be vital," Dr. Schnuck told us. Sam, Andy, Wendy, Stone, and I listened to the physician while holding our breaths. "If he makes it through the night, there's a slight chance Mr. Slippknott might pull through this."

"That doesn't sound very optimistic, doc," Andy said with a catch in his voice. Stone put his arm around his nephew's shoulders. I noticed tears running down Sam's cheeks, and I reached over to embrace her, as well.

"Sorry, folks," the doctor replied. "I wish I could give you a more positive diagnosis. We'd hoped suspending the antibiotic would prove beneficial, but so far it hasn't."

We huddled together and said a prayer on Bubba's behalf before we departed the hospital that evening. There wasn't a dry eye among us as we walked toward the exit. Sam sat in the back seat, directly behind me, and sniffled all the way home to the inn. I handed her the last few tissues in the box of Kleenex I'd found in the console. I needed to remember to put a new box in Stone's truck, as I had a bad feeling we might all need them before this ordeal was over.

TWENTY-SIX

Although I found it difficult to fathom that the cake Chena provided was tainted in any way, either intentionally or accidentally, I decided to call Hazel and Orpha on Monday morning for confirmation. Both octogenarians were members of our church. They were known to gossip and occasionally stir up trouble amongst the Bible study group, but they could both be counted on when the chips were down.

Orpha asked about Bubba and expressed concern for his well-being. She told me she had skipped lunch prior to the wedding ceremony and admitted to not only enjoying a first piece of the wedding cake, but another piece, as well. She assured me she'd only partaken in the second helping so as not to offend the bride and groom. "It did kind of look as if it was baked in some kid's Easy Bake Oven, you know."

"Yeah. My sentiments exactly, Orpha."

Orpha went on to say she hadn't suffered any negative consequences, and wasn't aware of anyone who had, but then again, she hadn't spoken to anyone except her proctologist since the ceremony. In fact, she'd skipped church Sunday due to the reason she'd had to call her proctologist in the first place.

"Oh, dear. I'm sorry to hear that." I could sense Orpha wanted me to inquire further about her health issues and knew it would be the polite thing for me to do. However, after minimal consideration, I decided I really didn't want to hear all about the itching and swelling of her hemorrhoidal tissue, or whatever else might have prompted that phone call to her doctor. I thanked her, wished her a good day, and called Hazel.

"The cake looked pitiful, and it smelled even worse, but surprisingly it didn't taste all that bad," Hazel said. "Although later on Saturday evening, I had a slight tummy upset and a rather severe case of dysentery."

"Dysentery?" I asked, not because I didn't know what it was, but because I'd never actually heard anyone use the term in the last century, or so.

"The runs, dear. I nearly pooped myself at church yesterday morning. And the fact Orpha didn't attend the service makes me wonder if she didn't have the same issue."

"I am so sorry, Hazel." I didn't mention that I'd just spoken with Orpha, and her friend did have some issue in that same general region. I was glad I had not face-timed Hazel, or she would've wondered why I had grinned so broadly at the news of her near accident. It's not that I normally found other people's problems to be comical, but I'll admit I *did* find her remarks rather amusing. Hazel's next remark, however, proved to be more shocking than humorous.

"No worries," she said matter-of-factly. "After a few capfuls of ammonia, I felt much better."

"Ammonia?" That sounded dreadfully risky, and I wondered if drinking the pungent-smelling compound had been an old tried and true home remedy I'd never heard about. I'd have thought it'd severally burn everything in its path. "Did you say you drank ammonia?"

"Yes. Ammonia. The pharmacist at the drug store recommended it. She told me the A-D variety of it is very effective against diarrhea and, thankfully, she was correct. I'll have to tell Orpha about it."

I stifled a chuckle. "I think you meant to say the pharmacist recommended you take Imodium A-D."

"That's what I said," Hazel insisted. "Ammonia A-D."

"Yes, of course." Although relieved the elderly woman wasn't downing ammonia to cure herself of the runs, I hoped she wouldn't recommend the corrosive compound to Orpha as a remedy. "I'm glad you feel better now, Hazel. And again, I apologize if the cake made you ill. I had no idea it—"

"Well, honestly, dear, I can't be certain it was the cake. It's possible it was the bowl of chili I ate after I got home. It'd been sitting on the stove for a few days, and—"

"Oh, dear!" I exclaimed. "Hazel, I don't think you should make a habit of leaving food out on the stove for days on end. You should always refrigerate it between meals."

"My mammy and pappy didn't even own an icebox, dearie, and they never got food poisoning from leftover chili."

Hazel sounded insulted by my advice about storing food in the fridge, and I didn't want to further antagonize her by explaining that earlier generations probably had stronger constitutions than people today. The fact that folks back then didn't have safe ways to store leftover food may have factored in to why the average lifespan had been much shorter than it was today. In fact, I was now amazed Hazel had made it into her eighties if she habitually ate food that'd been left on her stove for days. A lot of food-borne illnesses were passed off as the flu in her parents' days. When you hear someone say Great Aunt Mildred died in the midst of an influenza outbreak, she might have actually been killed off by a pot of stew gone bad.

The very thought made me want to clean out both of our refrigerators and start over with fresh food items. *That month-old, half-emptied bottle of mayo has got to go. The sooner the better,* I thought. *And the leftover fried chicken from two nights ago is as good as gone.*

After listening to a long, detailed story about a rumor Hazel heard involving a clandestine relationship between the choir leader and the organist's wife, I thanked her for her help. I assured her there'd be a second ceremony to make certain Wendy and Andy were officially wed, and we wouldn't forget to notify her of the date and time.

As I ended the call, Sheila joined me in the kitchen. We sat at the table sipping cups of strong Columbian brew, and laughed as I repeated the conversations I'd had with Orpha and Hazel. Suddenly something Hazel said came back to me. The cake *smelled* even worse than it looked. I thought back and recalled the distinct smell of Bubba's boutonniere.

Sheila handled the same boutonniere shortly after Bubba collapsed and had fallen ill. Raven had her face right next to the boutonniere for six or seven minutes as she administered CPR to Bubba, and she'd experienced an even more severe reaction. And Bubba, who'd had the longest and most pronounced exposure to the flowers, had been rendered comatose.

Could Bubba's boutonniere have had something to do with his current condition, along with the adverse reactions by everyone else who was in close proximity to it? I pondered that possibility for a few moments.

"Hey, did you hear what I said about that chimichanga that nearly killed me a couple of years ago?" Sheila asked. "You seem to be off in la-la land. Are you okay?"

"Sorry. Something strange just occurred to me." I told her what had happened to me the previous evening in the tub, and went on to explain my suspicions about Bubba's boutonniere.

"I'll admit I also took several sniffs of the box of bouquets and boutonnieres right before I grew faint and confused." Sheila took a long sip of coffee. "I think you might be on to something. But what do we do about it? Run your idea by the medical staff at the hospital?"

"Perhaps."

"Should we take it to the Rockdale Police Department?"

"No, for sure not that," I replied. "I'm not the local police chief's favorite person by a long shot. Let me run this theory by Stone and see what he says. We can speak to Detective Johnston, too, who will discuss it with the police chief only if warranted."

"All right. I trust both Stone and Wyatt's judgments," Sheila said. "Would you like a refill?"

"Does the Pope poop in the woods?"

Sheila looked at me oddly, laughing as she filled my cup, "I think you meant to ask, 'Is the bear Catholic?'."

I found Stone in the detached five-car garage that resembled an old-fashioned carriage house, bragging to Randy about his toys: a zero-turn Dixon mower with a massive fifty-four-inch blade, a heavy duty Graco power sprayer that could peel tar off the sidewalk, a Stihl chainsaw that could topple a sequoia in seconds, a Troy-Bilt snow blower that could blow an entire snowdrift into the neighbor's yard, and several other pieces of lawn maintenance equipment he sounded extremely proud of despite the fact he bitched about them every time he had to use them. I approached Stone with my suspicions while Randy listened in.

"That sounds a little far-fetched to me." Stone rolled his eyes and for a split second, I considered slapping them right out of their sockets. Naturally, I'd never act on an impulse such as that one.

"Maybe so. But do you agree it's possible?"

"Well," he said, "I suppose anything's possible, but I wouldn't say it was probable."

"I didn't ask you if you thought it was probable. Even I realize it's not likely. So, are you saying you don't think I should check into it? All I want to do is talk to Lily at the floral shop."

"I don't know, Lexie." Stone sounded reluctant, which came as no surprise. "I'm not certain it's necessary, or a good idea to infer the florist has done anything disreputable. I especially don't like the idea of you tackling this alone."

"I'm not inferring anything, Stone. I merely want to ask a few questions. And I'm sure Sheila will accompany me."

"Why doesn't that bring me any comfort?" Stone asked. He exchanged a knowing look with Sheila's husband. "Sorry, Randy, but having Sheila accompany Lexie doesn't make me feel less concerned."

Randy nodded his head in response. "There's no reason to apologize, Stone. Knowing the trouble these two can get into makes my blood run colder than a dead polar bear. You weren't around when they got kicked off an airplane in Sydney, Australia. Or, worse yet, the time they nearly got arrested for inciting a riot in downtown Kansas City. Fortunately for them, I'd once worked with the officer who had cuffed them and stuffed them in his patrol car."

"Hey! That's not fair!" I exclaimed. "Neither incident was our fault."

Both men turned to stare at me in disbelief. When neither made an effort to respond, I began to plead. "Come on, guys. We'll be very cautious and not put ourselves into any risky situations. And besides, if the flowers have anything to do with Bubba's condition, I'm sure it was just an accidental oversight, not an intentional act."

The two men exchanged another look. I truly considered reaching up and banging their two bullish heads together. Instead, I reminded Stone of his words from last night. "Besides, you did promise I'd have your blessing if I decided to look into the situation."

"But only under the condition it looked as if foul play was involved, and I don't feel as if there's any undeniable indication of that. Certainly nothing concrete enough that justifies accusing anyone of malicious intent."

"Listen, Stone. I only want to question Lily to see if she knows of anything that could have compromised Bubba's boutonniere. I have no intention of accusing her of anything."

"I suppose it couldn't hurt for you to speak with the florist. What do you think, Randy?" A clearly skeptical Stone asked his friend.

"It's your call, buddy. If you're okay with it, I am as well." Randy appeared resigned, as if he instinctively knew he'd lose any battle he engaged in with Sheila about joining me on my mission. "It's not like anything we say is going to make any difference, anyway."

"That's true. Well, okay. As long as Sheila is with you, and you ladies don't do anything dangerous, maybe I'll——"

I hadn't expected Stone to relent, so I was nearly bowled over when he caved. Not that it made any difference, as Randy had said.

It'd just be nicer if we didn't have to go behind Stone and Randy's backs to accomplish our mission. "Thank you. I'd best round up Sheila so we can get going."

Before Stone could respond, I ran out the door. I took the stairs two at a time and knocked on Sheila's door within seconds of entering the inn.

"What's up?" Sheila opened the door and her mouth dropped. I must have looked like a panting, crazy-eyed lunatic.

"Get your shoes on. We're going to Lily's-in-Bloom Floral Shop."

Sheila didn't even ask what I planned to do once we arrived there. She just snatched a pair of sandals off a shoe bench and headed for the stairs. "Let's go! I'll put them on in the car."

TWENTY-SEVEN

W hen we entered the shop, the florist was cussing like a "black Friday" shopper who'd just watched the woman in front of her snatch up the last Hermes Birkin purse at a rock-bottom price. When Lily recognized the two of us, she abruptly slammed the business phone's handset down on the base. That should have been our clue to leave without uttering a word. Instead, I explained the situation.

"Are you accusing me of putting something in the flowers that caused the best man to lapse into a coma?" Lily's normally fair complexion suddenly matched the color of the dozen red roses she was holding in her left hand.

"No, of course not," I assured her. "It's just that it occurred to us that everyone who was in close contact with Bubba's boutonniere suffered some degree of impairment. Me, included."

"And me, as well," Sheila added.

"You look to me as though you both are still motoring along quite splendidly under your own power," Lily replied. Gone was the polite, low-key manner she'd exhibited in the past. Her amicable personality had flown out the window like a mad cockatoo that had escaped its cage.

Sheila apparently thought it'd be better if *she* tried to reason with the incensed woman, instead of me. She was wrong.

"Listen, lady," Sheila began, "my friend is not accusing you of anything. We're just trying to determine if the boutonniere accidentally came in contact with something, such as a hazardous chemical, or a toxic substance that's used in the creation of floral arrangements."

"Are you two insane? The boy obviously suffered a heat stroke. I'm sure Raven, and you two, were affected by the brutal heat, as well. Raven told me she was sweating like a horse competing in the Kentucky Derby while she performed CPR on the young man. It's no small wonder Bubba passed out. Who in their right mind dresses the groomsmen in black for an outdoor wedding on one of the hottest days of the year?"

"Well, um——" I began, but stopped abruptly. How could I argue with Lily's valid point? I'd made the exact same one in my debate about the tuxedos with Wendy.

"Now get the hell out of my shop!" Lily's striking turquoise eyes bugged out as she pointed toward the front door. When neither of us budged, she hollered, "Both of you!"

"Yes, it was stifling hot. We aren't arguing that fact. But it's become abundantly clear it wasn't just the heat. Something in that boutonniere affected Bubba," Sheila replied. Her voice of reason was becoming increasingly accusatory. "We're just asking you if——"

"I said get out! Now!" As she screamed at us, Lily simultaneously picked up a large flower vase from the counter that had been intended for the dozen roses she'd angrily thrown to the ground. I didn't know if she simply meant to intimidate us—which incidentally did the trick splendidly as far as I was concerned—or if she planned to use it as a weapon against us. She held it over her head as if she were wielding a Louisville slugger rather than a lead-glass crystal vase.

"Let's get out of here before this whack-job adds us to her list of victims!" I grabbed Sheila's arm and practically dragged her to the door. I'm pretty sure she'd considered the idea of standing her ground and daring the woman to throw the vase. Knowing Sheila had always been a gifted athlete, my money would have been on her in the event of a floral shop brawl. But, I chose not to take the chance. I'd promised Stone and Randy we wouldn't do anything foolish, and provoking an irate woman yielding a potentially lethal flower vase probably fell into that category.

Having no evidence at all that Lily was guilty of negligence, and having promised Stone I wouldn't accuse her of anything, I shouldn't have made such a ruthless allegation. But it felt good to say it, especially after the way she'd reacted to our inquiry. Still, why had she reacted so defensively?

Out on the sidewalk, Sheila said, "She certainly acted like she had something to hide, didn't she?"

"You took the words right out of my mouth." We walked to the car in silence and strapped ourselves in. "Let's think about what our next step might—"

"Oh, crap!" Sheila exclaimed. Her outburst alarmed me. She frantically pawed through the overnight bag she called a purse.

"What's wrong?"

"I must have set my phone down inside the shop. As much as I hate to say this, we have to go back in there to get it."

"We?"

Sheila knew I was kidding and flashed me an ornery smile. As we unbuckled our seat belts, we looked up and saw Lily step from the floral shop and lock the front door. She rushed around the side of the building and, within seconds, pulled out of the parking lot in a silver SUV.

"Should we follow her?" I asked.

"No! At least, not until I get my phone back. You know I can't survive ten minutes without it."

Sheila wasn't kidding. She was exactly the type of phone-addicted person Stone had been griping about the previous day. I was often surprised her phone hadn't rooted into the flesh of her right hand.

"And how do you propose we retrieve your phone without breaking and entering? The chief of police would like nothing better than to throw my behind into a jail cell. Again! Didn't like it the first time, and ain't gonna like it any better the second. I'm not convinced your phone's not buried in the rubble inside your purse."

"I'm telling you it's not in there. I looked already." Sheila's response sounded defensive.

I took my own phone out of my fanny pack and dialed Sheila's number. Just then, the sound of a duck quacking came from inside the glove box of my car. I recognized the ring tone.

With a sheepish grin, Sheila removed her phone from the small compartment. "See? I told you it wasn't in my purse."

I looked at my friend and laughed. "You quack me up, girl."

"What's the hold-up? We're going to lose her if you don't step on it."

TWENTY-EIGHT

We began to follow Lily, trailing far enough behind so as not to draw her attention. Half an hour later, Sheila muttered, "I hope she hasn't set off on a trip to the Ozarks. The men are going to get concerned if we haven't returned home by sundown."

"If she hasn't stopped somewhere in the next ten minutes, I'll turn around and head home." I'd been having the same thoughts as Sheila.

I had just decided to give up when Lily pulled into a pothole-filled parking lot in a seedy section of Kansas City, Kansas. Fortunately, I'd had enough gas in Ladybug to cover the forty-mile drive. We watched as she climbed from the driver's seat of the SUV, grabbed a piece of paper off the floorboard of the back seat, studied it carefully, and returned it to its original location. Lily then walked stealthily toward the rundown building, glancing in all directions with each stride. It was clear she didn't want to be seen going into the shabby structure.

"What is this place?" Sheila asked. "And what do you think brings her here?"

"I have no idea, but I recognize this building." I thought about it for a few seconds before continuing. "You know what? I'm almost positive this is the abortion clinic I saw on TV the other day. The news report was about a protest scheduled here next weekend. A lot of 'right-to-lifers' have been trying to get this clinic shut down for years. According to the reporter, the police department is preparing for a riot-like atmosphere because a local 'woman's right to choose' organization plans to attend the event."

"Oh, my," Sheila said. "I'm certain both sides are passionate about their causes and bound to clash."

"You're right. The protest could easily turn violent."

"I wonder why Lily would come here. Do you think she might be spearheading one side or the other?" Sheila asked.

"Possibly. Or maybe she's just gathering information and plans to be either a protester or an anti-protester. Either way, it appears as if tailing her here was a ginormous waste of time as far as finding out anything regarding the boutonnieres."

"Which reminds me, shouldn't we text the guys to let them know where we are?"

"Hell, no!" I'm sure my expression was that of someone who'd just been asked if she'd like to test-drive a winged body suit by strapping one on and bailing off the new One World Trade Center building. "Are you nuts, girl? The less our husbands know about where our snooping mission took us, the better off we'll be. Have you never heard the phrase, 'what they don't know won't hurt us'?"

"No, not phrased like that, anyway. But you're probably right. I'm just not sure lying to them is a great idea, either."

"Who said anything about lying? We just won't say *anything*."

"Isn't that lying by omission?" Sheila asked.

"I like to think of it as a matter of sparing them a lot of unnecessary details and unnecessary worrying."

"And thus sparing us a lot of unnecessary, long-winded lecturing?"

"Good. I'm glad you see my point and agree that telling them where we went today is——"

"Unnecessary," we said in unison.

I glanced over at her dubious expression. "Trust me! This is not my first sleuthing rodeo by a long shot."

"All right. I'm in. Although, I am reminded of the old adage you often quote about God protecting children and fools." Sheila sighed dramatically before tacking on, "And we aren't exactly kids, you know."

"Nor are we fools." I didn't particularly like Sheila inferring I was a fool, or that she became one by association. I preferred to think of us as gutsy with a touch of spunkiness, rather than foolish. But I kept that thought to myself. It really wasn't a distinction I could argue.

"I assume you have a plan?" Sheila asked.

"Yes, my friend, I do. Did you happen to notice that after Lily placed that piece of paper back into her car, she never touched her key fob and her car never honked?"

"Well, not really. But so what?"

"Wendy drives the exact same model as Lily. When she locks it from either inside the car or with her key fob, it honks. Lily's car didn't honk, which means it's unlocked. Maybe if we hurry over there while she's inside, we can see what's on that piece of paper."

"What if she walks outside while we're doing that?"

"Don't worry," I assured her. "I'm good at improvising in sticky situations. Come on. Let's go. We may not have much time."

Clearly unconvinced, Sheila released another long sigh. "Oh. All right."

We hurried over to Lily's car and I quickly opened the back door. A shrill siren scared the crap out of both Sheila and me. Not expecting a car alarm to be triggered, we were both startled. As if I'd opened a cage and unexpectedly encountered a pissed-off rattlesnake, I instinctively recoiled, stepping back and tripping over Sheila, who was standing directly behind me. We both toppled to the pavement.

"Son-of-a b——" Sheila shouted.

I struggled to my feet, grabbed Sheila's arm and helped her up. "We've got to hide. Lily, and probably a few other curious individuals, will be out here in no time."

Sheila pointed to a side door of the clinic. "That's the closest place to hide. Hopefully, it's unlocked."

I was skeptical. Abortion clinics had a tendency to invoke strong reactions among people on both sides of the fence. Keeping a side entrance into the clinic unlocked was a recipe for disaster. But, we didn't have a better option at the moment. Before I dashed behind Sheila to the door, I looked down at the sheet of paper on the floorboard. "Doctor Angel DoGood" had been written across the top, with "August 27th at 10:00" and other information printed in smaller type below.

By taking those few seconds to gaze at the piece of paper, I didn't make it to the door before it closed behind Sheila. I chalked up her speed to the fact she'd been a track star in high school and still made a habit of running at least three miles every day. If anyone sees me running, I hope they call the police. I'm obviously being chased by something, or someone who's up to no good. Which explains why me catching up to Sheila would've been like a newborn zebra trying to chase down a cheetah!

As I reached the side door, Lily stepped from around the building having exited the front entrance. She glared at me with daggers in her eyes. I froze in my tracks. I then said the first thing that came to mind. "I think a buzzard landed on the roof of your car and set off the alarm."

"Yeah, of course it did." Lily continued to glare without blinking. Uncomfortable, I opened the side door and stepped inside. I expected to see Sheila waiting for me in a long corridor. What I didn't expect to see was a man in a white robe standing beside her with a clipboard in one hand and metal forceps in the other. Stitched across the breast pocket was *Dr. Angel DoGood*, a name that sounded highly facetious to me.

The doctor looked me up and down several times. I was curious as to why he was studying me with such a cynical expression, until he said, "Your friend says you're here to inquire about getting an abortion."

"I am?" I looked at Sheila, who shrugged, and then back at the doctor. "Um, yeah. That's right. I am. That's exactly why we're here. But, um, well, I can see you're in the middle of something, so we'll be on our way and I'll stop back by when you're not as busy."

"You're kind of old to——"

"Excuse me?" I replied curtly. I may look more like a patient needing a hip replacement than an abortion, but I didn't like being referred to as old, nonetheless.

"I'm sorry." His face flushed in embarrassment. "I meant to say you seem a little mature to be——"

"It is not unheard of for a fifty-one-year-old to get pregnant." I hoped my slightly protruding belly looked more like a baby bump than the quarter-pounder and fries I'd eaten for lunch when Sheila and I stopped at a fast food joint on our way to the floral shop.

"Well, no. But——"

"You know what?" I said, interrupting him. I gave him the most indignant look I could come up with. I don't know what made me say what I said next, other than pure orneriness. "Your attitude has made me have a change of heart, Doctor DoGood. I've decided to not terminate my pregnancy, after all. It might be nice to hear the pitter-patter of toddlers' feet again."

"Toddlers?" he asked in amazement. "As in twins?"

I bit my tongue so as not to laugh out loud.

"Triplets," Sheila said before I could respond. Her next few remarks were spoken with a heavy dose of venomous aversion. "My friend is having two girls and a boy. As you should know, that happens fairly regularly with those IVF treatments."

"You mean you *tried* to get pregnant?" The doctor looked at me now with a stunned expression, as if he'd been zapped with a tazer.

"Hell, yeah, she did!" Sheila replied. "It's early on in her pregnancy, of course. I'm curious, sir. Is Dr. Angel DoGood your real name? After all, I can understand why you'd use a fake one. But DoGood? Seriously?"

Rendered speechless, the doctor stood as motionless as a pillar of salt. Aware Lily had returned to the parking lot to shut off her car alarm, I thought fishing for information might prove useful. So before he could tell us to not let the door hit us in the keister on our way out, I said, "By the way, someone's car alarm is going off in your parking lot."

"Yeah, I know. I had a few minutes' worth of paperwork to do before I saw my next patient, and overheard my receptionist at the check-in desk make an announcement about it to the patients in the waiting room. The owner immediately went out to her vehicle to turn it off." His tone was terse, and before he turned and walked off, he dismissed us by pointing to the door we'd just entered a couple of minutes earlier.

"Bingo!" I said after the doctor had disappeared around a corner of the hallway. I grabbed Sheila's arm. "Let's get out of here."

"Amen to that."

TWENTY-NINE

"What did you mean by 'bingo'?" Sheila asked as we walked to my car.

"The doctor inferred Lily is a patient, not someone who's planning to be involved in the scheduled protest. She's apparently here to get an abortion."

"Not necessarily, Lexie. I'm not convinced he inferred anything at all. But, even if that's true, what does that tell us?"

"Just that it might have something to do with why she was so on edge when we walked into her shop earlier. I know I'd have been as tight as a size six girdle if I'd been preparing to head over here for an abortion. The only thing that puzzles me is that she and I discussed having children on the day we ordered the floral arrangements. I recall her saying that she and her husband, Joseph, had been married for three years and were trying to have a baby. Which begs the question, why schedule an abortion if you're trying to get pregnant?"

"Maybe the baby's not his," Sheila suggested. "Or Lily knows there's a possibility she'd gotten knocked up by someone other than her husband."

"Oh, goodness. I hadn't thought of that."

"In fact, Joseph might not even know she's pregnant. What if Lily's husband is Caucasian, but the baby daddy's not? Joseph would soon figure it out if the baby turned out to be of mixed-race. If the baby daddy is black, Asian, or even Hispanic, and the baby's features mimic the biological father's, it probably wouldn't sit well with Joseph. That'd be an obvious indication to him he wasn't the baby's real daddy."

"I guess that's possible, despite how unlikely it seems," I said. "I need to check in with the new librarian and see if Deb's getting along okay on her own now."

"Huh?" Sheila asked. My sudden change of subject had left her with mental whiplash. "What's that got to do with Lily and her possible pregnancy?"

"If Lily planned to get an abortion, her pregnancy is probably not public knowledge. Obviously. But if anyone knows the scoop about Lily's situation, it'd be Deb Custovio."

"I agree with your first remark," Sheila began, "but I seriously doubt the new librarian has heard about it through the grapevine. If there's anything to this improbable theory, her pregnancy would most likely be a secret Lily kept close to the vest, if you know what I mean."

"Yeah. I imagine you're right, but it wouldn't hurt to check it out."

We got into the car, clicked on our seatbelts, and I turned the ignition in Ladybug. She sputtered to life, coughed several times, shook violently a few moments, and then died. I tried again and heard nothing but a cranking sound. The third attempt yielded the same results.

"Stop, or you'll flood the engine. Open the hood," Sheila instructed, as she took a small bag of tools out of her purse and stepped out of the car. I wouldn't have been surprised if she'd also extracted a spare carburetor and water pump in the event she'd need to replace one or the other. She tinkered around under Lady-bug's hood for a few minutes, before hollering, "Try it again!"

This time the Volkswagen roared to life like a brand new car. There seemed to be very little my best friend couldn't do, and I was often amazed by her abilities. Sheila was great to have around during crisis situations and I considered this incident to be in that category. I wouldn't have wanted to explain to Stone and Randy why we needed assistance in an abortion clinic's parking lot that was miles away from Rockdale. As I put the car in gear, my phone beeped.

"*Where are you girls?*" I read the text I'd received from Stone out loud. "*Randy and I are getting hungry.*"

"Uh-oh," Sheila murmured.

"Relax. I've got this one." I'll admit my smugness was completely unwarranted, but it was seldom I was the one most apt to be able to pull our hides out of the fire. My skill sets were so vastly opposed to Sheila's.

I steered the car to the shoulder and sent Stone a return text. *We stopped to see a doctor. No worries though. Sheila feels fine now. Be home soon. We're having pizza for supper.*

I handed the phone to Sheila so she could read my text. Sheila gasped and the color drained from her face. "But. But. But…"

"Have you always had a speech impediment and I'm just now noticing it?"

Sheila saw no humor in my question. "I thought you said we weren't going to lie?"

"Did we see a doctor today?" I asked.

"Well, yes, if you count Dr. DoGood."

"Do you feel perfectly healthy at the moment?"

"Of course."

"Good. Then we didn't lie." I raised my right hand for a high-five, which Sheila ignored.

Instead of a high-five, she gave me a look that could most certainly burn a hole through an anvil. "We?"

"Yes. We."

"What am I going to say when Randy asks what was wrong with me?" Sheila's voice sounded wheezy, as if she had an issue with breathing all of a sudden.

"Tell him that out of nowhere you suddenly had trouble catching your breath, but it turned out to be just a symptom due to stress. That wouldn't be dishonest in the least. I mean, look at you. You're gasping for breath as I speak. You are seriously acting as if you swallowed an entire Brussels sprout down the wrong pipe. And if Randy asks where we went to see a doctor, tell him we stopped at a clinic. There are a couple of Urgent Care clinics in town, and I'm sure he'll assume we stopped at one of them. Again, you won't be lying. We did stop at a clinic."

Sheila's eyes widened, her mouth hung open, and she shook her head. She remained silent, as if she still couldn't catch her breath.

"Want me to slap you on the back, buddy?" After Sheila shook her head, I continued. "Then how do you feel about the Heimlich maneuver? If I can figure out how to perform it correctly, it'd probably dislodge that Brussels sprout that seems to be wedged in your windpipe."

I laughed, hoping a little humor would lighten the mood. Sheila didn't even crack a smile. I'm sure she was wondering what she'd ever seen in me that prompted her to befriend me. But then, she'd probably asked herself that on numerous occasions during the course of our friendship.

I glanced over at her again as she took a long, deep breath. After I watched her let it out slowly, I asked, "Hey, now that you're breathing properly again, why don't you make yourself useful while I drive home? Call Anthony's Pizzeria and order a large meat-lover's pizza. On second thought, order two. I am eating for four, you know. When you told the doctor I was having triplets, I was hoping my 'McBump' from our large lunch would fool him into believing you."

This time, against her will I'm sure, Sheila did laugh. She then picked up her phone to Google the pizzeria's phone number. "You're lucky I love you so much, Lexie. You do realize you are a terrible influence on me, don't you? Always have been, and probably will be until I take my last breath."

"I know, my friend," I replied in agreement. "And I wouldn't have it any other way. But do me a favor. Don't take your last breath until after you've written down the recipe for your famous punch. It will have to serve as your legacy, you know."

We both dissolved into laughter, then spent the rest of the ride home discussing Bubba's mysterious illness. We decided we might have better luck talking to Lily's assistant, Raven. She'd fainted, as well, and no doubt had more interest in what had caused both her and Bubba to fall victim to an unknown cause than her boss had. Hopefully, Raven would be more willing to discuss the possibility of contaminated flowers in Bubba's boutonniere. With any luck at all, we might even be able to find out what she knew, or didn't know, about the likelihood of Lily being pregnant.

When we pulled into the driveway, Stone and Randy were standing in the yard discussing which brand of zero-turn riding mowers they thought was the best. I could sense Stone was about to question us about our conversation with Lily. But after noticing the two square boxes Sheila was carrying, his train of thought was suddenly focused on pizza. Randy really must have been hungry too, as Stone had mentioned in his text, because instead of asking Sheila how she felt, his first question was, "Did you ask for extra cheese?"

"Yes, dear." Sheila looked at me and winked, as we followed the men through the front door of the inn.

THIRTY

"How are we going to get in touch with Raven?" Sheila asked after leftover pizza had been served for lunch the following day and the kitchen spruced up. The previous evening, Randy had accepted Sheila's explanation of why we'd stopped at "a clinic" without any further questioning. His lackluster response was probably due to the fact that we were all in a state of despair over Bubba's mysterious medical condition. The outcome remained in limbo and often caused us to lose sight of things going on around us. Then again, it could have been because Randy was experiencing severe heartburn from eating too much of the acid-rich pizza with extra cheese. I noticed he only ate one small piece for lunch before accompanying Stone to the hospital.

After they'd departed, I told Sheila about my first meeting with Raven. "I noticed a letter sticking out of Raven's purse, which she'd set on a coffee table in front me while trying to swab the coffee blotches off my shirt. She'd forgotten to take it with her when Lily asked her to fetch me a bottle of water. I wasn't being nosy or anything, but both the address the letter was sent to and the return address on the envelope were clearly visible."

Sheila raised her eyebrows at my last remark. Before she could question me, I continued. "She apparently lives in a studio apartment at the River's Edge complex in St. Joseph. I recall seeing that complex when we were on our way to the St. Jo Frontier Casino one day. Like the casino, River's Edge sits right alongside the Missouri River."

"Good thinking on your part," Sheila said. "Did you see which apartment she lives in?"

"Um. Yeah. Apartment 412, if I remember right."

"And if you don't remember right? Are we going to knock on a bunch of strangers' doors until we find the correct one?" Sheila had clearly not found the tone of my voice reassuring.

"Of course not, silly girl!" I was a lot better at this sleuthing stuff than my best friend gave me credit for. "I snapped a photo of the letter with my phone. You know, just in case I ever had a reason to remember where Raven lived."

"I'm sure glad you weren't being nosy or anything."

Before driving to Raven's apartment, we stopped at the Rockdale Library on our way out of town. I asked Deb how things were going for her as the new head librarian, and if she had any questions for me.

"No," Deb replied. "I think I have the hang of it now. Not that I don't enjoy having you come in now and then to visit."

"I enjoy that, too. Say, I was just wondering. Do you happen to know Lily Franks?" It was a metaphorical question, of course, because Deb knew everyone who lived in Rockdale; formerly, currently, and even a few who had plans to move there in the near future. I wouldn't be surprised if Deb handed out welcome baskets to every new family who moved to town.

She'd always appeared to me to be a senior citizen in a thirty-something-year-old body. As I'd trained Deb to run the library in my absence, I often had to slow down my speech and repeat things as if I were trying to teach a ninety-year-old how to shoot and post a video on YouTube. Naturally, before I could do such a thing, I'd have to have an eight-year-old teach the process to me. I listened now as Deb expounded on Lily's pregnancy.

"Of course I know Lily. I was so tickled to hear that she and her husband had finally gotten pregnant. It seems the IVF treatment worked, thank goodness. It's pretty effective, but also an expensive risk if it doesn't pan out," Deb said as she adjusted the wool sweater draped across her shoulders. It was as if she'd worn it if to ward off an unexpected August chill. Fortunately, Sheila and I were dressed in shorts, tank tops, and flip flops, because it felt as if the library's thermostat was set on eighty. I wiped sweat off my brow as Deb continued with her explanation. "Joseph worked a second job for over a year to save money for the IVF attempt, so the fact that it was successful is even more of a blessing. Why did you want to know if I knew Lily?"

"Oh, no particular reason. I just mentioned her name in passing since we saw her yesterday. She provided the flowers for Wendy's wedding."

"Oh, yes. They were gorgeous. She's fabulous at creating floral masterpieces, isn't she?"

"Absolutely," I said.

"Speaking of the wedding," Deb began, "how's that big fellow doing who collapsed during the ceremony? I heard Raven's illness was short-lived. Thank goodness."

"Yes, thank God for that. Unfortunately, Bubba's still comatose." I wanted to get back to the subject of Lily and the abortion clinic, so I reverted back to the original subject abruptly. "I hadn't heard about Lily's pregnancy, and she didn't mention it, but that is such welcome news."

"Yes, indeed. At just nine to ten weeks along, it's still too early to feel totally confident. Lily and Joseph are over the moon, of course, and we're all praying the pregnancy makes it to that oh-so-important first-trimester mark," Deb said.

The librarian's response had blown the frosting off my cupcake. Having seen Lily enter an abortion clinic the previous day, I would have expected her pregnancy to be neither public knowledge nor something she and her husband were "over the moon" about. I figured the easiest way to uncover the truth about Lily's visit to the clinic would be to ask Deb about it. And I was correct.

"We were surprised to see Lily going into an abortion clinic in Kansas City yesterday. I wonder why in the world she'd stop by there." I said this in a musing, rhetorical way, knowing Deb would rise to the occasion if she knew anything about it. I was not surprised that she did.

"Oh, well," Deb began with a self-satisfied smile, "that's because Lily is doing the flowers for Lydia Brown's wedding in mid-October. Lydia just started at the clinic as the receptionist for one of the doctors there. She works from ten to four, which she claims is six hours too many. I doubt she'll work there much longer. Too stressful for her, as you can imagine."

"Oh, yes. I can well imagine," I replied. Now we knew why the paper Lily glanced at in the parking lot said "Dr. DoGood, August 27th at 10:00". She hadn't stopped by the clinic for an appointment with the doctor, but to do business with his receptionist, who evidently arrived to work at ten. As a nice way of saying Deb must be the nosiest woman in Rockdale, I flattered her with, "I am forever amazed at how in tune you are with everything that's happening in this little burg."

"Thank you, Lexie. I have always found it's better to keep my ears wide open and my mouth zipped shut." As she spoke, Deb's expression looked like what you'd expect to see on Mother Teresa's face as she accepted a prestigious humanitarian award. I'd agree Deb's ears missed nary a thing, but I knew better when it came to her mouth being zipped shut. Her lips flapped more often than a hummingbird's wings. Whatever those wide-open ears of hers took in, her "zipped-shut" mouth was more than happy to let out—with whomever she could entice to listen.

"That's a very good policy, my dear." I decided our visit with the librarian had been enlightening, and we'd learned all we were apt to learn. "Sheila and I had best be going. I'll be praying for a healthy baby for Lily and Joseph right along with you, Deb."

"I'll pray too," Sheila interjected. "Can't be too rich, too thin, or have too many people praying for you."

THIRTY-ONE

We had no trouble locating the River's Edge complex. It was exactly where my unreliable memory had remembered it to be. However, it was a good thing I'd taken the photo of the letter in Raven's purse at our first meeting because she actually lived in apartment 241. If we'd come expecting to find her in apartment 412, as I'd incorrectly recalled, we'd have been sadly disappointed, as there was no apartment by that number in the three-story building.

We weren't surprised to find Raven at home, knowing she'd been scheduled to get off work at one o'clock. But we *were* surprised to see three pieces of luggage lined up in her entryway as she opened her door in response to our knock. All three looked as if she'd had to sit on them to get the zippers all the way to their closed positions. One suitcase had a small swath of yellow material sticking out from where the zipper had gotten stuck three-quarters of the way around.

"I was just leaving."

"That much is apparent." I replied good-humoredly as I glanced at the woman's matching red luggage.

After an exaggerated sniff, Raven answered. "I have a plane to catch at three."

"Going on a lengthy vacation?" Sheila asked. Her cheerful voice and demeanor could have won an Academy Award, considering the miserable state Raven was clearly in at that moment. "You deserve one after that traumatic experience on Saturday. You were so brave. We appreciate your efforts in resuscitating Bubba. So where are you headed?"

"Home."

"Home?" Sheila and I repeated in stereo.

"Yes. I've decided this place is just not for me. I miss my family and friends back home in South Carolina." She evidently missed them a lot, because her eyes were beet red and nearly swollen shut from crying.

I had scrutinized the photo I'd taken of the letter sticking out of her purse before rapping on her door. It was from a Carolyn Hobbs of Surfside Beach, South Carolina. Betting on a hunch, I said, "Going home to Surfside Beach, huh?"

Forget about having a Brussels sprout lodged in your throat! Raven's mouth instantly dropped open like she was preparing to stuff an entire head of cabbage into it. "How did you—?"

"Never mind, dear." I smiled warmly at her. "I'm just happy for you and glad to see you didn't suffer any permanent damage from your fainting spell at the ill-fated wedding. I'm sure you'll be happier back home on the east coast. Maybe you and your ex-boyfriend will even patch things up once you return. You know what they say, don't you? Absence makes the heart grow fonder, and sometimes causes the eyes to wander."

It was like tapping into a maple tree, as tears began to stream unchecked down Raven's cheeks. I realized too late I shouldn't have ad-libbed that last part I'd tacked on about the wandering eyes. Ad-libbing had never been my friend, yet I couldn't seem to stop. I felt remorseful as I watched the young lady sob. For a second, I considered searching for a bucket to place under Raven so the hardwood floor we stood on would not be damaged by salty water marks.

After we'd managed to calm Raven down, I said, "I know you

need to be going so you don't miss your flight. Before you go, can you answer one question for us?"

"(*Hiccup!*) I'll try, but (*sniff*) make it quick. I can't afford to (*hiccup*) be late. My last-minute airline ticket is non-refundable."

"Of course, sweetheart," I said. "Can you think of any reason the flowers in Bubba's boutonniere might have caused him and you, as well as Sheila and me, to have adverse reactions?"

"Well, (*sniff*) I do recall Lily telling me that (*hiccup*) certain flowers were lethally poisonous to animals, such as oleander, lily-of-the-valley, and belladonna, which is also known as (*hiccup*) deadly nightshade. The castor oil plant is particularly toxic, as its bean contains ricinolein, or ricin. Did you know that a number of flowers, like that poinsettia plant you probably (*sniff*) put on your kitchen table every Christmas can kill a cat if it ingests any of (*hiccup*) it?"

"Yes, I have heard that, now that you mention it." In an attempt to lighten the mood and seem less accusatory, I added, "However, there didn't appear to be any stray cats keeling over at the ceremony on Saturday. Do you know what flowers are poisonous to humans?"

"I don't know them by name, but there are a number of plants that can (*hiccup*) make humans very ill, and on rare occasions be deadly. Most, if not all, would have to be ingested to poison a person, however. I don't think many of them, if used in a boutonniere, are likely to make someone react the way (*hiccup*) Burlon did."

"Burlon?" Confused by her response, I watched as all of the color drained from Raven's face. If nothing else, her hiccupping stopped on a dime.

"Oh, yeah, um. Well, you see, I heard that Bubba's real name is Burlon. Bubba is just a childhood nickname that stuck, I'd guess."

"You'd guess that, huh?" I tried not to let my suspicions creep into my voice but failed miserably.

"I really need to go now. I'm running short on time, and I have to drop off my key with the front office before I catch an Uber ride to the airport." Raven grabbed two of her three suitcases and brushed past both Sheila and me so abruptly, she nearly knocked us down in her wake.

"What about your other suitcase?" Sheila hollered as Raven raced down the hallway.

"Don't need it. It's just clothes. I can buy (*sniff*) new stuff when I get home." And with that, Raven disappeared into an elevator at the end of the hallway.

"Should we chase her down and place this third suitcase in the Uber car with her?" I asked. "It looks like it has enough clothes in it to outfit a small African village."

"Can you move as quickly as she just did?" Sheila cocked an eyebrow at me as she spoke. "I set school records in track, and I know I couldn't have caught her even back then. She's hauling two overloaded suitcases, and I can't run that fast empty-handed."

"Yeah, I guess you're right. I couldn't run her down if she were running backward and carrying all three bags." I pointed to the lone red suitcase on wheels. "What should we do with that third bag then?"

Sheila shrugged her shoulders. "Let's take it down with us, just in case. The Uber driver may be running late."

"Good idea. If we can't catch her in time, I guess I could mail it to that Carolyn Hobbs who sent the letter to Raven. I have her address on my phone."

"Do you have any idea what that'd cost, girl? As Raven said, she can buy new clothes—probably for less than it would cost you to ship that heavy bag to South Carolina. Just take it home with you if she's already left," Sheila replied. "She abandoned it, so it's up for grabs in my opinion. I'm too skinny, and you're too short, but Wendy is about the same age and size as Raven. Maybe there are things in there Wendy could wear. Better than to let perfectly good clothes go to waste. Raven looked very stylish both times I've seen her."

"Yeah, you're right. Raven has great taste when it comes to clothes. In fact, Wendy would look quite fashionable in the ensemble Raven is wearing right now, don't you think?"

"Absolutely. Too bad she wore it today instead of packing it in this bag." As Sheila spoke, she yanked up the handle of the heavy suitcase in order to pull it behind her.

I shut the apartment door behind us, made sure it was locked, and then we headed toward the elevator that would take us to the ground floor.

A red Ford Taurus, with Raven securely ensconced in the rear seat, was pulling away from the curb when we stepped outside. We tried valiantly, but were unable to flag the driver down. Even at Sheila's insistence, I just didn't feel right about taking the bag of clothes home to Wendy. We ended up stopping at a local shelter for abused women on the way home. Wendy was fortunate to have a good income and never lacked for nice clothing. Rather than give the suitcase full of useful items to her, I felt better about donating the clothes to women who needed them a lot more than she did. We did, however, scrutinize everything in the suitcase before turning it over at the front desk of the shelter.

The only item we found of interest—other than a zebra-striped dress that would have been a real hit in that aforementioned African village—was a gold-plated, heart-shaped locket. The photo inside the locket was of a young couple, but a black permanent marker had rendered the man's identity a mystery. His face had been "redacted" from record. We didn't recognize the woman with the long dark hair, oversized eyeglasses, and blue eyes either, but we kept the locket just in case it might prove to be useful later on. Should the noxious flowers turn out to be the culprit, Raven might be considered a viable suspect, as she was the person most likely responsible for arranging the floral accessories. It occurred to us afterward, if that was the case, the bag and clothes might have been considered evidence, as well. At least we knew where we'd dropped the suitcase off if the authorities needed to reclaim it at a later date.

Tracking Raven down just in the nick of time had proven worthwhile. We now had a lot of new discoveries to chew over. For example, what was behind her apparent rush to leave town, or her unexplained familiarity with Bubba—or Burlon, as she'd referred to him? Thanks to the Internet, we'd also found out that her hometown of Surfside, South Carolina, was just a few miles south of Bubba's hometown of Myrtle Beach. *Coincidence?* I asked myself. *I think not.*

There was also the fact that Raven had said a number of flowers were toxic. Sheila and I planned to do some research on that subject later in the evening.

But the thing that confused us most was why Raven would try to kill Bubba, if indeed she did, and then work so furiously to save him. Her frantic efforts to resuscitate him seemed anti-productive if eliminating him had been her intention. She'd likely put her own health in jeopardy by performing CPR.

"Do you think there's any possibility that Bubba is the man who broke Raven's heart?" Sheila asked.

"I do. I don't believe in coincidences, particularly of this magnitude. Maybe doing CPR was designed to deflect suspicion away from herself in the event it was discovered his sudden illness had been a result of foul play."

"Could be," Sheila replied. "Maybe that's why she's so anxious to get back to Surfside Beach. It stands to reason she wouldn't want to be around if the authorities decide to question her."

I nodded my agreement. "And maybe what has recently happened to her ex-boyfriend has to do with why she moved here from South Carolina in the first place."

"Did Andy mention anything about Bubba's ex-girlfriend showing up at the wedding? Seems like he would have recognized Raven if she were engaged to his best friend at one time."

"Yeah, you're right. I hadn't thought about that. Andy showed no indication of recognizing Raven. But then, neither did Bubba. Maybe we're looking at Raven's sudden desire to hurry home all wrong. It may have nothing to do with Bubba. In fact, Raven may have had nothing to do with Bubba's illness to begin with. We may be overlooking some very crucial clue," I said.

"Wouldn't be the first time, buddy. We need to probe into this matter further, don't you think?" Sheila asked.

"I agree wholeheartedly." Agreeing wholeheartedly with Sheila had led to more than our share of mishaps and sticky situations, but, as usual, it didn't stop me from doing it once again.

THIRTY-TWO

Sheila and I sat together at my desktop computer and researched poisonous plants. She gasped as I was refilling our coffee cups and pointed toward an image on the screen. "Isn't this the palm of Christ flower that was in all of the floral arrangements?"

I looked at the screen. "Yeah. So what?"

"Palm of Christ is another name for the castor oil plant." When I didn't react immediately to Sheila's statement, she continued. "Don't you recall Raven telling us castor oil is one of the most toxic plants in the world? This article says its bean contains ricinolein, another name for ricin, as Raven indicated. And you know from watching television how deadly ricin can be."

"Wow!" I looked at the image on the screen again to confirm what Sheila had said. "Yeah, that's definitely the same flower. But according to Raven, it doesn't have a reputation for causing death among humans who've come in close proximity to it unless they ingested the flower, and I'm sure Bubba did not get so hungry during the nuptials that he began gnawing on his boutonniere."

Sheila nodded as she continued to read the details about castor oil plants on the website. "This also states that the inhalation of ricin can lead to respiratory distress followed by pulmonary edema, respiratory failure, and multi-system organ dysfunction. Weakness and influenza-like symptoms of fever, myalga, and arthralgia are also possible."

"What is myalga and arthralgia?"

Sheila read further before replying to my question. "Muscle and joint pain."

"Without being able to converse with Bubba, there's no way of knowing if he's experienced either of those symptoms."

"Do you think this could be the smoking gun?" Sheila asked.

"It could be the cause of everyone's adverse reactions, but I don't think 'smoking gun' is the correct term in this instance. I can't believe Lily Franks meant to kill anyone when she used the lovely red flower in the wedding boutonnieres and bouquets. This might be a case of accidental poisoning, you know, with no harm intended by the perpetrator. After all, Wendy chose the flowers, not the floral shop owner. But I do recall Lily being hesitant to include the palm of Christ, even though she didn't mention why. She only relented because Wendy insisted. Of course, she never expected anyone to ingest the flower, and probably couldn't imagine the toxin being inhaled to such a dangerous degree. Unless—"

"Unless what?" Sheila asked when I paused.

"What if someone intentionally ground one or more of the beans down to a powdery-like substance to dust the flower with?"

"You're right. And who would know better than Lily, and obviously Raven, that the castor oil bean can be deadly if turned into powder and inhaled? Perhaps that's why Lily chose not to mention why she was hesitant to include the palm of Christ blossoms in the arrangements. The idea of using it as a murder weapon might have already been forming in her mind."

I considered Sheila's comments for a few moments. "Nah. What motive could Lily have had to kill Bubba? What ties could she have even had to him that'd make her want him dead? Andy told me he's never been to Missouri before, and I can't imagine she's been to Myrtle Beach, either. If she has, what are the odds she met Bubba there? That's the part that makes no sense to me whatsoever."

"Yeah, me neither. I still think we're overlooking something or someone. Are you certain Lily used palm of Christ, or castor oil, plants and not something that's very similar looking?"

As Sheila spoke, I rifled through a stack of papers I'd gathered and stored in a large plastic envelope labeled "Wedding Stuff". I pointed to the receipt after locating it amongst the paperwork. "Yep. See? White orchids, palm of Christ, and baby's breath."

"Baby's breath?" Sheila asked. She was clearly puzzled.

"Yes. Why do you look so confused?"

"There was no baby's breath in Bubba's boutonniere."

"What are you talking about? I'm sure I remember them being used as a filler in all the flower arrangements."

"No. I don't think so. Not in Bubba's boutonniere, anyway."

We both stood up and practically sprinted to the kitchen. Inside the pantry, I opened up the spare refrigerator and withdrew the box of bouquets and boutonnieres. All three of the groomsmen's boutonnieres were missing.

"What in the world?" I looked at Sheila in astonishment. "We both saw Bubba's boutonniere in this box. In fact, we even touched and smelled it. I'm certain the other two were in this box, as well."

"As am I," Sheila agreed. She lifted the box up over her head and looked under it, as if she truly thought the three boutonnieres could be stuck to the bottom of it. "Where in the heck could they have gone?"

"Someone must have taken them. And you know what that means, don't you?"

"Yes. Someone did not want Bubba's boutonniere to be pegged as a possible murder weapon."

"Exactly," I agreed with a nod. "Hopefully, it doesn't turn out to have been an actual murder weapon. But the fact someone has gone to the effort to confiscate all of the boutonnieres makes it look like Bubba's boutonniere truly was intended as such. I'm still hoping against hope that Bubba wakes up and pulls out of his coma."

"Yes. Of course. This discovery definitely points toward foul play. Who'd ever conceive of using a boutonniere as a murder weapon?"

"I don't know. But it begs the question of why all three were taken," I added. "Could someone have been planning to take out all three groomsmen in the wedding party? And, if so, why?"

"Good grief!" Sheila exclaimed. "We really do need to notify the police department."

I thought it over for a moment. "Not yet. First, let's call Stone and tell him what we've discovered. If I call the police department, they will just scoff at my insistence that a murder was attempted and —"

"— may still prove to have been successful."

"Yes. But, I can guarantee you we'll need more evidence than this to get the police department to investigate it. I don't think my insistence that someone tried to kill the six-foot-eight best man with a flower will carry a lot of weight with the police chief. You'd think the department would appreciate all I've done to help them solve homicides in the past, but they don't. On the contrary, they appear to resent my intervention."

"Don't you mean 'interference'?" Sheila's mocking question did not merit a response. She quickly evaluated my expression and backtracked. "I'm just kidding. I know how valuable you've been in solving murders in this town, and they really should have your picture up on the wall at the police station."

I wanted to tell her they'd prefer to have it up on the wall at the post office under "Most Wanted". Instead, I repeated my original suggestion. "I think it's best if we discuss it with Stone first."

"You're probably right. I'm sure Stone will want to talk it over with the medical staff. They may be able to determine if any poison of the plant variety has actually been found in Bubba's system. Should we drive over to the hospital, Lexie?"

"No. I'll just call Stone to save some time. Then you and I need to make another visit to the floral shop."

"Oh, boy. I was afraid you were going to say that." Sheila rolled her eyes so dramatically, I was surprised they didn't get stuck in that position, as my mother always told me mine would do if I kept crossing them.

I picked up one of the bridesmaid's bouquets, which had been left behind, and held it up for Sheila to look at. "As you can see, the bouquets have baby's breath in them."

"I know, Lexie. But I swear to you the boutonnieres did not. They had a different white flower than these in the bouquets."

"Okay. I believe you. I've no reason to doubt your memory. It's always been sharper than mine."

"Well, I don't know about—"

I interrupted Sheila's attempt to placate me. "I have a plan."

"I'm sure you do." The sarcasm in her tone was not appreciated, and I told her so. I couldn't help but grin as I scolded her, though.

Sheila laughed before executing the sign of the cross. I assumed she thought this would save our bacon in the event my plan took a bad turn, even though neither of us were Catholic. I looked at her in disbelief. "Seriously, Sheila?"

"I don't think it can hurt us any. Let's go do something foolish and test out that theory of yours about God protecting children and fools."

And so off we dashed like moths to a front porch light and did exactly that. As it turned out, whether we proved the proverb right or wrong was a matter of opinion. Some would think what happened to the two of us that evening proved the adage was hogwash, while others would insist the fact we were still alive to debate the matter proved otherwise.

THIRTY-THREE

S peaking with Stone on the phone, I sensed he was distracted by
activity at the hospital. Nevertheless, I told him about the
disappearing boutonnieres and explained the toxic qualities of
numerous different flowers, including the potent poison associated
with palm of Christ, otherwise known as the castor oil plant. His
responses were short, and I could tell the significance of Sheila's and
my discovery was not sinking in.

Understandably, Stone was more interested in the fact Bubba
had been moved to a room because his condition remained
unchanged and space in the ICU was in critical demand.

"Does that mean they've given up hope he'll regain consciousness?" I asked when I realized he was too preoccupied to absorb
what I'd been trying to tell him.

"I'm not sure what it means, but I'm not happy about it. The
way I see it, he needs 'round the clock supervision. He's certainly
not going to get the attention he needs in a regular room."

"I agree. So, anyway, Sheila and I are going to—"

"Oh, good. Here comes Dr. Schnuck. I need to talk to him right
away."

"Okay. But, as I was trying to tell you, Sheila and I are—"

"Gotta go, babe. You two do whatever you need to do. I'll talk with you later."

Before I could even respond, Stone had ended the call. But not before instructing Sheila and me to "do whatever we needed to do", which was exactly what I'd hoped he'd say. Later the two of us could stop by the hospital and explain our concerns and recent discoveries to the medical staff. With any luck at all, we'd have more information to share by then.

When we entered Lily's-in-Bloom Floral Shop, we heard Lily conversing with someone over the phone in her office. She was crying as she spoke, making it difficult to make out her words. "I feel so bad" and "running out of time" were the only phrases I could decipher. I also thought I heard her say "put a new diaper on the iguana", but that's neither here nor there.

Standing outside her office, we practically had our ears plastered to the glass partition next to the office door. When Lily looked up and noticed our presence, she laid her phone on her desk, walked to her door, and closed it. It was obvious we were trying to eavesdrop on her phone conversation.

"Well, crap!" I said. "I guess while we're waiting, we can poke around the shop. We might accidentally stumble onto the missing boutonnieres."

"You think she'd be stupid enough to sneak into the inn to steal them and then bring them back to her shop?" Sheila asked.

"Maybe it never occurred to her that a couple of master sleuths like us would show up to confront her about them. She likely never imagined anyone would put two and two together and come up with three. Three missing boutonnieres that might have been tampered with, that is."

"Good point," Sheila conceded. "She probably figured if anyone even noticed the three boutonnieres were missing, they'd assume they'd been discarded and never give them a second thought."

We wandered around the shop, searching in every nook and cranny, to no avail. I turned to Sheila. "Most likely, if she did hijack the boutonnieres and bring them back here, she'd have hidden them somewhere rather than set them out in plain sight. Wouldn't you think?"

"Yeah, you're probably right. You don't think she'd try to preserve them for some reason, do you?"

"I would think that's the last thing she'd do. Why do you ask?"

"Because," Sheila began, "if she wanted to preserve them, she'd probably put them in the cooler. I think every floral shop has a cooler for preserving cut flowers and arrangements. Do you know where it'd be?"

"Yes." I pointed to the far corner of the shop. "When Lariat and I met Wendy here to order the wedding flowers, Raven told me there was a floral cooler across from the restroom. When I walked back there, I saw a metal door at the end of the hallway."

We walked to the cooler and after opening its heavy metal door, discovered it was about eight by ten feet in diameter. The entire compartment was galvanized steel, reminding me of the vault at our local bank. The shelving that lined the inside perimeter of the cooler held loose flowers, already constructed floral arrangements, vases of roses still in their bud stage, and other floral items. The aroma from the cooler was almost nauseating. I'm sure the fragrance of each individual flower was heavenly, but the cumulative effect was anything but.

Leaving the door open, we entered the cooler and began to search the shelves. We'd been looking for no more than two minutes when Sheila exclaimed, "Look! I found them. All three of them."

"Awesome. That's all the proof we need that Lily perpetrated the assault on Bubba."

"Exactly." Sheila clapped her hands in excitement. "Let's go confront her. When we present this evidence to her, there's no way she can deny her involvement."

THIRTY-FOUR

J ust as I reached for the three boutonnieres that had been placed in a see-through plastic box like you might find at a grocery store's salad bar, the door closed behind us. I rushed over and tried to open it, but found it locked. I banged on the door and hollered, "Hey! Open the door! It's locked, and we're trapped in here."

I stopped yelling and waited for the door to open. I might as well have been waiting for fossil fuel to turn back into dinosaur bones. I slammed my fist against the door several more times, yelling, "Help! Help us!"

Finally, Sheila grabbed my fist mid-slam and said, "No one's coming, Lexie. No one outside the shop could possibly hear us from inside this cooler. And if anyone is in the shop, they'd have surely heard you by now and let us out. And Lily would let us out if she hadn't closed the door intentionally to trap us in here in the first place."

"Do you really think she did this on purpose?" I had known the answer without even asking, but hoped Sheila would have a reas-suring response. I needed her to say something positive to calm my rapidly increasing hysteria, because my claustrophobia was beginning to kick in full force. No such luck.

"No, I think it was a gust of wind that blew it shut."

I looked at Sheila to see if she was serious. There had been no open windows or doors in the floral shop. Sheila picked up the plastic box filled with half-wilted boutonnieres, and said, "Duh. Of course she did it on purpose. She knew we were in here snooping around. If she had something incriminating to hide, like these boutonnieres, and knew we were on to her, she might have figured she had nothing to lose."

"True," I replied. "Especially if she'd already attempted to kill Bubba, and might still end up being successful. I'm sure she never intended to harm Raven, but couldn't have imagined Raven would end up with her nose practically buried in Bubba's boutonniere as she tried to breathe life back into him."

"Good point." Sheila spoke as her eyes darted around the cooler, looking for a possible means of escape.

On the inside of the door, we noticed a small keypad. The light on top glowed red, which, according to the legend on the bottom of the box, indicated the door lock had been activated. It also indicated that to override the system, we merely needed to punch in the four-digit pass code.

"No problem," I said. "There're only something like ten thousand possible combinations. You try the first five thousand, then I'll take over and finish up the last half."

"Not funny," Sheila said. "Let's try some of the obvious choices, like 0-0-0-0, 1-2-3-4, and so forth. The address here on Sycamore Street is 1-4-1-9. Try that."

"All right." After punching in the four digits, I said, "Nope."

"Lily on a phone dial would be 7-4-7-9."

"Okay...nope."

As Sheila listed off potential codes, I tried each one. Each time I tried, the light on top of the keypad flashed yellow, returning to red once the mechanism reset itself. After the sixth or seventh failed attempt, I said, "We might be in for a long night."

"It's four-thirty in the afternoon," Sheila said. "I wonder how long the oxygen in this cooler will last. Worse, I wonder how long it'll take before the CO2 level gets too high to be safe. We might be in for a shorter night than you think."

So much for hoping Sheila would have reassuring words to share with me. Just thinking that we might have a limited supply of oxygen to sustain us, and a limited time before an elevated carbon dioxide level killed us, caused me to hyperventilate. Now it was I who felt like I had a Brussels sprout lodged in my windpipe.

"What *(gasp)* are we going to *(gasp)* do?" I asked. "I already can't catch my *(gasp)* breath."

"That's just your imagination in overdrive, Lexie. We must have at least a few hours' worth of oxygen in here before it begins to get difficult to breathe. Try to relax. Take deep breaths and exhale slowly. In the meantime, I'll continue to punch in random four-digit codes. Who knows? I might get lucky and pick the code that unlocks the door."

"Good idea. I'll concentrate on calming my nerves." As Sheila suggested, I inhaled a deep breath and let it out slowly.

"Besides, Stone will probably know exactly where to find us, so don't panic at this point." Sheila's voice was as calm as a windless day on the coast. But she should have known me well enough by then to realize telling me to stop panicking was as preposterous as insisting I cease blinking until we'd been rescued. It was not only improbable, it was impossible.

"I disagree. I think panicking is warranted because I don't believe Stone understood where we were headed when I talked to him on the phone earlier. I agree we can't just sit in here and hope God whispers our location into someone's ear, but there's got to be another solution besides contacting Stone. Keep trying to crack the code while I think of a plan."

"No, Lexie!" Sheila was adamant. It was one of the few times I could ever recall her raising her voice at me. "You need to call Stone and own up to what's happened so he can make sure we get out of here before it's too late. We are in a life-or-death situation, you know."

"I know, but if we do that, we'll never hear the end of it. Getting

Stone to agree to let me look into this situation took an act of God. Or damned near, anyway."

"You would prefer to die?" The sarcasm in Sheila's tone cut to the quick.

"Of course not. Don't be so dramatic. We'll think of something."

"I already have. Call Detective Johnston. I realize you aren't crazy about having to explain how we got trapped in a floral shop cooler. I get it. But getting locked in here only goes to prove we had a valid reason for wanting to speak with Lily. It's not our fault we stopped by just to have a word with her and rather than being forced to come clean with us, she locked us in here. I don't think Stone and Randy can hold that against us. If anything, it shows evidence of guilt on Lily's part, and confirms our suspicions," Sheila said. Hers was the voice of reason and calmness in the chilly room. "If we call Wyatt, he'll have someone here to rescue us long before we run out of oxygen, I'm almost certain."

"*Almost* certain? Would you mind repeating that last remark with a little more confidence?" I tried to chuckle as I pulled my phone out of my back pocket, but couldn't quite muster up any counterfeit amusement. "But you are absolutely right. With the idea of being locked in a small, airless compartment overwhelming me, I hadn't been able to look at the situation clearly. We should be commended for our actions, not chastised. In essence, Lily's actions validate our reason for coming here to confront her in the first place. Finding the three stolen boutonnieres in this cooler are further proof of her wrongdoing."

"Exactly. So call the detective, and then Stone, so he and Randy won't worry about where we are."

"Uh-oh. I was afraid of that," I mumbled. I shook my phone as if I thought maybe a loose wire was keeping it from turning on.

That aforementioned "calmness" my friend had exhibited suddenly vanished like the West African Black Rhino. In a nearly hysterical voice, she asked, "Huh? Whaddya mean 'uh-oh'? You were afraid of what? What's wrong? Can't get a signal? Did you choose the cheapest phone service available again? Please tell me you forgot Wyatt's number, because we can find it via an online directory."

"I wish I could tell you that, but I know Wyatt's number like the back of my hand. You surely don't think this is the first time I've needed rescuing, do you? The problem is my phone's gone dead. I was so exhausted last night, I forgot to put it on the charger before I turned in for the night. No big deal, though. Just use your phone. Wyatt's number is (816) 555-0206."

"I can't use my phone. I stuck it in your glove compartment before we came into the shop."

"You what?" The panic and claustrophobia I'd been able to bring under control resurfaced like a blue whale coming up for air. "Good Lord, Sheila. Why do you keep putting your damned phone in my glove compartment? What good is it going to do you in there? Why even own one if you never have it on you in case of an emergency?"

"I was afraid I'd set it down and forget it, like I'd thought I'd done the first time we came here. You know how I am about losing things."

"Yes, I do. I'm the exact same way. That's why I wear a fanny pack and have been trying to talk you into doing the same for years. I left one too many purses in one too many restaurants before I finally got wise and switched over to a fanny pack. They might have gone out of style about the same time bell-bottom jeans did, but it stays attached to me at all times. So why didn't you just put your phone in your back pocket?"

Sheila turned around to show me that her skinny jeans were pocket free and looked as if they'd been painted on with a sprayer. Sheila was nothing if not current with ever-changing fashions. I wondered how much extra she'd had to pay for all of the strategically placed rips and tears in her trendy new denims. I also wondered if she regretted her choice of pants. I'm sure the nippiness of the floral cooler was seeping in through every nook and cranny it could find. I'd already tucked my slacks into my socks to keep the chill from sneaking up my pant legs.

"Your purse, then?" I asked. I was starting to panic about our dismal situation. "You couldn't have just put your phone in your purse? From now on, you are forbidden to put your phone in my glove compartment. If we live through this, that is."

"Hey! Chill out. How was I supposed to know we'd get locked in a cooler? Besides, I didn't have any room in my purse to put a phone. I have the new larger-screen model, you know."

I glanced at her purse, which she'd be lucky to be able to squeeze in one of an airplane's overhead compartments. I didn't mean to be snippy. It was just my nerves talking when I asked, "Do you have to check that purse every time you fly?"

Sheila merely shook her head and stuck her tongue out at me. She knew how moody I could get when I was scared spit-less because she'd witnessed the phenomenon on numerous occasions during the course of our friendship. "Just relax, my friend. Surely someone will realize we're missing and summon help. I'll try more codes on the security box."

"Fine." I saw no point in arguing, despite the fact I felt her efforts were futile. It could take hours to punch in the correct code from the over ten thousand possible combinations, and neither of us had told anyone where we were going. I'd tried to tell Stone, but he'd been so distracted, he'd probably already forgotten I'd even called. He likely thought Sheila and I were power-shopping at Wal-Mart. The only person in the world who knew of our precarious location was likely the woman who'd made certain we were locked into the nearly freezing cooler, in the first place. A lot of good that was going to do us.

Sitting across from Sheila with my back against a shelf, I listened to my stomach growl. I tried to take my mind off our impending demise by thinking about the items I'd have to put on the new to-do list for a re-do wedding ceremony. Unfortunately, it was a good idea that didn't work worth a tinker's dam.

On the bright side, I soon figured out why Sheila's phone wouldn't fit in her purse. The girl carried enough emergency food in her oversized bag to sustain an entire Girl Scout troop lost in a large Tibetan cave for at least a month.

With nothing else to do while we waited, we munched on beef

jerky, peanuts, chocolate-covered raisins, peanut butter and cheese crackers, Pringles, and even pastrami sandwiches. *Who carries emergency pastrami sandwiches in her purse? Besides Sheila, of course.* But on that evening, I was thankful she did. The comfort food was most welcome, even though the salty snacks made my throat dry.

"It's been three hours, Sheila. I'm sure I've gained at least five pounds since we walked into this cooler. I'm certain to die of dehydration if I don't succumb to hypothermia first. Did you happen to read the thermometer outside the door on our way in? It read thirty-five degrees. My teeth are chattering and my lips feel like they could freeze shut. We'll be lucky if we don't end up with frostbite."

"I wish I'd left some hand warmers in my purse," Sheila muttered under her breath. "I shouldn't have replaced them all with that big box of Milk Duds."

"You routinely carry hand warmers in late August?" I realized then Sheila would be the perfect contestant on *The Price is Right.* No matter what the game show's host asked for, she'd be almost certain to have it in her purse.

"Don't be snippy. I'm sorry I can't do anything about the fact it's frigging freezing in here, but…"

Just then, when I was certain Sheila's bag could not contain another single item, she reached into it and withdrew a flask. She handed it to me, and chuckled at my questioning look. "Here's some Jose Cuervo to ease your thirst and warm up your insides."

"Tequila? Are you nuts? Alcohol is a diuretic. The last thing I need is to be found dead in a floral cooler with an alcohol level over the legal driving limit. Did you know that alcohol may make you feel warmer because it widens blood vessels under the skin, but in actuality it lowers your core temperature, which makes hypothermia set in quicker?" Sometimes when Wendy blabbers on about how one of her victims died, I accidentally learn a few interesting facts whether I want to or not.

"To each her own," Sheila said. She then uncapped the flask and took a long swallow. How it didn't burn like liquid fire all the way down to her toes, I don't know. I was just relieved when she reached into her bag one more time and withdrew a bottle of water, which she handed to me. "Bottoms up."

"Oh, Thank God. I was afraid I wouldn't be able to open my mouth to talk before long."

"Yeah, that would have been awful," Sheila replied dryly. Her anxiety about our dire situation had turned her into a cranky-pants.

"There's no reason to be sarcastic. I want out of here just as badly as you do."

"Sorry. I'm just a teeny bit uptight." Sheila gave me an apologetic smile, and added, "Drink your water sparingly. It's the only bottle I had and we might be in here for a long while yet."

Her comment reminded me of something. "When Wendy, Lariat and I were here several weeks ago, I could've sworn Lily told Raven to get me a bottle of water out of the cooler. I don't see any bottles in here now."

"Maybe their supply ran out, or they have a separate drink cooler."

"Thanks for pointing out the obvious." I hadn't meant to be surly, but the thought of impending death had a tendency to make me a 'teeny bit uptight' too. "I'm wondering how much oxygen we have left."

"Me too. The carbon dioxide level has to be fairly elevated by now too. I know I'm starting to feel sleepy. How about you?"

I nodded, and we grew silent for a while, both of us lost in thought about the predicament we'd found ourselves in. I began thinking about Sheila's earlier remark regarding Lily hiding the three boutonnieres. I reached over to where Sheila had set them down and picked up the plastic box. Gazing at them, I realized Sheila's memory had been spot on. I held them up for Sheila to study. "What do you see here?"

"As I told you earlier, I see no baby's breath. What I do see are white orchids, the palm of Christ blossoms, and lilies-of-the-valley being used as filler. Why?" Sheila asked.

"That's what I thought. Wendy specifically requested that baby's breath be used as the filler, which is quite common in boutonnieres, bouquets, and other flower arrangements. But, as you pointed out, this is not baby's breath, but lily-of-the-valley."

"Okay," Sheila said, drawing the two-syllables out like the word was seventeen letters long. "So maybe Lily ran out of baby's breath and substituted lily-of-the-valley. So what? These boutonnieres are just as lovely, either way. I doubt Wendy even noticed the difference."

"That's not my point. Don't you remember? Raven included lily-of-the-valley in her list of poisonous flowers yesterday, along with the castor bean plant and several others."

"Oh, good grief. That's right. And when we Googled the flower last night, it said that the entire lily-of-the-valley plant can be deadly and contains lethal traces of convallatoxin, which intensifies the heart's contractions."

"Yes. It also said it can cause the heart to slow down, potentially leading to coma and/or death. Doesn't that sound exactly like what happened to——?"

"——to Bubba!" We finished the sentence in unison. We looked at each other in shock.

"It's beginning to look as if Lily used as many toxic flowers as they could in the boutonnieres," I said. "Although I'm pretty sure the bouquets had baby's breath in them."

"They did." Sheila studied me for a few moments as if concerned about my mental state. But then, I was too. "Don't you remember that we confirmed that before we left the inn? That's why I noticed they used a different filler for the groomsmen's boutonnieres."

"Oh, yeah. That's right. Sorry, my mind feels a little foggy all of a sudden."

"Yeah, mine too." As she replied, I noticed Sheila's worried expression had changed to one of fear. I reached over and patted her leg.

"Don't worry. We'll make it out of here somehow. Don't lose faith." To take her mind off our dire situation, I reverted back to the topic of the toxic flowers. "The boutonniere was pinned to the groomsmen's lapels, practically right below their noses. What if

Bubba accidentally inhaled too deeply and some of the toxin from both poisonous flowers got into his lungs?"

Before responding in a whisper, Sheila's eyes darted from side to side, as if she were afraid the flowers in the room would launch the rumor mill into motion before her speculation could be investigated. "You know, it's possible Lily made the substitution for nefarious reasons, rather than simply because she'd run out of baby's breath. However, that scenario seems far-fetched now that I've said it out loud."

"I don't know why you're whispering, but you're exactly right. There's another aspect of this to consider as well. When Wendy, Lariat, and I ordered flowers for the wedding, Lily ordered Raven to get back to work filling orders. What are the chances it was Raven who substituted the lily-of-the-valley for the baby's breath? Could she have sprinkled a ground-up castor bean on Bubba's bouton-niere, as well? Raven knew both flowers to be poisonous, and she had a possible motive to kill the person who we now suspect broke her heart. I'm positive it was Raven who pinned the boutonnieres on the groomsmen prior to the ceremony. It sounds to me like it could have been a crime of passion, so to speak."

"You're right. In which case," Sheila deduced, "it's conceivable that Lily Franks had no idea about the substitution. Truthfully, either one of them could be responsible for Bubba's illness."

"Yes, but if Lily didn't know about it, why would she lock us in this cooler? Could she somehow be in cahoots with Raven?" I asked, thinking out loud. "And if so, why?"

"I don't know. I can't imagine she'd put her own neck on the line for an employee who had only been working for her a couple of weeks. This whole thing makes no sense," Sheila said. "I think once we get out of here, we need to go directly to the police station, despite what they think about you and your propensity for getting involved in police cases."

"Yeah. As much as I hate to admit it, that's exactly what we need to do. In the meantime, we should write our suspicions down on a piece of paper, which I'll hide in my shoe, or something. You know, just in case, we don't…"

"Make it out of here alive?" It was a question requiring no response, and when I failed to make one, Sheila added, "Yeah. I guess you're right."

"You must have a pen in that big bag of tricks, don't you?"

"Um, no. I think I took it out to make room for more Slim Jims."

"Swell." I didn't have a pen either. I'd only put what I considered to be the bare necessities in my fanny pack before I'd left the house, which, unfortunately, had not included a writing instrument. The entire contents of my fanny pack included a tube of lip gloss, a tin box of breath mints, my driver's license and a few credit cards, thirty-seven dollars in cash, and a cell phone that was as useless to me at that moment as a pet rock.

I removed the half-eaten Slim Jim I had just stuck in my mouth and glared at it as if it were the enemy. I then threw it and my empty water bottle across the tiny metal compartment in frustration. Sheila looked at me as if I'd pitched a live hand grenade into the corner of the room. "What are you doing?"

"Sorry, but I drained the entire bottle without thinking. Now it's gone right through me and I have to pee. I'm also beginning to feel really drowsy. I think I'll take a nap."

"I'm having trouble keeping my eyes open, too. But I think we should try to stay awake. Why don't you pee in that empty bucket on the bottom shelf? I'll probably have to do the same before long."

"All right. But I think I'll wait until I can't hold it any longer. I wouldn't be surprised if you had a roll of toilet paper in that humongous purse of—"

"Oh, my!" Sheila suddenly exclaimed in alarm. The terror in her voice unnerved me. She jumped to her feet. "Do you feel like I do? Like you're on the verge of losing consciousness?"

It quickly became clear we were in an even more perilous situation than we'd realized. Not only were we subject to a limited amount of remaining oxygen, the near-freezing temperature in the cooler, and a gradual increase of the CO_2 level, we now seemed to have another problem we hadn't considered.

"Kind of. Have you noticed an odd odor?" I asked.

"Yeah, now that you mention it. I smell something with a bitter aroma to it."

"That's it. That's what I smell, too. I think it's the flowers. Whatever it is, I agree it would not be wise to go to sleep. You don't happen to have a board game or two in your purse, do you?" I asked. The glare Sheila bestowed on me was all the answer I needed.

In a desperate attempt to stay awake, we decided to play a game called "Twenty Questions", where one player thinks of a person, place, or thing, and the other gets to ask twenty yes-or-no questions in order to come up with the correct answer.

"Does this person have more than fifteen tattoos?" Sheila asked in a sleepy voice.

Before I could say "yes", because my latest *People Magazine* had reported Angelina Jolie as having seventeen of them, Sheila's body slid down the wall like a glob of hot wax. When I couldn't wake her, no matter how hard I tried, I began to weep.

"I'm so sorry, my friend. If I haven't told you lately, I love you," I said with a sniffle. I prayed her unconscious mind could hear my words of deep sincerity. "And, by the way, I did not select the cheapest phone service provider this time."

I'd barely finished my remark when I felt myself slipping into oblivion. I felt bizarrely happy, because I would not have been able to deal well with survivor's guilt if my stubborn relentlessness ended up taking my best friend's life and spared my own.

THIRTY-FIVE

"Lexie? Wake up. Come on, baby. Wake up."

I'd heard Stone's voice call to me just before opening my eyes. It seemed as though his voice had come from a long way off. My throat felt dry and scratchy, as if I'd just awoken in a recovery room following a tonsillectomy. As I looked into the worried eyes of my husband, I wondered how much time had passed. The last thing I remembered was sobbing about the fact I might have gotten my dearest friend in the world killed.

With an enormous sense of relief, I soon heard Randy talking to Sheila and questioning Lily, who stood outside the cooler in the hallway. I thought I heard Wyatt's voice, as well.

"Is Sheila all right?" I asked Stone. "Where are we?"

"We found you two here in the floral shop's cooler. I think you'll be fine, but Lily's called for an ambulance to transport you both to the hospital to be checked out."

"Oh, no. Do we have to go? Each visit to the emergency ward gets more and more humiliating."

"Yes, I'm afraid so, darling. Lily said you might have taken in too much of a dangerous gas called ether-something."

"Ethylene." Lily leaned into the cooler and provided the name

212

for him, which at the time I thought an odd thing to do for someone who'd just tried to use it to murder two women. But then I realized, if the jig was up, she'd need to feign concern to make it appear as though the event was merely an accident.

In a pretentious manner, Lily went on to explain how ethylene oxide occurs. "It's a toxic gas flowers put off naturally as they age. Prolonged exposure to the gas can cause fatigue, dizziness, confusion, and occasionally even death. Some of the more expensive coolers have a filter to filter out the gas. Sorry, but this cooler has no filter because the cost of the fancier model is out of my league."

Strangely enough, Lily *did* sound sorry. Not sorry about what had happened to Sheila and me, mind you, but sorry we were still alive and kicking. I was pushing hard against my temples in an effort to alleviate the throbbing. "That must be why my head feels like a helium balloon about to explode. To make matters worse, I can't feel my toes on either foot."

"What in the world were you two doing?" Stone asked. Lily tilted her head, clearly as interested in my response as Stone. "You had to know it wasn't safe to lock yourselves in a cooler."

"Of course we know it's not safe to be locked in here. But... well...we...just..." I began, struggling to explain our presence in the floral cooler. I was barely whispering as I explained. "We had to. We'd found evidence of what likely happened to Bubba and we needed to confirm it before taking it to the police department. His condition was not an accident, Stone. We're convinced it was due to foul play."

From Stone's expression, you'd have thought I'd told him Sheila and I had read hippos killed more humans every year than any other animal, so we'd gone swimming in a small lake with a pod of them to find out if the statement was true.

"What does locking yourselves in a floral cooler have to do with confirming evidence of foul play?"

"We didn't lock *ourselves* in here, Stone."

"No?" he asked impatiently. He was clearly not buying any of what I had to say. "Go on."

"We just stepped in here for a few seconds, not expecting that someone would lock the door behind us." As I whispered, I cast an accusatory glance Lily's way. "It took a number of hours for the gas to build up enough in our systems to affect us."

"You two have been in here for over seven hours. It's a wonder we didn't find two dead bodies when we opened the door." Stone sounded almost angry they *hadn't* found two dead bodies. It was as if he thought we deserved to have succumbed to our own stupidity. That this thought even crossed my mind made it clear to me the effects of the gas had not completely abated yet. I could barely work up enough energy to take a full breath, so I didn't try to respond. I figured it was best to let him vent his frustrations. I knew once he got it off his chest, he'd be as malleable as a flat bicycle tire.

"It's after midnight," Stone said. "We've been worried sick about you. We weren't sure if the two of you had been abducted, or involved in an accident on some rarely traveled back road. It would never have occurred to Randy and me to look in a floral shop cooler, for goodness sakes! You're lucky we found you in time, considering you told no one about your plans to come here."

Stone's last remark prompted me to rally up the oomph to respond. "I did so tell someone. I told you! Don't you remember speaking with me? I explained to you about how all three grooms-men's boutonnieres had been confiscated from the pantry refrigerator. We found out they contained not one, but two toxic flowers! I really need to speak to Wyatt privately about our suspicions. Lily Franks needs to be interrogated by the police." I whispered, as Lily stood just outside the cooler door. Fortunately, she was having an exchange with Wyatt and paying no attention to my conversation with Stone. "In fact, someone needs to step outside the cooler to keep an eye on her before she locks the entire lot of us in here."

Stone stared at me oddly, as if trying to judge my sanity. Apparently, he came to the conclusion I was completely bonkers. He made no response other than a look that spoke volumes all by itself.

"Stone, she locked Sheila and me in here to do away with us because she knew we were on to her. There's nothing to stop her from locking that door again, leaving us all to die while she flees the country."

"Oh, jeez. You are in worse condition than I realized. Wyatt is outside in the hallway with Lily. I think he can take care of the situation if Lily tries to lock us in here." Stone's response was heavily laced with sarcasm, which I didn't appreciate. He turned away from me and asked the detective if the ambulance was en route to the floral shop.

"They should be arriving any second," Wyatt replied. "In fact, I think I hear sirens in the distance."

I pulled Stone's head down toward my mouth. "This is not the ethylene talking, Stone. We think either Raven or Lily, or possibly both, targeted Bubba on purpose, if not all of the groomsmen. We know for a fact it was Lily who locked us in here, which makes her our number-one suspect. She has nothing to lose at this point, and that makes her very dangerous."

"Honey, lay your head on my lap. Try not to talk. You're not making any sense, and talking is not going to help your headache subside any time soon. As I said, Wyatt is outside with Lily right now. I don't think there's much chance she's going to overpower Randy or me, much less Detective Johnston. Besides, after I contacted Lily to ask her if she'd seen you two, she rushed back here to her shop. She told me when she saw your car parked behind the building, she had a bad feeling you two had gotten locked in this floral cooler. She had it open before we arrived. She was nearly hysterical when we arrived, having just discovered both you and Sheila lying unconscious in here."

"She 'had a bad feeling'? Yeah, right. She *knew* we were in here and was likely faking her concern," I said in defense of my theory. "If she was distraught, it could have been because she'd been caught before the gas had eliminated us for good."

With an expression of pity, Stone tenderly stroked my forehead. It was clear he thought the toxic gas had made me cuckoo for cocoa puffs. With my lips pressed up against the denim of his blue jeans, I mumbled, "I'm glad you guys thought to look for us here."

"We didn't," he replied. "It was Rapella who suggested we search the floral shop. She and Rip stepped into the Inn around nine-thirty to ask about Bubba and say goodnight. Randy and I told them you two were missing. We had already called Wyatt, who put out an all-points bulletin on you girls. With Ladybug parked behind a dumpster in the rear of the building, it went undetected by the police officers who were patrolling the streets and responding to the APB. Why did you park your car there, anyway?"

"There were no available parking spots when we arrived." Actually, I hadn't even looked for a spot on the street, as we'd been trying to be less conspicuous at the time. We were afraid Lily would make a sprint for her SUV the moment she laid eyes on us. After all, she'd made a quick getaway the last time we confronted her.

"Well, whatever." Stone sounded unconvinced.

As absurd as this may sound, I was a little ticked off that he didn't believe my response, even though it wasn't exactly truthful. I wisely kept my aggravation to myself. "How did Rapella know where we were?"

"She told us she'd overheard you talking on the phone, discussing the groomsmen's boutonnieres. She said, 'If I were in Lexie's shoes, I'd go to the floral shop to confront the owner.' Why didn't you tell me someone had taken the boutonnieres out of the fridge?"

I did! In fact, Rapella overheard me talking on the phone to you, you numbskull! I laid my head on Stone's lap and sighed. It seemed pointless to remind him I had told him about the missing boutonnieres on the phone earlier, and in return his response had been that Sheila and I should do whatever it took. It truly was my fault. I'd known he was preoccupied at the time and barely taking in a word I was saying to him. I had actually thought his distracted state of mind might be to our advantage. I certainly couldn't blame Stone for being worried about us when we hadn't shown up at the inn by well past suppertime. I felt fortunate to have a man who always put my welfare ahead of his own. *Thank goodness Rapella was paying attention to our conversation, or things might have turned out much differently.*

As Sheila and I lay side-by-side in the back of an ambulance a few minutes later, I reached over and clasped her hand. "Sorry, pal."

"No need to apologize, Lexie," Sheila said. "We were in this together, weren't we?"

"Yes. And I appreciate you being my sidekick on what turned out to be an ill-advised mission. We might be dead right now, you know, and it would have been all my fault."

"Don't fret about it," Sheila said. In an effort to lift my spirits, she added, "I wouldn't have held it against you. Because, after all, I'd have been dead."

We both laughed and then simultaneously put our hands on our temples and groaned. "Please, Sheila, don't make me laugh!"

"Okay, I won't. Oh, hey. Did Wyatt tell you that Lily didn't lock us in the cooler?"

"No." That should have been welcome news. For some reason, it wasn't. For one thing, it blew my theory that Lily was the perpetrator out of the water, and for two, I sensed my friend was about to tell me getting locked in there was our own stupid fault. Which is exactly what she did. "If she didn't, who did?"

"No one. When she hung up the phone, after the conversation we overheard, she—"

"You mean eavesdropped on?" I said with a chuckle that only made the jackhammer inside my head pound harder. "Oh, God, that hurts!"

"Yeah. I know what you mean. You need to not make me laugh, either. My head feels like a titanium *piñata* someone's been banging on for an hour. One more whack, and it's—"

"So who locked us in the cooler?" I interrupted. I didn't have the patience to listen to a lengthy description of Sheila's headache. Considering how excruciating my own head felt, I already had a pretty good idea about hers.

"No one," she repeated. "In her explanation to Wyatt, she said that after she ended her phone call, she had grabbed her purse, locked up the office, and headed home. She looked around and, when she didn't see us, she assumed we had decided not to wait for her to finish the phone call and left. She hadn't even walked back to the cooler because she knew it had an automated system installed on it. To make sure she never left the door open overnight, risking all of her stock stored inside it, she had a system installed that automatically closes the door and locks it after two minutes of it being opened. As we'd thought, the code box inside is for safety purposes. In the event she or any of her employees got locked inside, they just had to enter the pass code to override the system. The pass code, incidentally, is 0925. Her niece was born last September twenty-fifth."

"Well, crap. How would we have ever figured that one out, not knowing Lily's birthday, much less her niece's? Do you know if Wyatt happened to ask Lily why the cooler has a locking mechanism on it, to begin with?"

"Actually, he did. She told Wyatt her shop was burglarized a few years ago, and although only cash from the register was taken, the thieves trashed the place—destroying all of her fresh flowers, vases, specialty arrangements, and other supplies—before they left. That incident convinced Lily to have the security system installed on the cooler to protect her stock, which amounts to thousands of dollars."

"Makes sense, I guess." I groaned as I put pressure on my temples with my hands again, trying to alleviate the throbbing.

When I lowered my arms to my sides a few moments later, Sheila reached over, picked up my left hand, and gave it a squeeze. "I think we should rest now. I'm feeling light-headed again, and my headache is getting worse by the second."

"Yeah, mine too."

After our conversation concluded, we remained silent until we reached the circular drive behind Wheatfield Memorial Hospital, which led to the emergency room—the place I now plan to claim as a second home on our income taxes.

THIRTY-SIX

"Hey there, Ms. Starr," the emergency room physician said in greeting after entering the curtained-off cubicle. "We were beginning to think you'd moved away, having not seen you in here for several months."

"Yes, well. Very funny." I could feel my face flush. "I'm still living in Rockdale. Visiting the ER is a bad habit I'm trying to break, Dr. Jifi."

"That's good to hear," he responded while he scanned my chart. "Says here you've been exposed to ethylene gas and a high level of carbon dioxide. Your blood work showed trace amounts of each, but both tend to dissipate from your system quickly once you've return to breathing clean air. Another hour in those frosty conditions and we'd likely be talking about amputation right now. All of your toes and a few fingers on Mrs. Davidson's right hand were beginning to show signs of frostbite. You two ladies are very lucky to have been rescued when you were."

"Yes, thank God for our friend, Rapella Ripple. When will we be released?"

"You should be good to go in no time."

"That's good. Is Sheila doing all right?"

"Yes, she's fine. It was wise to come in to be evaluated, but neither of you appear to have sustained any lasting ill effects."

"Just curious, Doc. We were locked inside a floral cooler, surrounded by flowers, a few of which are considered toxic. Would an over-exposure to, say, castor oil and lily-of-the-valley plants, show up on a tox screen?'

"There's no indication we need to run a tox screen on either one of you ladies."

"I realize that, Dr. Jifi. But there is a patient on the fifth floor of this hospital, named Bubba Slippknott, who has been in a coma for several days. Sheila and I discovered both of the flowers I mentioned were present in a boutonniere pinned to his lapel when he lost consciousness, and I'm wondering if inhalation of either flower could have caused that to happen."

Dr. Jifi was making notes on the chart in his hand. I wasn't sure he'd even heard what I'd just said, but I didn't want to interfere with what he was so intent on doing. Finally, he looked up, and replied, "Unless Mr. Slippknott decided to chow down on his boutonniere, it's highly unlikely the presence of toxic flowers would cause him to fall into a coma. Most flowers are only considered to be potentially lethal if ingested, not merely inhaled, so the odds of those flowers causing your friend to lose consciousness are extremely low. You can get dressed now and the nurse will be back in a few minutes with your discharge papers. Your friend has already received hers."

Soon after, I was dressed and waiting impatiently for the nurse to return. Sheila poked her head in through the curtains and I motioned her to come in and have a seat on the bed next to me.

"Randy's getting the car," Sheila told Stone, who had also entered my cubicle.

"I'll go check on Bubba's condition before we head home," Stone replied. "You can keep your partner in crime company in the meantime."

"I think he meant to say 'partner in crime-solving'," I said after Stone was out of earshot. I then reiterated what Dr. Jifi had just told me about the poisonous flowers in the groomsmen's boutonnieres. "The doctor agrees merely inhaling those floral toxins would not cause someone to slip into a coma, except maybe in very rare cases."

"That explains why none of the other groomsmen were affected by them. The retired cop in Randy made him question Lily while we were waiting for the ambulance. She told him that Raven ran out of baby's breath with two boutonnieres to go, and they didn't have time to get any more, so Lily instructed Raven to substitute with lily-of-the-valley sprigs in all of the groomsmen's boutonnieres so they would be consistent and look as if they were planned that way."

"That makes sense," I said. "And, after all, we didn't even notice the substitution at the ceremony. It wasn't until we were locked in the cooler that we even made the discovery."

"*I* noticed there was no baby's breath in the boutonnieres, if you remember right."

After a few seconds of reflection, I did recall her telling me that, which was what had prompted us to run to the pantry, and in turn, discover the boutonnieres had gone missing. I nodded and motioned for her to finish her story.

"Lily also admitted to feeling concerned about the substitution when Bubba collapsed and fell into a coma. When Raven fainted, she panicked. Afraid the flower swap or the palm of Christ, which she admitted she had reservations about including, could have had something to do with it, she decided to come to the inn the following day while no one but your guests were there. She also admitted to Randy she knew taking the boutonnieres was wrong, and feels very bad about doing so."

"I'll bet. She must have talked to the Monaghans. They're Andy's aunt and uncle from his mother's side of the family, and came from Thompsonville, Texas, for the wedding. "

"Yes," Sheila replied. "According to Lily, she told Nanette Monaghan she wanted to try and preserve the flowers so the young couple could reuse them when the rescheduled wedding ceremony took place. She said Nanette showed her to the pantry in the kitchen and then went back to packing her bags, leaving Lily alone with the flowers. She removed the boutonnieres and took them back to the floral shop, hoping no one would ever make the connection. Lily felt certain Nanette would have departed before you returned home and that you'd never be the wiser. She planned to replace the lily-of-the-valley sprigs with baby's breath when the next order came in, and sneak the boutonnieres back into the pantry fridge somehow. She knew she couldn't be held responsible for the palm of Christ since Wendy had insisted upon them."

"She must have been tense enough to snap a crowbar in half. No wonder she was so uptight when we showed up at the floral shop two days in a row."

"Yes," Sheila said. "She also told Randy she'd never met anyone in the wedding party, besides Wendy, and had no reason whatsoever to want to harm Bubba or anyone else."

"Did she mention anything about the abortion clinic?" I asked.

"No, but then the subject never came up. Randy didn't know anything about us following her there. Remember? We were supposedly at the Urgent Care clinic to find out why I was suddenly having trouble breathing."

"Of course," I said with a rueful smile. "You seem to have made a habit of having breathing issues in the past several days. You should probably see a doctor about that, buddy."

"No. What I should probably do is get on my horse and get the hell out of Dodge." When Sheila noticed my expression of concern, she added, "Don't worry. I was just kidding. I'm in this for the long haul—until we uncover the truth about Bubba's illness, or you get me killed. Whichever comes first."

I thought about shoving Sheila off the rolling-gurney bed. After all, she was already in the emergency room. Instead, I put my arm around her and gave her an appreciative hug. "I won't let that happen, Sheila. We won't be doing anything else that will place us in harm's way as we investigate this situation. I promise."

"Famous last words. Besides, Lexie, I'm beginning to believe the entire thing was an innocuous fluke. Perhaps a health issue Bubba has that has yet to be diagnosed. At this juncture, I don't really think anyone intentionally tried to hurt him. Do you?"

I was saved by Nurse Rosalie from having to admit I still

harbored suspicions the situation wasn't as "innocuous" as Sheila wanted to believe it was. Rosalie arrived with my discharge papers, and I couldn't get out of that cubicle fast enough. A notion had been flitting through my mind that I wanted to check out. I had a hunch who was behind Bubba's sudden illness, and I could hardly wait to find out if my intuition had merit.

THIRTY-SEVEN

I didn't climb out of bed until ten o'clock, having not returned home from the hospital until almost three in the morning. The headache remained, although it wasn't nearly as overpowering as it had been earlier.

I took a long hot shower and got dressed. When I made it downstairs at ten forty-five, Sheila, Randy, Stone, Wendy, Andy, Samantha Slippknott and the Ripples all sat in the parlor, as if in the midst of a symposium. Rip and Ripple had decided to hang around a few days in case any last-minute guests dropped in to book a suite at the Alexandria Inn. If that situation happened, they offered to watch over the guests so Stone and I would not be encumbered with duties involving our lodging facility. Also, the Ripples reasoned, if the wedding was rescheduled in the near future, they would still be around to attend the ceremony. I was very appreciative of their offer and already felt as if Sheila and I owed our lives to Rapella for her quick thinking the previous evening.

Stone motioned me toward a loveseat and poured me a cup of strong Columbian brew from an antique sideboard cabinet, on which I usually kept a pot of fresh coffee when the inn had guests on the premises. Stone must have brewed a pot that morning in my absence.

After inquiring about both Sheila and Bubba's conditions, I asked what the group had been discussing. By the expression on Sheila's face, I wasn't sure I wanted to hear the answer to my inquiry.

With a reproachful scowl, Wendy had glanced from me to Sheila. "We've come to a mutual agreement that neither you nor Sheila should be involved with Bubba's mysterious illness any longer. It's just not worth taking the risk of either of you getting hurt or worse, as in the case of what almost happened with you two overnight."

Stone took over from there. "The medical staff is baffled and is considering the possibility of transferring Bubba by life flight to the Mayo Clinic in Rochester, Minnesota. It sounds as if his fate will soon be out of our hands, so there's no reason to delve deeper into what put him in this condition to begin with."

Bubba's fate never was in our hands, I wanted to say. *It's been in God's hands all along. But why would transferring Bubba to a better-equipped facility lessen the need to find out what actually happened to him? If his condition was due to foul play, wouldn't we all want to see whoever was responsible brought to justice?*

I looked around what was, for the most part, a disapproving group. After studying everyone's expressions, I decided against voicing my true feelings. It was obvious only Sheila, and possibly Rapella, would back my desire to continue the investigation into the list of potential suspects. Therefore, rather than rattle everyone's cage, I asked, "Am I correct in assuming we are all in agreement about having Bubba transferred?"

Following a chorus of "Yes", "You bet", and "Absolutely" responses, I turned to Andy. "Is Raven Kostaki the woman Bubba was dating before he decided to call off the engagement?"

Andy gave me a puzzled look. "No, but his ex's first name, coincidentally, *was* Raven. Raven Hobbs. Why do you ask?"

Raven Hobbs? I thought. *The letter Raven received was from a Carolyn*

Hobbs. Oddly, it was addressed to Raven "Kostaki". If Raven Kostaki was actually Raven Hobbs, the sender was clearly in on the ruse. Who, if not Raven's mother, would be most likely to support her daughter in an attempt to win back the love of her life? But would her mother condone a potentially lethal assault on the ex-fiancé? I highly doubt it. No mother wants to see her offspring pull a stunt that could land her son or daughter behind bars for the rest of their life.

"I don't believe it's a coincidence, Andy. Is his ex's mother's name Carolyn, by any chance?"

"Yes. Why? What are you saying?" Andy asked.

"The two Ravens are one and the same. It's apparent now that Raven Kostaki's real name is Raven Hobbs. What I can't figure out is why neither you nor Bubba recognized her." Although I didn't mention my hair fiasco out loud, I thought about how Yvonne had dyed it pink. That's when I realized anyone can change her physical appearance if she wanted to remain incognito. "I'll bet Raven changed the color and style of her hair to disguise herself and perhaps altered other physical characteristics."

"Raven Hobbs didn't have breasts nearly as big as Raven Kostaki's." Andy looked at Wendy sheepishly. "Sorry. It was hard not to notice those big melons of hers."

"Breast size is easily augmented," I said.

"But Raven Hobbs had riveting light blue eyes. I don't recall that Raven Kostaki did," Andy said. After his remark, I thought back to the locket Sheila and I had found in Raven's suitcase. I'd have bet anything the girl in the locket's photo was Raven herself, before she altered her appearance. I vividly remembered her startling blue eyes in the photo. It had most likely been Bubba's face that had been eradicated from the photo with a black marker.

"Maybe you don't recall the color because you weren't looking at her eyes," Wendy said jokingly to her fiancé.

After everyone stopped chuckling, I said, "Raven's eyes were dark brown at the wedding, but colored contacts could easily change her eye color from blue to brown."

"Speaking of which," Andy said, as if trying to convince me the two Ravens couldn't possibly be the same individual, "Raven Hobbs wears large purple-framed eyeglasses."

"We just talked about her wearing colored contacts, which would eliminate the need for eyeglasses."

"Yeah, that's true. But Raven Hobbs has long brown hair, straight as an arrow." Before I could respond, Andy added, "I guess she could have had it cut, permed, and dyed blond with blue streaks. The problem with that theory, though, is that Raven Hobbs is extremely thin. Raven Kostaki, on the other hand, could stand to lose a few pounds."

"Do I need to explain how comfort food like ice cream and potato chips can become a girl's best friend after a heartbreaking end to her engagement?" I asked.

Wendy piped up then with a remark directed at her fiancé. "If you were to stand me up at the altar, I could be a spokesperson for Weight Watchers by January."

Andy stood motionless, as if in deep thought. "You know, now that I think about it, you might be right. I can see where Raven Hobbs could have transformed herself into an entirely different looking woman and changed her last name in order to remain anonymous. You'd think she'd have changed her first name too, though, since Raven is such an unusual name."

"Fooled you, didn't it?" At Andy's reluctant nod, I continued. "Besides, changing 'Raven' to a pseudonym might have been harder for her to do, since one's first name is such a personal thing. What I don't understand is, why did she move here, and what could she have hoped to gain by poisoning Bubba?"

Wendy gasped audibly. "You think Raven poisoned Bubba?"

"I think I can explain why she might have wanted to harm him," Andy said. "Raven Hobbs is a calculating, crazy bitch. Her mood changes are epic, and terrifying!"

"Oh, come on, Andy," Wendy said with a snort. "Tell us what you really think about her!"

After we all chuckled at Wendy's wisecrack, Andy added, "It wasn't just me who tried to talk Bubba out of marrying her. All of his buddies did. After Bubba broke up with her, she went berserk. She started stalking him, along with any girl he showed an interest in. It didn't take those chicks long to realize dating Bubba wasn't worth putting up with his unpredictable ex-fiancé."

"Wow. Interesting," I replied.

"I can honestly envision Raven moving here and getting a job she knew would bring her into close contact with Bubba in a place he'd never expect to run into her—whether to try to win him back or teach him a lesson. With Raven, either option is possible. I can also see where she might think she could win him back by completely modifying her appearance. She probably doesn't understand that although attraction might begin here," Andy said, pointing to his chest. "True love takes place in one's heart. Raven might transform herself to look like a supermodel, but it wouldn't have changed the way Bubba felt about her."

Andy's words were so poignant that my eyes grew misty, as did nearly everyone else's in the room. Stone patted his nephew on the shoulder. "Well said, son."

"I agree," I added. "It appears as if Raven had a motive to hurt, or even kill, her ex-boyfriend. We now know it was she who put together the flower arrangements and created the boutonnieres, as well. I wonder if there's something else she could have added to Bubba's bouquet in hopes of harming him. I need to go speak to Lily right away and—"

"No!" The voices of multiple people resonated across the parlor.

"Forget Lily. I'll go talk to Raven one-on-one," Andy volunteered. "I know Raven better than anyone here, so I know best what to ask to get to the bottom of this. Bubba's my best friend, after all, and was only here in Rockdale to be the best man at my wedding. Besides, Lexie, you need to take it easy today."

"You'll have to call her if you want to speak to her, Andy. Raven has gone back home to Surfside Beach. She flew out yesterday."

"And you know this how?" Wendy asked. Her tone was scathing. She had always been my toughest critic when it came to the murder cases I'd gotten myself involved in.

"Doesn't matter. The point is, something compelled the young woman to flee the area, which I think is incriminating all by itself." I know I probably sounded full of myself as I spoke, but I was proud of the effort Sheila and I had put forth. It had led us to the discovery that our number-one suspect had left the area.

"You *would* find it incriminating," Wendy began, but Andy interrupted, for which I was grateful.

"Then I'll go talk to Lily," Andy said. "Or, better yet, I'll call Raven if someone can find her number online for me."

Randy perked up suddenly. To this point the retired police officer from Merriam, Kansas, had only taken in the conversation without commenting. "If anyone speaks to Raven, it should be Detective Johnston or another detective in the local police department."

"I think we need to talk to Lily before we confront Raven or speak to the police," I suggested, to which Randy concurred.

Rip, who was also a retired law officer, offered his opinion. "I agree as well. Let's wait until we have more evidence before we contact Rachael, Rayleen, or whatever this girl's name is."

"It's Raven, dear." Rapella corrected her husband, who was known for his inability to recall people's names. He'd referred to me as Lisa, Lacy, Leslie, and even Melissa once—and that was just in the last couple of days.

Rapella then turned to Andy. "You need to be by your best friend's side in case he awakens from his coma. Why not let Rip and me go have a talk with Lily? We've been involved with the investigation of several murders ourselves, and with the information you've just shared about Raven, we can easily take care of this matter with the florist."

"Thanks Rapella. I *would* like to be there if Bubba…" Andy choked up and took a short pause to collect himself. "I mean, I want to be there *when* Bubba wakes up."

"Rapella, I could always join—" Sheila began before Rip cut her off at the quick.

"No, Shelby. You need to take it easy today too."

Rapella cast an exasperated look at Rip and shook her head. "Sheila, Rip's right. You and Lexie both need to rest. Do you realize how close you came to dying in that cooler? Please, let the rest of us take care of things today. You girls have done more than enough already. With the information you've already gathered, we should be able to connect the dots without your assistance."

"Thanks, Rapella." I tried to sound sincere. She had likely saved my life and Sheila's the previous night. I appreciated Rapella's concern, but I hated to be forced to the sidelines just as the loose ends were about to be tied together. It would be like getting within spitting distance of the peak of Africa's Mount Kilimanjaro and having someone say, "You head on back down now. I'll take the last leg of this journey alone and let you know how it goes."

Just then, Stone's phone rang. It was Detective Johnston. After a few short responses, Stone ended the call and placed another. At the conclusion of the second exchange, he said, "It looks as though the plot has thickened. Wyatt decided to turn the three boutonnieres Lily confiscated into the CSI lab. They showed not only traces of ricinolein and lily-of-the-valley plants, but also a heavy dusting of sulfur powder. And, Lexie, he told me to let you and Sheila know you can stand down now because they'd be taking over the investigation."

Stone looked at me as he spoke. I knew he was waiting for a response, so I gave him an unenthusiastic nod. Stone then continued to speak. "I also just spoke with Dr. Schnuck. He told me he now believes Bubba's acute allergy to sulfur is the main, but not sole, factor behind his current condition. He seems to think that between Bubba's mild asthma condition, the toxic flowers in his boutonniere, his peanut and sulfur allergies, and the heat and excitement of the day, the perfect storm was created. The cumulative effect was powerful enough to overwhelm Bubba's system and take him down. According to Dr. Schnuck, it doesn't look particularly promising for his young patient, and he doesn't anticipate Bubba ever regaining consciousness."

There was a collective gasp in the room. This was not the news we'd hoped to get from the lead physician on Bubba's case. With crestfallen expressions, we all focused on Stone's words as he continued.

"Dr. Schnuck said it was very clever of you and Sheila to figure out the significance of Bubba's boutonniere and insist it be tested. Knowing about the sulfur he inhaled could be the best shot they have at saving Bubba's life. They've decided to hold off transporting him to the Mayo Clinic."

"If Raven's responsible, where would she have acquired sulfur powder?" Wendy asked.

"You can buy it at a lot of places," Rip said. "I know sulfur is found in a lot of fertilizers."

"You can buy it over the counter at any pharmacy," Randy added. "I sprinkle it in my socks when I plan to work outside on the lawn. Sulfur powder makes a great chigger repellent."

"As a rancher, I can tell you it's also found in cattle feed," Andy said. "I'm sure Raven knew all about Bubba's allergies. She probably hoped that, between the two poisonous flowers and the sulfur powder, it'd be enough to take him out."

"Or maybe," I said, "just enough to teach him a lesson. The fact that she tried so valiantly to save him after he stopped breathing makes me think she never actually meant to kill him. After all, Raven worked up a sweat performing CPR. If not for her heroic efforts, I think Bubba would have died on the spot."

"That's true," Andy replied. In a weak attempt to bring a little levity into the conversation, he added, "Then again, she'd probably have done just about anything to get her lips on his one more time."

We all discussed the quickly unraveling mystery behind Bubba's sudden and tragic collapse at the wedding. I felt some measure of relief knowing the police department was now involved in the case. But, knowing they'd be starting their own investigation did not mean that Sheila and I were to going to just sit around polishing our nails and eating bonbons, hoping they soon discovered who was behind the vicious assault on Bubba Slippknott. If not for the two of us, the police would not even realize an investigation was warranted, and I still had one more thing I wanted to check out.

It seemed as if Sheila and I had been grounded for the day. I wanted to use the time to peruse the six or seven video clips I'd taken with my phone on the day of the wedding. I had a feeling there might be something in one of those clips that might incriminate Raven and help lead us to the truth behind Bubba's mid-nuptials collapse. I could not have been more spot on.

THIRTY-EIGHT

Once the parlor had cleared of everyone except the two of us, I motioned Sheila toward a small table that guests of the inn used to play cards, Yahtzee, and other games. Currently, part of the table was occupied by a thousand-piece, half-finished jigsaw puzzle depicting a lighthouse on a rocky coastline. Over the course of several weeks, at least a dozen different guests had spent time at the table working on it.

After we were both seated, I said, "I know it seems as if Raven is the obvious suspect in Bubba's illness, but for some reason I don't think we've properly eliminated every possibility. For example, I keep thinking back to the gleeful expression on Lariat's face after Bubba had been hauled away in the ambulance. I also recall him warning Wendy at the floral shop that fresh flower arrangements would keel over faster than someone suffering from heat stroke if left outside during the reception. Odd coincidence, don't you think? Although it most likely was just an ironic analogy, given what happened at the ceremony."

"Yes, but it could have also been the seed that planted an evil plot in Lariat's mind. If so, maybe he'd intended for Detective Johnston to get the tampered-with boutonniere."

"Perhaps. Lariat was open with me about having had run-ins with the detective, and that Wyatt wasn't one of his favorite people. However, I don't think Wyatt has a sulfur allergy. And it's the collective opinion of everyone we've spoken with that neither man would've been overtaken by the toxic flowers unless they were ingested."

"True. You don't think Lariat's jubilant expression could've just been a result of over-indulging in my infamous spiked punch?" Sheila asked. "It's legendary for knocking unsuspecting folks on their behinds. I swear I saw him refill his cup three or four times before the ceremony even began."

"I'm not surprised. I saw you do the same," I joked. "And I did consider that possibility. In fact, I thought at the time the punch might be why he stuck around for the actual ceremony. I'd expected him to make sure everything was in order and then head on out."

"Yes, but I thought the same thing about Raven and Chena. Chena hung around after delivering the cake, as well, presumably to help serve it. Annie was present to shoot the wedding ceremony, of course. But Lily left after the flowers were delivered. Why wouldn't Raven, Chena, and Lariat have done the same thing?" Sheila seemed to be thinking out loud as she considered the possibility of one of those three service providers having been involved in Bubba's collapse. "I just can't wrap my head around what motive Lariat might have had, or what he'd stand to gain by harming Bubba, or Wyatt, or really doing anything that might make the wedding ceremony be anything but a smooth operation and a testament to his good work."

"Good point." I had to agree. Screwing up the ceremony would've reflected badly on the wedding planner. "Maybe we're not giving Lariat credit where credit is due. Perhaps that's exactly why he *did* hang around—to make sure everything ran smoothly so he'd give us no reason to post anything but rave reviews about his services. For all I know, that's what every wedding planner does. Being present throughout the entire wedding festivities may be considered part of their services."

"Could be. I honestly don't believe Lariat was behind the assault on Bubba. I know if I had purposely carried out the sulfur-dusting plot, I'd vamoose as soon as possible. I wouldn't want to be present if, and when, my scheme worked and my victim keeled over."

"An out of sight, out of mind, kind of mindset?" I asked. At Sheila's nod, I added, "I have to agree. I'd think the perpetrator would feel as though they'd draw less suspicion if they weren't present when Bubba collapsed. Perhaps we should concentrate on people with at least some degree of motive who left before the ceremony commenced—for instance, Lily and Annie."

"Lily truly doesn't appear to have a motive to harm Bubba. I feel as if we can safely eliminate her as a suspect. Don't you?" At my nod, Sheila continued. "And Annie Frieze? What motive could she have?"

I explained how Annie had lost out on a twenty-five-thousand-dollar first-place prize due to Wendy's tie-breaking vote in the photography contest. "She won a turkey instead."

"A turkey?" Sheila replied with a laugh. "Hell, I'd be pissed too."

"And she's a vegan." I could hardly get it out without cracking up, and soon Sheila and I were both laughing so hard our eyes began to water.

"Oh, hey!" Sheila exclaimed so excitedly, I thought she'd been struck by a sudden epiphany that would solve the mystery.

"What?" I asked, as keyed up now as she appeared to be. "What just came to you?"

"Came to me?" Sheila looked confused. "Nothing 'came' to me. I just found one of the last two pieces that would complete the lantern room on the lighthouse."

"Seriously?" I asked. I hoped I didn't sound as irritated as I felt. My friend could have headed home five minutes after the thwarted wedding ceremony. Instead, she and Randy had hung around to help us out. I deeply appreciated their friendship and support, so I knew I had to curb my impatience. "Good eye. Now I need you to focus on the problem at hand."

"Oh, sorry." Sheila flashed me a whimsical grin. I wasn't surprised that with almost no effort whatsoever, she'd picked the correct puzzle piece out of a large group of randomly-shaped pieces. Sheila had always had a keen mind when it came to intricate brainteasers. She was an absolute wizard with Sudoku puzzles, which is something I could struggle with for a week of Sundays and never solve. That's why I knew instinctively she'd be a good partner when it came to solving the mystery of Bubba's collapse. As she absentmindedly sifted through the remaining puzzle pieces, Sheila said, "I guess you do have a point. We really shouldn't disregard the fact Annie might want a little payback. And what better way to repay someone who'd cost you a prestigious award and a hefty twenty-five-thousand-dollar prize, than to screw up the biggest day of their life?"

THIRTY-NINE

After listening to the detailed description of my first encounter with Annie, Sheila still seemed unconvinced. "Honestly, Lexie, I've yet to find anyone in our suspect pool with a strong enough motive to harm—or kill—Bubba."

Before she spoke again, Sheila carefully inserted the last piece of the lantern room into the jigsaw puzzle on the parlor table. Once again, she had miraculously reached into a pile of about three hundred similar looking pieces and withdrew the correct piece. "What about the Custovio sisters? Who invited them? Didn't you tell me that like Lariat, Yvonne also had a grievance against Wyatt? Could he have been the actual target, rather than Bubba?"

"No, I don't think so, Sheila. Yvonne doesn't have an evil bone in her body. She can definitely be too salacious at times, but she's a good person at heart. Besides, Wendy told me she felt obligated to invite Yvonne and added her sister, Deb, as her plus-one. Any date Yvonne might show up with would likely cause a stir, if you know what I mean."

"From what you've told me about your hairdresser, I understand Wendy's concern."

"Your idea that perhaps Bubba wasn't the intended victim does bear thinking about, Sheila. At this juncture, we can't be positive it was Raven behind the sulfur scheme."

"If it turns out Raven isn't our perpetrator, who else could it possibly be? And if Bubba wasn't the intended victim, who was?"

"I don't know the answer to either of those questions, but that's what we're trying to figure out. I'm hoping one of the video clips I took at the wedding might give us undeniable evidence of the perpetrator's guilt. I'd forgotten about taking the videos until this morning when I tried to drag my bone-weary keister out of bed."

"I know the feeling well," Sheila said with a heavy sigh. "My headache is only just now easing up. How's yours?"

"Completely gone. I think the ibuprofen I took did the trick."

We went through the video clips one by one, paying close attention to everyone's movements. The first two were of the entire wedding party being arranged into groups by the photographer. All business, Annie ordered members of the wedding party around like a drill sergeant. Nothing appeared to be amiss in either video clip, and Bubba looked the epitome of good health.

The third clip showed Chena carrying the lopsided wedding cake over to the cake table and setting it down. She almost looked as if she were trying to hide behind it. Then again, I wouldn't have wanted anyone to know I'd baked it either, especially for the amount she'd charged.

After arranging the cake with the least pathetic side facing the crowd, Chena spoke to someone barely visible through the scope of the video's lens. The person, who seemed to be shorter than Chena and wore a black shirt or jacket, clearly made a remark that set the cake decorator off. Chena responded back angrily and literally spat in the person's face. I couldn't help but wonder if any of the spittle landed on the cake, which had enough strikes against it already.

"Oh, yuck!" I exclaimed. Sheila and I looked at each other in dismay before returning our attention to the video. Chena waved away the guest in black before removing a cake cutter, a large box of plastic forks, a stack of small cake plates, and a plastic cake topper depicting a bride and groom from a large reusable shopping bag.

"I'm glad she chose not to use that tacky cake topper," Sheila said.

"Believe it or not, she did. I removed it before Wendy had a chance to observe the cake. As it was, she was horrified by the cake's appearance, anyway. A plastic couple who look like Ken and Barbie on top of it would've put her over the edge."

We both chuckled before returning our attention back to the video clip. We watched as Chena placed things in order and then walked away, out of the field of vision. Like the previous two videos, there seemed to be nothing out of the ordinary—other than the spitting episode—so we moved on to the next one.

Video four showed a throng of guests surrounding the refreshment table. We watched Orpha White, Hazel Hallberg, and a half-dozen other people exchange small talk while replenishing their appetizer plates. Henry Clay, a member of our church, piled at least half the shrimp rollups on his plate. Obviously, the rollups hadn't been tainted in any way or Henry's obituary would've been printed in that morning's *Rockdale Gazette*. The only death mentioned in the paper was that of a Billy goat named Pepe. Sadly, Rockdale High School, otherwise known as the home of the fighting rams, had lost their school mascot to old age.

Video five showed Lily and Raven placing a large floral spray on the serving table located on the back patio where the after-wedding reception had been slated to take place. All the individual tables were adorned with smaller silk arrangements Lariat had provided. Toward the middle of the clip, Lily handed the box of bouquets and boutonnieres to Raven, and then turned to walk toward the parking lot. At the end of the clip, Raven carried the box to the far end of the refreshment table and set it down in order to free her hands to complete another task.

We replayed the clip several times, but didn't detect anything abnormal. Neither Lily nor Raven's actions appeared at all unusual. We were becoming disenchanted, having hoped for something solid enough to base a murder charge on—or at least attempted murder. I skipped the fifteen-second sixth video clip and moved on to the seventh, which was the lengthiest and final one. I had been filming it when Bubba collapsed.

We watched in dismay as the cleric, Bob Zimmerman, asked if anyone had any objection to the union between Wendy and Andy. A second later, Bubba Slippknott passed out and fell over backwards. Reverend Bob's amused expression clearly showed his belief that the best man had been acting out a practical joke. His expression soon morphed into one of horror when he realized it hadn't been a hoax, but that something terrifying had happened to the now unconscious young man.

The video then showed what looked like pure chaos erupting. A few panicky guests began running around aimlessly, while others stood perfectly still as though they were frozen like popsicles on sticks. Next, we saw the bride ripping off her veil and rushing toward the fallen best man and, finally, a highly distraught-looking Raven running over to Bubba and dropping to her knees to begin administering CPR. Raven looked nothing like a woman with murder on her mind, but rather like someone who wanted nothing more than to save the man lying in front of her. Just then, the video stopped.

Sheila and I could only stand to watch that clip once, but we were both convinced nothing in it revealed malice on anyone's behalf—in particular, Raven Hobbs.

"Dang it!" I said. "I really hoped we'd find something that would implicate a murder suspect in one of these videos."

"Me, too," Sheila agreed. "If it was Raven who tried to kill Bubba, she deserves an Oscar for that performance in trying to save his life. Oh, wait. We forgot to look at the sixth video, not that I expect it will show anything of any significance."

"I guess it couldn't hurt to check it out."

And we did. We were horrified, astonished and, yes, oddly delighted, to discover something in that final video clip that convinced us who was behind the tragedy that had befallen Bubba.

We were alone in the inn. Cindy Travis and Evelyn Horan, both from California, would be checking into the inn later in the afternoon. They'd be attending a local dog show the following day. In our quest to be as accommodating as possible, we'd arranged for Ms. Travis's two canine contestants to have clean, comfortable bedding and a feeding station in the inn's garage.

Everyone else was either at the hospital or, in the Ripples' case, speaking with Lily at Lily's-in-Bloom Floral Shop downtown.

There was only one thing for Sheila and me to do. We quickly got ready and were on our way within ten minutes. With any luck at all, we'd return to the inn before anyone even realized we'd left the premises. We were determined to confront the would-be killer and nail down a confession from the individual, which we would then drive directly to the police station. Or, at least, that was the plan.

We were nearly, but not one-hundred percent, certain who the perpetrator was and how the crime had been committed. The question of why this individual would carry out such an evil deed, however, remained unanswered. Sheila and I vowed not to rest until it was.

FORTY

"Can you explain this video to us?" I asked as I set my camera down on the counter in front of the surprised woman. She watched in horror as the video clearly depicted her pulling a small plastic bottle of ground yellow powder out of the front pocket of her black jumpsuit. She then opened the bottle and liberally coated one of the boutonnieres with the powder, shook it to let the powder settle deep into the cut flowers, and set the boutonniere she'd tampered with down amongst the other bouquets and boutonnieres. Each one had a white name tag attached to the main stem, but, without enhancement, the tag was unreadable in the video.

"What do you think this is going to prove?" The woman tugged repeatedly on her left ear lobe as she spoke, a nervous habit I'd noticed the first time we'd met in her shop.

"That you intentionally poisoned Bubba Slippknott, and now his life hangs in the balance. You may very well end up being guilty of first-degree murder." I spoke matter-of-factly as I studied her intently, so as to judge her countenance when she faced the truth.

Her emotions were difficult to evaluate. Her expression morphed from surprised, to horrified, and finally to confused, all in the space of ten seconds.

With the proof staring her right in the face, she snatched my phone off the counter and ran toward the bathroom in the rear of her shop. With her long strides, even Sheila couldn't have caught up with her in a foot race.

"No sense in trying to delete the video," I hollered out to her. "I've already sent copies of it to Detective Johnston and the chief of police."

I hadn't actually sent the video to anyone other than Sheila. We had taken this measure in the event something happened to the original copy. But it didn't hurt to let Chena think the jig was up and the authorities were prepared to arrest her on attempted murder charges at any second, a charge that might later be upgraded to premeditated murder.

"What we don't understand," I began, "is why you'd want to harm Bubba. What could possibly persuade you to poison a man you'd never even met before? Or did you and Andy's best man somehow share a history we're unaware of? You might as well spill the beans, Ms. Steward. It's just a matter of time before you leave here in handcuffs."

Although Chena didn't know it, we'd neither notified the police, nor any other living soul for that matter, and no one would be showing up at the bakery shop to cuff the cake decorator. But Sheila did have the voice recorder app activated on her phone, which we planned to take straight to the police station after we'd secured Chena's recorded confession.

The ploy worked. With her head bowed down, Chena returned to where Sheila and I stood and sheepishly laid my phone on the counter. With tears glistening in her eyes, Chena looked up and began to speak.

"It's not what you think," she began. "I know the video shows me sprinkling sulfur powder in the boutonniere, but I truly had no intention of harming Mr. Slippknott. As you correctly stated, I'd never even met the man, nor did I know he had an allergy to the substance."

"So, what was the point?" Sheila asked.

"What you don't see in this video is that, after I put the box of flowers back down on the table and walked away, that young floral assistant named Raven walked up and detached all of the name tags. She tossed the tags in a trash receptacle, picked up the box, and then walked over to the wedding party gathering together for their group photos. Without name tags, Raven selected the bouquets and boutonnieres at random and pinned them on to the groomsmen and bridesmaids. Admittedly, the bouquets were identical, as were the boutonnieres, except, of course, for the one that had been dusted with sulfur. It hadn't occurred to me Raven would do that, or I'd have never attempted the prank I was trying to pull."

"I don't get it," Sheila said.

"Neither do I," I said. "What prank are you referring to? Causing Bubba to have a severe allergic reaction was what you'd considered a prank?"

"No. Don't you see?" Chena asked. "I didn't know Bubba was going to get the boutonniere I'd sprinkled with sulfur. I thought that—"

Chena stopped to pull a tissue out of the Kleenex box on her desk. I finished her sentence for her, as the truth had just dawned on me. "You intended for Gunnar Wilde to get the boutonniere you tampered with. Let me guess. Gunnar also has a sulfur allergy, doesn't he? Dr. Schnuck at Wheatfield Memorial told us it was not an uncommon allergy. Many people are allergic to sulfa, sulfur, and/or sulfites."

"Yes, I suppose so," Chena replied. She sniffled and blew her nose loudly before continuing. "But Gunnar's allergic reaction to sulfur is not nearly as severe as Bubba's apparently is. Gunnar uses sulfur in the mix he feeds his cattle. It's an essential nutrient required for the normal growth and reproduction of bacteria in the rumen of cattle."

"Rumen?" I was curious. I recalled the doctor saying that sulfur had a wide variety of applications. This was not one of the ones he'd mentioned, but Andy had informed us at the pow-wow that morning it was sometimes found in cattle feed. I listened as Chena explained further about the importance of sulfur to the digestion tracts of bovines.

"The rumen is the first paunch, or stomach, of a cow. The rumen receives the food, or cud, from the esophagus, and the bacteria helps digest it and pass it on to the second paunch called the reticulum."

"Is it true cattle have four stomachs?" Sheila asked.

"No. They have only one, but their stomach has four compartments, each serving a different function in the digestion process."

"Wow! You know a lot about cattle," Sheila said. She sounded quite impressed, despite the terrible "prank" Chena had tried to pull off.

"Yes. Gunnar and I went together for over two years before becoming engaged. Then Mattie Hill came waltzing in and stole him away from me." In the time it took her to verbalize two sentences, Chena's demeanor changed from one of great sorrow and regret to one of overwhelming anger and bitterness. I felt obliged to defend my daughter's best friend, who was like a daughter to me.

"If Gunnar was happy, he wouldn't have even looked at another woman, let alone Mattie Hill. It's certainly not Mattie's fault Gunnar ended your engagement. I'm sure he'd have never even noticed Mattie if not for the fact he believed a future with you was not in the cards. You should consider it a blessing. Better to find out now that the two of you weren't meant to end up together than after you and Gunnar were married. Divorce is an awful thing to go through. An unhappy marriage would be even worse."

"I realize that, but he broke my heart, nonetheless. It still hurts to see him so happy with another woman, particularly a beautiful one like Mattie. I can't help but feel jealous of her." For a tall, athletic woman, Chena suddenly looked fragile. I almost felt sorry for her. I listened as she continued to explain. "I just wanted to get back at Gunnar without really causing him any permanent damage. I knew from experience that when he inhaled too much of the sulfur when he fed the cattle, he immediately broke out in hives. He was usually very careful around the sulfur, but he still suffered from overexposure to it on occasion. I guess I just wanted to embarrass him, even though it wasn't even close to the level of humiliation he'd caused me. You see, the hives would make his face turn red, and cause itchy raised bumps to form. The reaction he has to sulfur makes him look miserable, but also hysterically funny."

"People tend to look miserable when they *are* miserable, and that doesn't sound hysterically funny to me at all," I said. "But I do understand how the mix-up in boutonnieres occurred, and that you didn't intentionally mean to bring any harm to Bubba."

"I would never have even considered such a thing had I known how it would turn out."

I made a scoffing sound. "I'd have thought that would have gone without saying."

"Yeah, no shit," Sheila added.

"Okay, okay. I know what I did was horrific. I'm so sorry it turned out the way it did. I am scared beyond belief that Bubba will die, and I'll spend the rest of my life behind bars."

"Mostly the latter, by the way it sounds." I was in no mood to cut Chena any slack. Whether Bubba was the intended target, or not, his life remained in limbo due to a mean-spirited, thoughtless act this woman had perpetrated.

"No!" Chena exclaimed in earnest. "Truly, Lexie, my main concern is that Bubba regains consciousness soon and suffers no long-lasting effects from my impulsive, jealous prank. I couldn't live with myself if he dies. I would gladly sacrifice my life if it would save his." Chena began to cry, and I felt as if her concern and grief were sincere emotions.

I could physically feel my heart softening just a bit. Goodness knows I too had an impulsive trait. That impetuousness I'd been born with had gotten me into life-threatening situations on numerous occasions. The difference was it was always my life I put on the line, not that of an innocent bystander. "If you step up to the plate and confess to your actions, you may do time, but not for the rest of your life."

"Okay." Chena shrugged as she spoke. "I'll probably turn myself in sometime this week."

"It'd be in your best interests to do it today, young lady," I said. As I responded to Chena's noncommittal remark, I felt my melting heart instantly turn back into stone. "Telling us you'll 'probably' turn yourself in sometime this week ain't gonna fly. We have recorded your confession and Sheila and I will be turning you in ourselves if you don't do so immediately. We're not giving you a bye just because you accidentally assaulted the wrong person. We're only offering you an opportunity to make the outcome better for yourself. But that offer has a time limit on it and the clock is ticking as we speak."

Chena turned toward Sheila, as if for support, who nodded before speaking. "Listen to her, Chena. You should take advantage of the opportunity Lexie has afforded you. If I were you, I'd waste no time going to the police station if you want to get a reduced sentence. I can assure you, the longer you wait, the worse the outcome will be."

"Oh, all right." Chena then turned back toward me and said, "You know, I nearly tried to price you out from the beginning because I wanted nothing to do with this particular wedding. I should have paid heed to my gut instinct."

"Yes, you should have," Sheila and I said in harmony. Then I added, "You nearly did price me out, if you recall."

"Believe it or not, I gave you a fair price, even if the cake didn't turn out quite as nice as I'd have liked."

"It was god-awful, Chena. The lopsided concoction looked as if it were thrown together by a demented monkey. I should have—"

"Okay. Okay. I'll admit it *was* a royal mess, and I'm sorry." Chena dabbed at tears as she spoke. "As I was saying, there was a reason I didn't want to be anywhere near the wedding. I knew Gunnar and Mattie standing up as groomsman and maid of honor for Wendy and Andy would be something I couldn't bear to watch."

"So why didn't you just drop off the cake and split?" Sheila asked.

"I wanted to, but I couldn't. It was kind of like the train wreck about to happen in front of you that you can't take your eyes off no matter how awful you know it's going to be. The sulfur prank was a spur-of-the-moment thing to begin with, not a premeditated act."

"How's that, Chena?" I asked.

"Well, knowing the cake table was being set up on the lawn, I brought that small container of sulfur powder to sprinkle in my socks in case there were chiggers in the lawn. I am highly susceptible to chigger bites. They make me miserable. I swell up and itch like crazy for days. I'm a little ashamed to say this, but chiggers have almost the same effect on me as sulfur has on Gunnar. Sulfur, believe it or not, is a great deterrent to chiggers."

"So, I've heard," I said dryly. I'd hazard to guess Chena didn't find her own suffering "hysterically funny", but I kept the thought to myself. Instead, I told her about Sheila's husband. "Randy uses sulfur powder for the very same purpose you do—to repel chiggers."

"It's very effective. Try it some time," Chena advised. "So, anyway, as I was setting up the cake before the wedding, Gunnar walked up to me and asked, 'Did you actually charge Andy and Wendy for that pathetic-looking cake?' And then, to add salt to my wounds, he added, 'It looks horrendous!'"

"Well, that was admittedly very rude of him." *It was true, but not exactly polite,* I thought. Gunnar had obviously provoked his ex-girl-friend intentionally. It sounded as if he'd inadvertently induced the tragic event that had felled his fellow groomsman.

Sheila and I had deduced that the person dressed in black in the video clip, who was the recipient of a spit bath from Chena, was Yvonne Custovio. We'd assumed she'd walked up to the cake table and made some remark about sleeping with Chena's current boyfriend, or something of that nature. She seemed to take great pleasure in stealing other women's lovers. The fact that the person Chena had spat on was shorter than Chena had made us mistakenly assume the individual was female. Only now we realized that individual was Gunnar Wilde. Like Gunnar, Yvonne had short, curly, dark brown hair, of which only a small portion was visible in the video clip, and she'd worn a black blazer to the wedding.

I was amused by the fact Chena had failed to mention she'd spat on her ex-fiancé after his cutting remark about the cake. She didn't know I had captured her confrontation with Gunnar at the cake table on another video clip we hadn't shown to her. "I guess I might have felt a desire for a little payback, too, Chena, if I'd been in your shoes. But to cause anyone physical harm is unforgivable in my opinion."

"I know. You're right, Lexie. It was a horrible thing to do, and I greatly regret my decision."

"I would hope so. So what happened next?"

"Well, right after he walked away, I looked over and saw Raven put the box of flowers down on a table. I recalled the sulfur in my pocket, and the inspiration to exact a little retribution against him hit me. So, when I thought no one was looking, I sprinkled some of the sulfur powder in the boutonniere marked with Gunnar's name, as you saw in the video. But after I saw Raven remove the name tags a few minutes later, it was too late to do anything about it without admitting what I'd done. However, I felt sure that if the wrong groomsmen did end up getting the boutonniere with the sulfur in it, he'd be unaffected by it. It never occurred to me it'd end up on the lapel of someone who not only also had an allergy to sulfur, but a severe one, no less. I know I should have come forward right away, but I was afraid to. I knew if Bubba was to pass, and it sounds as if he still may, I'd be in deep trouble."

"From what you've told us, I don't think you'd be charged with anything more than aggravated assault or, perhaps, manslaughter, if Bubba doesn't pull through. Although likely the chief cause, the sulfur is one of only a number of factors in what took Bubba down. His is a complicated case. I do know for certain, as I've already told you, it'd be in your best interests to turn yourself in as quickly as possible and explain to the police what you just told us."

"Will you go with me?" Chena asked. "I'm scared to death. I may need you two to hold me up as I confess to the police."

"Absolutely," Sheila and I agreed in unison.

I was aghast at what Chena had done, but I felt sorry for her in an odd way, too. Even knowing my words would fall on deaf ears, I'd plead to the police chief to go easy on her as harming Bubba had never been her intention. She really hadn't intended to cause great injury to anyone, even Gunnar.

I felt Chena's pain as she'd explained the heartbreak she'd experienced. I knew how true the old adage about the best laid plans of mice and men going astray could be. I've had well-constructed plans go astray more times than I could count. But to even attempt such a prank was beyond contemptible.

And to be perfectly honest, I wanted to see the expression on Chief Smith's face when he discovered his nemesis—the co-owner of a bed-and-breakfast and volunteer librarian—had been instrumental in solving another local crime. I knew it'd be a bitter pill for the man to swallow. And, oh, how I'd enjoy watching him as he tried to choke it down.

This mysterious case of marriage and mayhem had been unraveled and the perpetrator, such as she was, would be brought to justice. Whatever that justice might entail, I hoped it would be fair. Chena didn't appear to be a malevolent person by nature. How many of us have made ill-advised choices based on affairs of the heart? Fortunately for most of us, the results were much less traumatic. Chena's actions may have been intentional, but they were hardly premeditated. If anything, Chena was guilty of a crime of passion, which is exactly why there is a third-degree murder charge in our justice system.

FORTY-ONE

September 1, 2018

B ubba awakened from his coma on the fifth day following his collapse at the originally scheduled wedding ceremony. He spent another day in the hospital recuperating and regaining some strength. Appearing weak and gaunt, but otherwise healthy, he'd been allowed to leave Wheatfield Memorial Hospital earlier that morning, on October first, in order to participate in Wendy and Andy's rescheduled nuptials.

Bubba was more than gracious once informed about what took place during his five-day coma. In Chena's defense, he'd jokingly said, "After all, it could have been the handful of peanuts I ate that put me over the edge. That was my own fault. I knew very well I was prone to having allergic reactions to nuts."

At the news the sulfur-laced boutonniere had been intended for him, Gunnar had remarked, "I feel bad for Bubba, but it looks as if I dodged a bullet. My face swells up like a road-killed possum after I've inhaled too much sulfur."

Bubba heard about Gunnar's reaction to the news while Andy and his three groomsmen were getting dressed in their rented white

JEANNE GLIDEWELL

tuxedos for the repeat ceremony. Evidently, Lariat had felt superstitious about ordering black tuxes again. To Gunnar, Bubba had said, "Like me, it appears as if you dodged another bullet when you ended your former engagement. Sounds like both our exes are vindictive bit—"

Before he could finish his response, Andy cut in. "Hey, fellows. Get your bowties tied and your jackets on. The ceremony starts in ten minutes, and I don't want it delayed for even a minute. I'm not going to let our tickets to the all-inclusive resort in Cozumel go unused. They let us reschedule our honeymoon stay the first time, but they might not be as understanding a second time. Not to mention, my beautiful bride will have all our heads on a platter if this ceremony doesn't go off without a glitch!"

For the second ceremony, Andy and Wendy were both wearing the matching his-and-hers watches Stone, a former jeweler, had created as his wedding present to them. He had combined twenty-four carat gold bands with small peridots surrounding the face of the handsome timepieces. The couple had both celebrated their birthdays in the last four weeks, and peridot was the birthstone for August. If not for Bubba's unfortunate health crisis, they would have celebrated an August anniversary, as well.

Lariat, despite his drinking problem, had turned out to be a really upstanding guy. He'd made all of the arrangements for the second ceremony solely on his own with Wendy and Andy's blessing, and at no additional cost. I believe my blessing—not to have to deal with any of the details or decisions—goes without saying.

Lily had felt terrible about the mix-up with the flowers. She'd never imagined anyone might have an adverse reaction to the toxic flowers in the bouquets.

The doctor assured us the flowers alone would not have caused Bubba to slip into a coma, and I passed this on to Lily. It was the sulfur that had most likely turned the tide, and not in his patient's favor. Regardless, Lily said she wouldn't feel right charging for the flowers. She credited all of the cost of the floral arrangements back to Wendy and Andy. Lariat supplied enough silk flower arrange-

ments for the second ceremony, including bouquets and boutonnieres, that the need for fresh flowers was eliminated.

Best yet, Chena, who could not have been any more appreciative of the fact that neither Bubba or the local police department
pressed charges for her ill-advised practical joke, supplied a beautiful
three-tiered cake at her own expense. She'd included all sorts of
frills and extras we hadn't ordered on the first go 'round and, fortunately, the plastic bride and groom topper was nowhere to be seen.

My wedding present—hiring a wedding planner for
them—seemed pitiful in comparison to the gold watches Stone
gifted Wendy and Andy with, so I also purchased a honeymoon
package from the resort where they had reservations. The package
consisted of two bottles of champagne, a dozen chocolate-covered
strawberries, a fresh fruit basket, a couple's massage at the hotel's
spa, and dinner for two at the top notch on-site steakhouse. The
package and pertinent vouchers would be in their suite when they
arrived at the resort, and I hoped they'd be pleasantly surprised by
my gesture. After a week of non-stop worry and stress, both of them
could sorely use a few days of rest and relaxation and a bit of
pampering by the hotel staff.

The afternoon of September first was overcast. The temperature was at least fifteen degrees cooler than it had been the previous
week, which was appreciated by everyone in attendance. For once,
Lariat Jones appeared to be stone-sober. I thanked him for all he'd
done, and told him I wouldn't hesitate to recommend him to others
who were in search of a wedding planner—or a doily tatter, for that
matter.

In response, Lariat said, "I still can't believe Yvonne recommended me. She was driving me home from a party a while back
because I was too trashed to drive my bike. She must've been in a
real hurry to get rid of me, because she got stopped by Detective
Johnston. He clocked her doing fifty-eight in a thirty-mile-an-hour
construction zone, and from what I've heard, she lost her driver's
license over it. That's why her sister drove her here today. The
detective told me he'd better never catch me behind the wheel of a

moving vehicle in the condition I was in that night. He said he'd be keeping an eye out for me."

"Yeah, and you better believe him, too, or you'll find yourself in the same boat Yvonne's in," I told Lariat. "I don't want to hear you being lauded on the evening news for being an organ donor either, no matter how honorable a thing that is to do. Frankly, no one on the waiting list deserves a pickled liver anyway."

"Hey now! And here I thought I'd grown on you!" Lariat exclaimed. But he knew by my warm smile that I was kidding.

"Surprisingly enough, you have. Tell you what, Lariat. I'll promise to start drinking only decaf coffee after noon if you'll promise to never drive drunk again. And that means no drinking at stop signs either."

"All right, Lexie. It's a deal. I guess I really have been pushing my luck long enough. I had a close call the other day, in fact, which kind of made me see the light."

"Then that close call might have truly been a life-saver." I kissed Lariat on the cheek before he walked toward the refreshment table. I sensed his soberness would be short-lived as he came to a halt in front of Sheila's punch bowl.

As though sensing he'd just been the topic of discussion, Wyatt approached me then. "Hey, Lexie. Let's hope today's ceremony goes off without a hiccup. I'm not sure any of us could take a repeat of last week's attempt at getting Wendy and Andy officially married."

"Amen to that," I replied.

"And speaking of getting hitched, Lexie, I'm thinking about proposing to Veronica."

"All right! It's about time, Wyatt," I replied with a playful punch to his shoulder. "I'm so happy for the two of you."

"But first I want to make sure you're okay with helping us plan the wedding." Wyatt gazed at me with such sincerity, I thought he was serious. I'm sure my face flushed as red as the silk rose bud in Wyatt's boutonniere before he finally laughed. "I'm just kidding you, Lexie. But I think I will speak to Lariat about it this afternoon."

"Then you better do so now before he gets too deep into Sheila's high-powered punch." After congratulating Wyatt on his decision to propose to his long-time girlfriend, I walked away to mingle with the crowd before the exchanging of vows commenced. I headed in the opposite direction, knowing if I didn't give a proper welcome to Hazel and Orpha, I'd be the main topic of discussion amongst the church grapevine at tomorrow's service.

After I chatted briefly with the church ladies, I walked over to greet Dr. Schnuck and several other physicians who'd been on Bubba's medical team at the hospital. They had attended the second ceremony to support their former patient and, I suspect, to keep a watchful eye on his still tenuous condition.

"Hi, Lexie." The doctor who had treated me in the emergency room after Sheila and I had been locked in the floral cooler had apparently crashed the wedding, too. "Glad to see you're in the pink. How's your friend doing?"

"Sheila's fine, as well. Thank you for coming."

"I'd heard from one of the ER nurses that Sheila had also been seen in the emergency room the same day as Bubba was admitted. Is she trying to beat your attendance record?" Dr. Jifi asked. "That would be no easy task, you know."

After laughing politely, I replied, "Oh, Lord, I hope not. I feel bad enough she got ill from something at the wedding."

"Yeah, right." The doctor said dryly before laughing boister-ously. "She can blame her own spiked punch for her 'illness'. I was told by her attending nurse that your friend's blood alcohol level was well above the legal limit. Good thing she had her husband as a designated driver to haul her to the hospital."

"Are you saying Sheila's dizziness and confusion were caused by her being—?"

"Plastered?" He cut in with a chuckle. "Yep. But the nurses didn't want to embarrass her in front of her husband, so they told her she'd probably been affected by too much heat exposure."

"That doesn't sound very professional for a hospital, but I understand why you did it." Even I had to laugh at his remarks. Sheila's punch had not become infamous by being insipid. It could literally drop a grizzly in its tracks if the animal imbibed just a bit too much.

In fact, I now had to wonder if that's not what had made me feel as if I might pass out in the tub that same evening. Not only had I devoured a couple of cups of punch at the ceremony earlier in the day, I had downed two large glasses of it while putting the wedding items away before bathing that night. And to think I'd been pointing my finger at Georgia's shrimp rollups and Chena's wedding cake, when in actuality it had likely been a conglomeration of several fruit juices and four or five different types of liquor; a formula that even I, as the punch's creator's best friend, will never, ever be privy to. It was a recipe for fun, frolicking, and, yes, disaster. It was also one Sheila would take to the grave with her. I just hoped that wouldn't happen for many, many years.

It'd been a worrisome week, for sure. But Bubba had come through the ordeal unscathed, for the most part, and everything had fallen into place as far as the wedding do-over was concerned. We were all extremely grateful on both counts.

As Wendy's favorite country-and-western star, Bryan White's, classic hit, "God Gave Me You", reverberated from the stereo speakers, the crowd of wedding guests watched in reverence as the bridesmaids were escorted up the aisle by the groomsmen.

It was customary for the audience to rise collectively to their feet when the bride was led down the aisle by her father or another designated honoree. In this case, that honoree was Stone, my husband and Wendy's stepfather.

However, despite the longstanding tradition, the crowd let out a group gasp and leapt to their feet as the maid of honor, Mattie Hill, headed up the aisle arm-in-arm with Bubba Slippknott.

Exactly one week prior, the odds of Bubba surviving his sudden health crisis had appeared dismal. His appearance today felt as if it could be due to nothing less than divine intervention. I sent up a heartfelt prayer of appreciation to God for stepping in when all hope had seemed lost.

The crowd went wild at the sight of the beaming best man, and the pandemonium continued until Stone turned his stepdaughter over to his nephew to be united in holy matrimony.

Never before had I seen a crowd clapping, cheering, and whistling loudly during a wedding procession. It was almost as if a world-renowned rock star had crashed the ceremony, making an unannounced visit to surprise the guests.

I'd also never seen a bigger smile on my daughter's face, and I'm certain anyone looking my way would have said the same about me. I later discovered that Annie had actually captured my expression in a candid photograph. It was an expression of a relieved mother who was thrilled beyond belief.

"And, now," Reverend Bob began, "finally, I might add, I pronounce you man and wife. Andy, you may kiss your bride."

Those were the most welcome words I'd heard in a long, long time.

The End

A RIP ROARING GOOD TIME

A RIPPLE EFFECT COZY MYSTERY, BOOK 1

"We ain't getting any younger, you know. Aren't you about ready to hit the road?" I asked Clyde "Rip" Ripple, my husband of nearly fifty years.

"Don't get your bloomers in a bunch, my dear. All I need to do is get the jacks cranked up and the antenna cranked down and we'll be ready to roll. We have plenty of time to get to the Alexandria Inn in time for the party."

"Well, get to cranking, buster. I'm anxious to get the Chartreuse Caboose on the road." I had nicknamed our RV this after we'd hand-painted it that color one weekend in a fit of boredom. We'd highlighted it with a few scattered yellow sunflowers for a little added flare. If nothing else, it was easy to locate in a crowded campground.

We'd already eaten breakfast and as usual, I heard a chorus of snap, crackle and pops before I'd even poured the milk on our cereal. It was just part of being a senior citizen, as was the prune juice we drank to wash down the whole-wheat toast that completed our morning meal. Bacon, eggs and pancakes loaded down with butter and maple syrup had gone by the wayside when our cholesterol levels achieved "walking time bomb" status. They were just a fantasy now, as were a lot of other things we'd always enjoyed in our younger days. Even our sex drives were more often in "park" than not. Still, for both being sixty-eight years old, we felt we had a lot more active lifestyle than most folks did at our age. We made sure there was never any room on our schedule for bingo and potluck dinners, staples of many senior citizens' social lives.

Rip and I, Rapella Ripple, are full-time RVers, crisscrossing the country in our thirty-foot travel trailer. We both retired at sixty-two years old, the earliest we could draw our social security benefits. Rip spent his entire career in law enforcement, first as a beat cop, then as a detective, and finally as Captain in our south Texas hometown of Rockport.

I, on the other hand, have had a vast array of full- and part-time, positions involving dozens of different occupations. It's not that I'm a high-maintenance, incompetent, or difficult employee, it's just that I bore easily. I've quickly tired of doing everything from pitching magazine subscriptions, where I made random phone calls and was rudely hung up on ninety-nine out of every hundred calls before I could even spit out a full sentence, to working as a clerk at a stained glass art gallery, where the "You break it, you buy it" policy applied more often to me than the customers.

My favorite occupation was short-lived—a taste-testing job at a local ice cream factory, which I was forced to quit when I developed both lactose intolerance and a double chin. But lest you think I'm flaky or unreliable, of all of the many jobs I've had, I've only actually been fired once. And that was due to an unpleasant customer I was serving at a local restaurant who took it personally when I referred to her rowdy young son as an obnoxious spoiled brat who should be put in time-out until he graduated from college. Let's face it, some people are entirely too sensitive.

We found retirement to be less than it was cracked up to be after a full year of sitting on the couch staring at a TV, speaking to each other only briefly during commercials. Fortunately, we could watch the same shows every other month and not remember whether or not we'd ever seen them before. The most excitement we were apt to have in an entire week was visiting a nearby park to feed the pigeons, at least until one of us felt the need to go home and take a nap.

When it finally dawned on us that our rear ends were beginning to take root in the plaid fabric cushions of our couch, we decided enough was enough. After all, we were retired, not dead.

Within a month, we had sold our home, given away most of our belongings, purchased a travel trailer, and hit the road. We made no plans, followed no schedule, just let each day take us wherever it might take us, which on a couple of occasions was less than fifteen miles down the road.

Sometimes we moved daily from one RV Park to another, from one state to another, when we got a wild hair up our you-know-whats. At other times we would rest a spell and recharge our batteries—and I mean *ours*, not that of our trailer, or the truck we used to pull it with—and we'd stay in one park for several months at a time.

We would often work as what is commonly referred to as "workampers" to keep busy and receive free site rent in exchange for helping in the RV Park office, cleaning shower houses, doing lawn work or whatever needed to be done. As you'll no doubt come to realize, "free" is my favorite word. Occasionally we're even paid a small chunk of change on top of our free rent, which comes in handy with the outlandish price of gas these days.

But right now we actually had a schedule to keep. In the Cozy Camping RV Park in Cheyenne, Wyoming, just a couple of weeks prior, we'd met Lexie Starr, her husband, Stone Van Patten, and her daughter, Wendy. Lexie and Stone had been celebrating their one-year anniversary during Cheyenne Frontier Days. When another camper was found murdered, Lexie and Wendy had become involved in the case, and I'd ended up involved as well, to the extent we gals nearly *bit the big one* in the process of discovering the identity of the killer.

Two days after our new friends headed home to the Alexandria Inn, a bed and breakfast establishment they own in Rockdale, Missouri, I'd received a phone call from Lexie. The call resulted in

Rip and I preparing to head east in order to attend a thirtieth birthday surprise party for Wendy at their inn.

There was an RV repairman in Rockdale who we'd arranged to have do some repairs on our trailer while we were there. Lexie had insisted we stay at the inn as their guests while our trailer was in the shop. Along with the word "free," I was also quite fond of its cousin, "guest." My favorite thing about being sixty-eight was the senior citizen discount that came with it.

Less than an hour later, we had Wyoming in our rear view mirror as we crossed over the Nebraska border. I had a feeling this trip would turn out to be one we wouldn't soon forget. Call it a premonition, or just a fit of fancy, but it was a feeling I couldn't shake. I was anxiously looking forward to finding out if there was anything to it, because boredom was nipping at our heels once again and I was more than ready for a little excitement.

A RIP ROARING GOOD TIME
Available in Paperback and eBook From Your Favorite Bookstore or
Online Retailer

ALSO BY JEANNE GLIDEWELL

A Lexie Starr Mystery Series

Leave No Stone Unturned

The Extinguished Guest

Haunted

With This Ring

Just Ducky

Cozy Camping

Marriage and Mayhem

The Spirit of the Season

Lexie Starr Cozy Mysteries Boxed Set

A Ripple Effect Cozy Mystery Series

A Rip Roaring Good Time

Rip Tide

Ripped To Shreds

Rip Your Heart Out

Ripped Apart

The Ripple Effect Cozy Mystery Boxed Set

Soul Survivor

ACKNOWLEDGMENTS

Thank you to my wonderful editors, Alice Duncan, of Roswell, New Mexico; and Judy Beatty, of Madison, Alabama. Without them, I'd look like the writer who, as a kid, paid her big sister to complete all of her English and grammar assignments throughout her years of public education.

I'm also extremely grateful for my proofreaders, Shirley Worley, of Shawnee, Kansas, Sheila Davis, of Fairway Kansas and Sarah Goodman, of Olathe, Kansas. Without these kind and incredible ladies, I'd look like the writer who, as that same kid, spent every school day sitting in the corner with a cone on her head.

And, finally, a big thanks to Nina Paules of eBook Prep, and Brian Paules of its sister company, ePublishing Works. Without this remarkable pair, I'd likely still be beating down publishing house doors, trying to get my foot firmly wedged inside one of them.

ABOUT THE AUTHOR

Jeanne Glidewell, lives with her husband, Bob, and chubby cat, Dolly, in Rockport, Texas, on Salt Lake, just off Copano Bay.

Besides writing and fishing, Jeanne enjoys wildlife photography and traveling both domestically and abroad.

Jeanne and Bob owned and operated a large RV park in Cheyenne, Wyoming, for twelve years. It was that enjoyable period in her life that inspired Jeanne to write a mystery series involving a full-time RVing couple--The Ripple Effect series.

As a 2006 pancreas and kidney transplant recipient, Jeanne is an avid advocate for organ and tissue donation. Please consider the possibility of giving the gift of life by opting to be an organ donor should you no longer need them. Becoming a living donor is the most selfless, heroic act of kindness ever, and you'd be gifting someone with something you don't really need but is crucial for the recipient to continue living. Too many people on the organ transplant list die unnecessarily every day.

Jeanne is the author of a romance/suspense novel, *Soul Survivor*, seven novels and one novella in her NY Times best-selling Lexie Starr cozy mystery series, and four novels in her new Ripple Effect cozy mystery series. She is currently writing *Ripped Apart*, the fifth book in the Ripple Effect Series.

JeanneGlidewell.com